A RECIPE FOR A ROGUE

KATHLEEN AYERS

Join my newsletter at www.kathleenayers.com and get a free ebook **The Study of a Rake.** Be the first to know about new releases, bonus chapters and more!

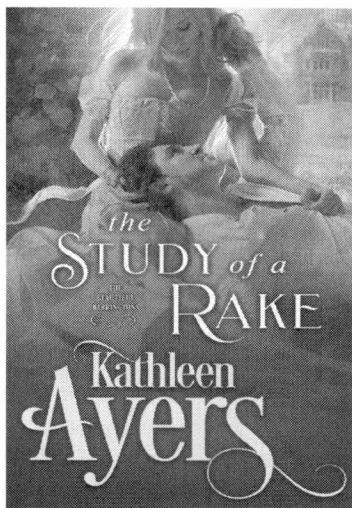

PROLOGUE

The Barrow, Duke of Granby's estate, 1840

Miss Rosalind Richardson watched the proceedings of the house party as the guests strolled through the Duke of Granby's exquisite gardens, careful to keep herself hidden behind an exotic-looking plant with pink, papery blooms. It was somewhat cowardly to take advantage of Granby's assortment of shrubs in such a way, but her mother had left her little choice. Avoiding the Earl of Torrington and refusing to further their acquaintance was the only option at present. Viscountess Richardson had decreed Lord Torrington would make her only child a fine husband.

Rosalind heartily disagreed.

She didn't want a husband, especially one like Torrington. Oddly enough, the earl had little in common with the usual type of gentlemen her mother sent her way.

But that made avoiding Torrington no less imperative.

Mother had been speaking of him for months, though Rosalind hadn't actually set eyes on the man until a few days ago at this bloody house party. Usually, when faced with one of Mother's chosen prospective suitors, Rosalind had no trouble keeping her eyes lowered, the timbre of her voice barely above a whisper, generally giving the impression she had only half a brain. But Torrington . . .

With a sigh of frustration, Rosalind adjusted the bodice of her gown and nearly fell into the flowering plant she stood next to, wincing as a thorn pricked at her skin. Leave it to Granby to fill his garden with hostile shrubbery. She supposed it suited his overall demeanor. A colder, more austere gentleman Rosalind had yet to meet. Frigid was a word that came to mind when considering His Grace. Like a mountain of ice. She had no idea what her cousin Andromeda Barrington saw in him.

But back to the problem of Torrington. The earl was far too attractive, even with the boredom etched on his features when they had been introduced. His hand had seemed uncommonly warm when Rosalind's fingers made contact. A hum of awareness had floated over her skin.

None of the others had ever caused a similar effect.

Their initial meeting, even while she'd attempted to calm her rapidly beating heart, had still been awkward. *Stilted.* Mainly because of Rosalind's surprise at his appearance. Meanwhile, Torrington had barely flicked a gaze in her direction, which somehow made things worse.

She had quickly resolved to keep her distance from him, reminding herself that outside of him being handsome, he was still a prospective suitor chosen by Lady Richardson and thus deserved to be dismissed. Just like all the others.

Rosalind doubted Torrington truly minded, not when the likes of Meredith Clare, Beatrice Howard, and Rosalind's Barrington cousins were in attendance. Against such a beautiful palette, Rosalind faded into the woodwork.

Just as she wished.

Eventually, Torrington would forget about Rosalind entirely. If only her mother would give up so easily.

While Rosalind kept her distance from Torrington, her mother redoubled her efforts to entice Torrington with the dubious charms of her daughter. Last night over dinner, Lady Richardson had felt the need to regale the entire table with Rosalind's talent at the harp, an instrument for which Rosalind possessed little to no skill. She'd only learned an instrument to please Cousin Amanda, the Dowager Duchess of Averell. Rosalind had nearly collapsed into a grateful heap upon hearing Granby didn't have a harp at his estate, else Mother might have asked her to play.

Torrington, from the look of sheer boredom on his face, obviously couldn't have cared if Rosalind spoke ten languages and had the ability to lead a charge of Hussars. If he'd had an opinion on her harp playing, he hadn't expressed it. Instead, he'd taken the opportunity to study Rosalind rather intently over a forkful of roasted pheasant, a mocking half-smile on his lips.

She'd quickly lowered her gaze, pretending absorption in her slivered carrots.

Immediately after dinner, Rosalind had pled a headache and retreated to her room. She'd had no desire to encounter Torrington in the drawing room where he might question her about playing the harp. If not that, Mother surely would have insisted Rosalind and Torrington be partners for charades or some other ridiculous game. The house party was nearing its conclusion, which only stoked Mother's determination.

Thus, Rosalind found herself hiding in Granby's garden.

She gave another exasperated tug at her bodice. The rise of her bosom was determined to flow over the gown's modest neckline no matter the adjustments she made. There was so . . . much of her that there was always a danger *something* might . . . pop out at an inopportune time. A good corset

3

took care of the worst of Rosalind's flaws, but not all. Of course, a tightly laced corset also served to push *things* upward and keep her permanently breathless.

Rosalind was plump and would always be so, no matter the assortment of reducing regimens her mother forced on her. Which explained the sheer number of older gentlemen Mother found suitable for her daughter. Mother insisted only a more mature man would appreciate Rosalind's well-rounded form.

Ugh.

There was an art to avoiding marriage, one Rosalind had perfected as much as she had the chocolate toffee cake she'd made for her cousin's birthday last year. There was true skill in molding flour, sugar, fruit, and vanilla into a symphony of taste, just as there was in convincing a gentleman she'd be unsuitable as a wife.

Baron Delong, who had groped her every time she was in his presence, had been the first. Rosalind had kindly explained to him that his yellow, toothy smile made her think of a rabbit, and then she'd giggled endlessly, to his extreme displeasure. Lord Chambers, she'd taken into her confidence, explaining that her most fervent desire was to enter a convent. Rosalind had convinced Mr. Gaberly she was too stupid to even name the street on which she lived, giving the impression she was a simpleton. There were a few others, of course, but in the end, each of those gentlemen had slunk away, explaining to Lady Richardson that her daughter didn't suit.

Mother despaired. Rosalind was nearly on the shelf.

But Rosalind didn't desire to be some titled lord's brood mare, a convenient, demure wife whose only purpose was to produce an heir. She had ambitions of her own. Plans. None of which would come to fruition if she were distracted by a husband.

"Are you hiding from Cousin Winnie or Lord Torrington?" Lady Andromeda Barrington, or Romy, as she was called, whispered from behind her.

"Both." Rosalind nodded. "I don't see Torrington out there with the others. Do you suppose he's gone and lost himself in the woods as a form of self-preservation? I would hardly blame him for attempting to escape my mother. I've been trying to for years."

Romy giggled. "When Cousin Winnie compared your harp playing to the music of angels last evening, I nearly choked on the pheasant. I love you dearly, Ros, but your plucking of the strings isn't the least heavenly. Now those gooseberry tarts you made. *Those* were divine."

"The only real talent I possess. Turning flour and sugar into something delicious. Mother disagrees, as you know."

"The daughter of a viscount isn't supposed to toil in the kitchens, Rosalind, with bits of dough stuck to her hands. It's *unseemly*," Romy stated, sounding remarkably like Rosalind's mother. "Nor as a duke's daughter am I supposed to know how to do more than embroider a rose on a handkerchief or something else equally useless."

"Yes, but you've found a way around things, haven't you, Romy? Why shouldn't I?"

"I quite agree. I shall be your biggest supporter."

Romy designed clothing. Gowns. The most delectable frocks. If she wasn't the daughter of a duke, Rosalind's cousin would be the most sought-after modiste in London. Romy had refused to allow society to dictate her life. She had secretly formed a discreet partnership with Madame Dupree, a dressmaker of some renown. If anyone ever found out it was Romy who crafted the ensembles of half the ladies in the *ton* and not Madame Dupree, the scandal would be enormous.

Rosalind wanted to emulate her cousin. Using dough instead of fabrics.

"I dream of an establishment," she said. "One that provides exquisite baked goods to all the finest homes in London, not only those with titles. I don't want to limit myself."

"Agreed. The titled are a fickle lot and always short of funds. Give me a wealthy merchant's wife who will pay her bills promptly over a countess whose husband is gambling away their fortune any day," Romy mused.

"Exactly. Gunter's has been the choice for years, but I think they could do with a little competition. The problem is, I need a way to stand out, so to speak. A reason for patrons to prefer my pastries and cakes over those of a much more established institution. And of course, I must be discreet. If Mother caught wind of my ambitions, she'd wed me to the likes of Lord Cheshire in an instant."

Cheshire was nearing sixty with a terrible case of gout. He'd professed on more than one occasion how delightful he found her full figure.

"Then you need be exceptionally discreet, Ros."

Rosalind nodded. The idea to enter trade had been taking form in her mind since her first season. She did not want to marry but needed a means to support herself. Her own Madame Dupree was among the bakers and coffee shop owners in London. She was certain of it.

"There *is* room in London for another such establishment, I think," Romy said. "Another place to take a young lady for hot chocolate and such."

"Exactly. I can also fill orders for weddings, balls, dinner parties, and the like."

"Maybe even Elysium. Leo appreciates a finely baked scone. You should ask my brother when he returns from his business in America."

Elysium's proprietor was Leo Murphy, Romy's bastard half-brother. Part gambling hell, part pleasure palace, Elysium boasted a French chef who served dinner and other assorted delicacies to Leo's patrons. Every lord losing his purse should be granted a decent biscuit. That was Leo's philosophy. And there was no reason why Rosalind couldn't provide that biscuit.

"The idea has merit," she said. "You don't suppose my custards and cakes would be used for improper purposes on the second floor, do you?"

Romy rolled her eyes. "I should never have told you about the things I witnessed when I snuck into Elysium. If Leo ever finds out, he'll be furious." Her eyes took on a faraway look. "There were a great many feathers in those rooms, Rosalind. Scarves attached to the bedposts. I suppose it isn't out of the question that a custard could be put to good use." She laughed. "You've such a vivid imagination—a rather naughty one for a well-bred young lady."

"One only has to listen at the door when your brothers are sharing a drink to get all sorts of ideas, as you well know." Or be born the daughter of a former rake. Rosalind's father, Lord Richardson, had kept quite an extensive collection of . . . illustrated instruction manuals. Books explaining and depicting a variety of sex acts. The trunk containing her father's erotic treasures had been stuck in a far corner of the attic, forgotten when Rosalind and her mother had moved into the house they now inhabited. Bored one day when she was fifteen, she'd explored the attic and come across the trunk. She wisely had not informed her mother of the discovery.

"Or perhaps I merely read a lot."

Romy shot her a speculative glance. "I suspect a little of both."

A different young lady might have tossed the lot of erotic tomes in the fire. Or perhaps refused to allow herself to become aroused at the depiction of such carnal pleasures.

7

Unfortunately, Rosalind was not such a girl.

There were times when she thought of herself as tinder, merely waiting for someone to strike the flint of her inherited wicked nature. Memories of her father were muted at best; he'd died when she was still a child. But she remembered overhearing him flirt with the upstairs maid. Or standing far too close and giggling with one of Mother's friends. Lord Richardson had once cut a swath through London, and Rosalind suspected he'd never reformed, at least not completely.

Torrington had that in common with her father. He was also reputed to be a former rake.

"At any rate, I suppose I'll eventually need to take a lover to satisfy my curiosity," she said blithely to her cousin. "One with whom I can form a relationship of mutual understanding. I'm at the very end of my third season with no offer of marriage in sight."

"You're rather proud of that."

"Unlike you, I've never desired marriage or romance. I shall be happily put on the shelf soon enough, like a jar of old beets one has forgotten. Eventually, Mother will give up. And then I can finally spend the rest of my days doing what I wish, making biscuits and scones. Cakes." A wistful note entered her voice.

"Cousin Winnie is not going to allow you to remain unwed. The very idea is absurd. Perhaps you should seriously consider Torrington."

"Absolutely not." A tingle ran down her skin at the mention of the earl. Yet another reason to avoid Torrington. He had an unsettling effect on Rosalind.

"He's handsome with all that silver sprinkled in his hair. Wealthy. Intelligent. I find him charming."

Rosalind shot her an accusing look. "Have you struck up an acquaintance with him?"

"Stop looking at me as if I'm a traitor. You never said I had to avoid him."

"For the sake of unity with me, I thought you knew your avoidance of Torrington was expected. You've never struck up a friendship with any of my other potential suitors."

Romy gave an airy wave of one gloved hand. "Well, they were all terrible, as you well know. One or two even smelled bad. Torrington is lovely."

"Lovely? A man his age, with his past, has perversions. Is that what you want for me, Romy? An older rogue peppered with perversions?"

"Peppered with—" Romy snorted. "Torrington isn't so old as all that, and he's terribly good-looking. I admit, when I first heard Cousin Winnie mention Torrington would be at this house party, I had a notion of some elderly, gout-ridden gentleman with bad teeth."

"You're thinking of Lord Delong. Or possibly Cheshire. But in all fairness, that seems to be the usual sort who pay me interest. Ancient lords needing a brood mare."

"You aren't a horse. And Torrington is quite dashing," Andromeda insisted. "Surely if you must wed—"

"Must I? I disagree. If I am successful in my venture, I'll be able to support myself."

"What about love? Affection? Friendship, at the very least?"

A nauseating sensation made its way through Rosalind's mid-section, settling like a ball of hardened dough in her stomach. Probably the unbelievably dry scones she had been served with breakfast. Or possibly this conversation.

"I will have my cakes and tortes. My tarts and toffees. My love for pastry will outlive any false declarations of affection."

"But—" Romy opened her mouth to object.

Rosalind held up a hand. "Even if I were remotely inclined to wed, which I am not, Torrington is *twice* my age. I've no desire to play nursemaid to an ancient husband as my mother did." A vision of Lord Richardson, withered against the sheets while Mother fed him broth, flashed before her eyes.

"Your father was many, *many* years Cousin Winnie's senior. Torrington is barely older than Tony." Romy scoffed. "And you've never once mentioned finding my brother ancient."

"He's a duke. It would be disrespectful." The Duke of Averell, Rosalind's cousin and Romy's legitimate brother, was so blindingly beautiful, he often didn't look real, more as if he'd been painted by a master artist. If Tony wasn't her cousin, she might well swoon in his presence. Most women did.

"You've spoken only a few words to Torrington, Ros. Avoided him at every opportunity. I think you're afraid you might like him and can't bear the thought since Cousin Winnie finds him suitable."

"Be honest with me, Romy. If my mother finds Torrington so acceptable, in all likelihood there is something terribly wrong with him. Perhaps he has seven toes on each foot. Or his hair isn't his own."

"I'm fairly certain it is. I doubt that head of curls is a wig."

"Well then, what about the fine figure he cuts? Probably the result of cleverly placed padding and some whalebone around his middle to make his waistcoat fit. Every man his age possesses a paunch, yet Torrington does not. Something else I find highly suspect."

Her cousin snorted, unable to rein in her laughter. "I know the look of a padded coat and a man wearing what amounts to a corset, Rosalind. I do not believe that to be the case with Torrington. Perhaps he is merely fit."

Well, what did Romy know? Her specialty was gowns. Dresses. Riding habits. Not gentlemen's clothing.

"*I* think Torrington pads his shoulders," Rosalind said, turning from her cousin to view the terrace once more.

Mother was chatting with their hostess, Lady Molsin, the Duke of Granby's aunt. Every so often, her chin tilted as she took in the gardens, probably looking for Rosalind.

"A gentleman his age doesn't fill out a coat quite so well without assistance," she stated firmly. "I'll wager there are two small pillows, one tied to each arm, masquerading as muscle in addition to padding his shoulders." Rosalind kept her gaze fixed on her mother and took a step forward, pausing when she heard the sound of silk tearing. "Romy, can you help me? I think Granby's shrub is attacking. My skirts are caught."

"Rosalind."

"I will be watching with great interest to see if one or both of Torrington's shoulders begin to slope and slip down to his elbow." She laughed. "Didn't that happen to a dance partner of yours once?"

Romy cleared her throat. Loudly. *"Rosalind."*

"I think I'm caught on a thorn." Rosalind tugged on her skirts once more, still laughing, amused at a vision of Torrington's broad shoulders disappearing to become bulges at his wrist, perhaps. "Torrington's valet has probably bound his mid-section tightly in some sort of contraption to account for the pleasing fit of his waistcoat."

Mother was walking to the edge of the terrace, her head turned toward the sweeping lawn.

"Perhaps yards of muslin wrapped tightly, more likely a masculine version of stays. Can you imagine a lord, even Torrington, grabbing onto a bedpost while a red-faced valet struggles to lace him?" A snort left her. "At any rate, my skirts are quite stuck, Romy. I am in desperate need of help lest I tear my gown." This time, when her cousin didn't answer, Rosalind looked behind her, the smile on her lips faltering.

Well, this is embarrassing. Nearly as bad as the bit about the harp.

Torrington, in all his dreadful silver-tinged handsomeness,

was standing beside her cousin. Rosalind's backside, much wider than she wished it to be, was pointed in his direction. The side of his mouth lifted just slightly in a mocking smile, making his mustache twitch and drawing attention to the curve of his mouth.

"Lord Torrington," she stuttered. "I didn't realize you were in the garden."

"Apparently not, Miss Richardson." He glanced at the outline of Rosalind's well-rounded backside with a lifted brow.

Rosalind immediately straightened. It was only a gown. A tear could be mended. Her embarrassment could not.

"Lady Andromeda." Torrington made a small polite bow. "I do hope I'm not interrupting your discussion."

"Not at all, my lord," Romy replied smoothly. "My cousin and I were just speaking of how lovely the duke's gardens are. Your interruption is timely, as it happens." She kept her eyes averted from Rosalind and waved vaguely in the direction of the house. "Because I must speak to Lady Mildred, and I've just caught a glimpse of her on the terrace. There is a matter of some urgency I must discuss with her."

Rosalind shot her cousin a horrified look, a silent plea not to leave.

"My lord." Romy bobbed politely to Torrington before sailing away leaving Rosalind to her fate.

Traitor.

Heat suffused Rosalind's cheeks as she looked at Torrington. Given the splotchy way in which she blushed, she was moments from resembling a rotting strawberry. At least the girth of her backside was no longer pointed improperly in his direction.

"The gardens are lovely, are they not?" Torrington's voice had a smoky quality, as if he'd been in bed all day and had only now awoken. The sound sifted pleasurably around

Rosalind's insides and along her thighs. Why couldn't Torrington be more . . . unappealing? He *was* handsome. Distinguished, with bits of gray scattered about his dark curls and through his carefully trimmed mustache. The brush of his beard, clipped short, lined a chiseled jaw. Torrington had an air about him. Not arrogance, exactly. But confidence. Self-possession. And there was a sense of amusement hovering about his shoulders, as if Torrington found the entire house party slightly absurd.

He *was* splendid. That was the truth of it. Rosalind hated that even she could see it.

"Lovely," she agreed, trying to remain composed as she tugged once more at her skirts. "Granby's gardeners are quite skilled."

"My understanding is that the duke does much of the gardening himself," Torrington said. "He has an interest in horticulture. There's a greenhouse"—he motioned to the left —"where I'm told His Grace putters away with dirt and pots."

"Fascinating." The gray strands in his close-cropped beard sparkled in the sunlight. Forcing her gaze from his jaw, Rosalind pretended to study the plant currently holding her hostage.

"Can't avoid me at the moment, can you?" He leaned over, the curve of his full lips twitching once more at her discomfort. He seemed about to burst into laughter at her predicament. "The bush is far too small to hide behind."

"Avoid? Hide? I'm not sure I understand what you mean, my lord. I merely sought some fresh air in the company of my cousin."

A low, amused sound came from the depths of his chest. "Oh, Miss Richardson. You desire at this very moment to toss yourself into a bed of thorns rather than converse with me. We were introduced upon my arrival, but you've kept away from me as if I have the plague ever since. I believe this might be our lengthiest conversation to date."

"We conversed over dinner last night."

Another burst of laughter, rich and melodic hovered in the air. "Agreeing with me that the pheasant is overdone doesn't constitute conversation, Miss Richardson. What did you think of the carrots?"

"Undercooked," she caught herself saying. "Far too crunchy."

"And I thought the potatoes over seasoned. Too much rosemary. And the trifle?"

Rosalind gave another tug at her skirts. "I didn't care for it. The sponge cake had deteriorated from an excess of sherry."

Torrington nodded. "You enjoy good food."

"I think it painfully obvious." She gave a wave down the side of her body.

His eyes flicked down her figure with something that looked very much like approval.

A low, warm hum started up her spine.

"Now, about the harp playing. Lady Richardson spoke so poetically of your skill. Do I have a recital to look forward to? Or do you even play? I would guess you merely pluck at the strings and pretend."

' "I pluck." Rosalind looked down at her slippers. Perhaps Torrington adored music. The fact she did not could serve to make her uninteresting. "I've no musical aptitude to speak of, if that satisfies your curiosity, my lord. You will not be subjected to a recital of my non-existent talents as the duke's music room does not possess a harp." She looked back up at him. "My mother is prone to exaggerate my talents, my lord."

"Undoubtedly." The smile stayed fixed on his lips as he took her in.

Rosalind's mouth hardened as she focused on one of the

brilliant pink blooms right in front of her nose. Very pretty but lacking in scent. Odd, papery petals. Exotic in appearance. The bush gave her something else to think about besides Torrington being so close.

"I think we are both aware of Lady Richardson's machinations, my lord," she finally said.

"Machinations?" His dark brows lifted. "You make her sound positively Machiavellian. Perhaps you'll apprise me."

Torrington probably wielded that smoky timbre like a weapon against every woman in London. Rosalind did not mean to be counted in that number and told the insistent hum along her arms to cease. She lifted her chin. "May I speak plainly, my lord?"

"I assumed you were, Miss Richardson."

Rosalind's lips tightened. Her irritation at Granby's shrubbery, her mother, and Lord Torrington was growing by leaps and bounds. "My lord, I do not know what my mother has done to bring you here—"

"To the garden?" he interrupted, forehead wrinkling in confusion.

Rosalind gritted her teeth so hard, she thought one might crack. He was purposefully annoying her. He knew full well Mother was matchmaking. Any gentleman would have to be blind and deaf not to notice. "I meant, my lord, your attendance at this house party. Surely you know she seeks to make a suitable match."

"She does? I hadn't realized Lady Richardson wished to remarry."

Rosalind scanned the area around them, looking for something she could toss at Torrington and perhaps knock the sarcasm from his possibly padded shoulders. "Your manner would give any young lady pause, my lord."

Torrington was looking down at her with far too much interest from eyes she'd taken to be brown but were another color entirely. There were striations of amber floating in the depths, giving the orbs a more golden hue. The same color of the earrings her mother had insisted Rosalind wear to dinner the other evening. The amber of his eyes shimmered as the sunlight caressed his cheeks.

Lovely.

"So, you admit to deliberately not furthering our acquaintance, Miss Richardson."

"I didn't see the point, my lord. We are obviously not suited to each other."

"How on earth would you know? You've spent the entire house party scurrying away from me like a frightened rabbit." Torrington's gaze shifted, landing firmly on her mouth.

"I don't believe I've ever scurried."

"Regardless, I'd like to know what I've done to offend you other than being someone your mother wished for you to meet." A curl fell to dance against his cheek, and he absently pushed it away, only to have it return a moment later.

Rosalind blinked. Torrington was far too distracting. Highly unsuitable for her in every way she could possibly imagine. Surely, he had no real interest in her. Rosalind was far from being the most stunning lady in attendance, and she'd purposefully made herself so boring he couldn't possibly find her the least entertaining. "I see I must be blunt with you, my lord."

"I doubt you can speak any other way. Go on."

Her lips pressed together. The flippant way in which he spoke to her, as if he knew her far better than their brief acquaintance allowed, annoyed Rosalind. Perhaps Torrington required a more direct dismissal from her. "Lady Richardson is matchmaking and wishes me to wed."

"But you do not share her opinion." The low purr of his voice buffeted her skin. "Is it me you object to then, Miss

Richardson? Or marriage in general?" He held up a hand. "I'm merely curious."

"Both, my lord. I'm sorry to say I do not find you the least appealing. There is nothing about you which draws my interest."

Torrington gave her a thoughtful look. He pushed back the curl again. "Really?"

"Forgive me, my lord, but it is true." Rosalind looked away as the lie stuck in her throat. She did think Torrington appealing, which, in essence, was the problem. "I've never found older gentlemen to be attractive. I find mature men to be . . . repulsive." Rosalind swallowed. "And there is the matter of your past."

"My past?"

"My father was a former rake, my lord. There is no reason to repeat history, so to speak." Rosalind kept her voice steady. "I've no desire to be a brood mare for an aging rogue in need of an heir." She repeated the words she'd said to Romy. "That may be unkind to say, but it is the truth."

"Your candor is appreciated."

"I would make a poor wife, my lord."

"I don't doubt it." He stared at her mouth again with great interest. "Repulsive?"

Rosalind's fingers sank into her skirts, grasping at the fabric. A strange sort of energy hung in the air between them, sparking along her skin with alarming frequency.

Torrington watched her with the same amused smile he'd had earlier. "I don't think I've ever had a woman refer to me as repulsive."

"I must apologize for being so direct, but you *did* ask." She composed herself. It hadn't taken nearly as much effort to dissuade the other gentlemen who'd approached her. Torrington must have an incredibly large ego that he couldn't suffer the rejection of a young lady he barely knew in her third season. "There must be dozens of ladies in my position who would be grateful to be under your consideration—"

"Hundreds, Miss Richardson. Possibly thousands." Torrington took a step closer, the awareness of his much larger form making her pulse kick up. "None of them seemed to mind the pillows masquerading as muscle beneath my coat."

Oh dear.

"Is your corset laced tightly? I think mine might be." He patted the flat plane of his stomach.

It sounds so much worse when he says it.

Cedar, leather, and clean linen invaded her nostrils as he leaned over her. Torrington's scent. Intoxicating. Rosalind inhaled deeply, or as much as she could. It was becoming more difficult with every passing moment to maintain the lie that he was repulsive when her entire body was tingling at his nearness.

"I happen to like gooseberry tarts, Miss Richardson. There is a trick to making the pastry flaky. I wonder if you know it."

He heard everything.

"My lord, you are—" she whispered, not daring to finish her thought. *An earl who should know nothing about pastry making.* She opened her mouth to ask Torrington how he'd know such a thing when the edge of his nose trailed along the curve of her cheek.

Rosalind's heart beat harder. Louder. Was he going to kiss her?

"Repulsive." Torrington's mouth was barely inches from her own. "Unappealing in every way. Your disgust is quite clear."

The featherlight touch of his mouth on hers sent a wave of sensation down the length of Rosalind's body. Her breasts began to ache, straining against the confines of her clothing, begging for his attention. Heat, the sort not caused by a warm fire or a cup of tea, bled down between her thighs. "What are you doing?" she whispered.

"I am attempting to make a point, Miss Richardson," he murmured softly over her lips. "Can you guess what it is?"

Oh, yes. Rosalind had a very good idea.

Torrington's mouth closed more firmly over hers with exquisite patience, gently coaxing the flame he'd lit so effortlessly inside her to burn brighter. The tip of his tongue traced along the seam of her lips, urging her to open for him.

A whimper came from Rosalind. A frantic, eager sound. Everything she'd gleaned from those books of her father's, some of which she'd examined several times, flooded her mind. She felt combustible, like a small plump pile of kindling, so dry the wood thirsted for the flame stretching toward it. Rosalind's lips parted, her tongue darting out to tentatively touch his.

A low growl came from Torrington. His mouth on hers became urgent. Possessive.

Lightning struck Rosalind, traveling over the small space where the tops of her breasts skimmed the edge of his coat. The sensation lapped between her thighs, drawing heat up between her legs. Surrender erupted from between her lips. Rosalind's hands slid up the expanse of Torrington's chest, palms stretched over his torso, her fingers running over his arms.

No padding. Not a bit.

What would it be like to have Torrington's mouth on her body? Feel all that warm, cedar-scented skin brush against hers?

The chirping the birds circling above their heads dulled. The conversations of the guests lingering on the terrace became more distant. Her mind tried to form a coherent thought and failed.

Torrington's mouth slowly retreated, and Rosalind found her lips chasing his, a small cry of regret escaping her. The fabric of his coat slipped through her fingers.

He took a firm step back from her. Surprise glinted in his eyes. The ragged sound of his breathing mixed with that of a pair of bees buzzing near the rose bushes. Torrington stared at her, his palms flat against his thighs, fingers pressing into the fabric of his trousers.

He'd never once touched her.

The sensation of being set aflame slowly ebbed from Rosalind's body. Her fingers fluttered in the air, wanting to grasp his coat once more. Not to mention her mouth, which could still feel the press of his.

"My lord—" she choked out.

"I've made my point, I think," Torrington said, his gaze never leaving her face. "As you have made yours, Miss Richardson. I'll take your opinions to heart. Had you asked, I would have told you I am not in the market for a wife. Or a brood mare as you so charmingly put it. You have been misinformed. I fear your efforts to dissuade me were wasted."

Mortification filled her. "I see." Rosalind jerked her chin and dipped politely. There was little else she could do save committing matricide. "Lord Torrington."

"Miss Richardson." He inclined his head. "I doubt we'll speak again. Enjoy the remainder of the party." Torrington's face was incredibly composed, giving nothing away. He did not apologize for taking liberties with her. Perhaps he wished to forget he had.

Rosalind forced herself to look away from his broad-shouldered form as he marched in the direction of the terrace to rejoin the other guests. Laughter erupted from somewhere near the French doors leading inside. She looked up and saw Lady Beatrice holding court, her fingers fluttering over the arm of the Duke of Granby.

Beatrice Howard didn't stand a chance of becoming a duchess, at least not Granby's duchess. Granby's intentions lay in a different direction. Rosalind couldn't believe no one else saw it.

Torrington jogged up the steps to the terrace, bowing in greeting to Granby and the others standing near the doors. He didn't turn or look in the direction of the gardens.

Rosalind had managed to ruin her mother's plans once again. Except this time, she didn't feel victorious. She gave her skirts a vicious tug, no longer caring if she ripped the silk to shreds. It would be best if she returned to her room quickly before anyone noticed her.

Or she gave any more thought to Torrington.

London, a few weeks later

The overly extravagant ballroom of Lord and Lady Ralston was full to bursting, but that was hardly a surprise. Every event they hosted resulted in a mad crush. Invitations to *this* ball, the finest of the season, were highly sought after. Tonight, even more so since Lord Ralston meant to announce the engagement of his daughter to . . . well, *someone*. Rosalind searched for the name and came up with nothing. The future groom was likely one of the eligible dukes swirling about the ballroom. Or possibly a marquess.

Lady Ralston had high aspirations for her daughter.

She tapped her foot in time to the music, watching, without envy, the young ladies twirling about the dance floor. She didn't want to be here tonight. Balls had only been enjoyable, very briefly, in her first season. The smell of pomade hovering in the air nearly caused one to choke. The press of moist silk from the crowd, nauseating. Dozens of fans waved in the air, pausing ever so often to conceal whispers or sidelong glances. Gentlemen strutted about, filled with their own self-importance, while the finest debutantes this season held court.

Tedious.

This entire ball was a study in excess, something Lord and Lady Ralston did not lack. Lord Ralston was sinfully wealthy, his daughter's dowry enormous. This house, one of the few in London with a ballroom of this size, was utterly lavish. You'd think, with such an abundance of gold, Lady Ralston would have spent some of her coin on decent refreshments.

Nothing on the refreshment table was the least appetizing. Rosalind had taken a small sample of everything as a form of research and had been appalled by the abundance of tasteless fare.

This is exactly why I will be successful.

A surge of hope swelled in her chest at the thought. She had finally secured a partner for her future endeavors. Or at the very least, succeeded in the *possibility* of securing such a partner. All it had taken was a sudden rainstorm and Rosalind's need for a strong cup of tea and a biscuit. A meeting more fateful than accidental.

Mr. Rudolph Pennyfoil was the owner of the small café Rosalind had dashed into, seeking shelter. He was a baker of solid family and sound ambition. Over several cups of tea, Pennyfoil and Rosalind had struck up a conversation, mostly to do with preparing currant scones. The connection between them had been instantaneous, solidified by their mutual love of dough. When she'd visited again the following day, he'd been shocked to discover Rosalind was a viscount's daughter and had grown reticent once he'd realized she was the cousin of the Duke of Averell. Still, he had allowed her to visit his workspace. Yesterday, Rosalind had gently voiced her plans, imploring him to consider a partnership with her. He'd yet to give her an answer.

Pennyfoil was a necessity for Rosalind. The daughter of a

viscount, truly any young lady of good breeding, could not go into trade on her own. Or at all. If her plan was to work, no one could know she and Pennyfoil were partners. Not only would there be a scandal, but Mother would put a halt to the proceedings, crushing Rosalind's dreams beneath the heel of her slipper. Rosalind would find herself wed in a trice with no say in the matter, especially now that the rumors about Romy's hobby were circulating about London. As it was, Mother was growing ever more suspicious as to why her daughter couldn't secure a match.

She glanced in the direction of her mother, sitting ramrod straight, hands clutched in her lap, beside the Dowager Duchess of Averell. She and Cousin Amanda both held up their chins, daring anyone to besmirch the Barringtons.

Romy stood on the other side, a fierce look on her beautiful face, defying the gossip being bandied about the room.

Rosalind abruptly looked away.

A wave of guilt assailed her for the unintentional part she'd played in the drama and rumor clinging to her cousin's skirts. She'd apologized profusely though Romy insisted it wasn't Rosalind's fault. How could Rosalind possibly have known Beatrice Howard would discover Romy's sketches at Granby's house party? One of which was for the very ballgown Beatrice had commissioned from Madame Dupree.

Nothing good at all had come of that blasted house party.

Especially not the unexpected, impossible kiss Rosalind had shared with Torrington. True to his parting words that day, he and Rosalind had not spoken again for the remainder of their stay at Granby's estate. Torrington had kept his distance. She'd kept hers. It had all been very civilized.

Mother had not been pleased. Rosalind had been subjected to a dramatic wringing of hands while being chastised for her lack of effort in securing Torrington.

Now, she despaired of Rosalind ever making a match.

The only thing I wish to make is a cake.

Rosalind shifted against the wall, attempting to get comfortable and knowing it would be impossible given the tight lacing of her corset. She was quite breathless standing near the dance floor but didn't dare take a seat for fear she might faint. The pinch to her mid-section was much worse when seated. A fainting Barrington cousin, one who toppled right out of her chair, would only add to speculation about her family.

The mood in the ballroom suddenly shifted. The hum of dozens of voices, like bees fleeing their hive, filled the air.

Rosalind's eyes caught on a gentleman nearly a head taller than every other man in the room, frost practically gilding his immense shoulders.

The Duke of Granby circled the ballroom, plodding about like some angry giant, gaze fixed firmly on Lady Andromeda Barrington. His eyes slid over the others in their group.

Mother, defiant. The dowager duchess, murderous. The Duke of Averell, grim.

The Marchioness of Hertfort appeared to the left of Rosalind, rich purple skirts swirling about her ankles. Diamonds sparkled at her throat and wrists and from the small tiara perched on her head. Lady Hertfort made her way over to Lady Richardson and the dowager duchess, looking down her nose at Lord and Lady Foxwood as she passed.

The parents of Lady Beatrice Howard sniffed at the cut.

Beautiful and elegant, Lady Hertfort could easily have been mistaken for royalty with her bearing, she was a marchioness, after all.

Lady Hertfort was *also* the Earl of Torrington's sister.

How Lady Richardson and Lady Hertfort had become such close friends was anyone's guess. A shared love of match-making, perhaps, because it was rumored Lady Hertfort despaired of her brother's bachelor state.

A pair of broad, decidedly *unpadded* shoulders came into view, waved forward by Lady Hertfort.

Rosalind looked down at her slippers, the brush of awareness causing her breath to hitch slightly. If she could have escaped the awkward greeting that was only moments away, she would have. But she supposed she and Torrington would be forced to speak to each other.

"Rosalind, dear." Mother's voice carried to Rosalind from her chair. "Come greet Lady Hertfort and Lord Torrington."

Rosalind told the ridiculous fluttering in her chest to cease. Torrington had never had any real interest in her. Yes, he'd kissed her, but only to prove a point. They could certainly be polite to each other, at the very least. There wasn't any reason for them not to be.

He wasn't looking for a wife.

She didn't wish to marry.

Hopefully, he'd forgiven Rosalind the insults she'd dealt him.

Pasting a bland, slightly bored look on her face, lest her mother sense how her heart thudded softly because of Torrington, she approached Lady Hertfort.

"Lady Hertfort, how lovely to see you again."

The marchioness had eyes very like Torrington's. Brown with bits of amber sparkling in the depths except hers were devoid of amusement and far more shrewd than her brother's.

Torrington's eyes landed on her. "Miss Richardson." He took her hand.

A spark of warmth slid down her fingers and around her wrist. For a brief moment, she was back in the garden with Torrington, being kissed to within an inch of her life.

Torrington gave no hint he recalled their previous encounter, or that it had been the least bit memorable. His expression remained impassive. Bored, if she were being honest.

Rosalind lifted her chin and focused on the spice cakes she would make with Pennyfoil tomorrow. Mother thought she would be walking in the park with Romy.

"You look quite parched, Rosalind," Mother said in a meaningful tone, her eyes shifting to Torrington. "My lord, would you be so kind as to escort my daughter to the refreshment table? It's such a terrible crush, I'm certain she would have difficulty finding her way there and back without your assistance."

Dear God. Could her mother be any more obvious? Rosalind's cheeks reddened, the sensation of the horribly blotchy blush inching itself across her face.

"There's no need." Rosalind rushed to assure them all, glancing at Torrington.

Lady Hertfort gave a sigh somewhere to Rosalind's left. "I'm thirsty as well, Torrington. Perhaps you can bring me back a glass?"

If Torrington was annoyed at either his sister or Rosalind's mother, he gave no indication. His handsome features stayed blandly polite. Bowing to her mother, he intoned, "It would be my greatest pleasure, Lady Richardson."

Somehow, Rosalind doubted that was the case. Nevertheless, short of causing a scene, she had little choice in the matter. Dutifully taking Torrington's arm, Rosalind gave a weak nod to her mother and Lady Hertfort. Torrington's muscles tensed beneath her fingers, and the warmth of him seeped through her gloves.

It seemed ridiculous to have ever accused Torrington of padding his arms or any other part of his body.

He led her in the direction of the refreshment table, artlessly steering her along the edge of the dance floor, not bothering to engage her in stilted conversation. Finally, unable to take one more moment of this uncomfortable encounter, Rosalind halted next to a large potted fern at the edge of the ballroom, a spot hidden from her mother, who was doubtless watching.

"We may dispense with this, my lord. I'm not the least thirsty and the other refreshments Lady Ralston has put out for her guests aren't the least appealing."

He raised a brow, a curl laced with silver falling over his forehead. "Does anything appeal to you, Miss Richardson? Because I have my doubts."

Rosalind purposefully ignored the sarcasm. "I only meant, my lord, that the biscuits and small cakes are disappointing."

"Not the sort you would provide, if you were in the business of doing so."

Torrington had overheard far more than she'd wished him to at Granby's. The fact that he recalled her words disturbed her even more. "Eavesdropping is a terrible habit," she murmured. "I realize I have no reason to ask, but I would appreciate—"

"Don't worry, Miss Richardson," he said, interrupting her. "I've already surmised you would rather be fondling dough," his voice dipped, "than anything else."

A shocked puff of air escaped her. "What an inappropriate thing to say. You are—"

"Ancient and repulsive. Yes, yes, I'm aware. No need to explain further." He took her elbow and pulled her once more in the direction of the refreshment table as if anxious to rid himself of her company. "*Cuisiner pour les Rois.*"

Rosalind struggled to keep up. "If you are attempting to be charming, my lord, you may cease. I don't speak French."

"You've declared yourself immune to my charms. I'm only seeking to give you some friendly advice. *Cuisiner pour les Rois* is what you need. A collection of recipes for pastries and other desserts. One of a kind. More exquisite than you can possibly imagine. No one in London has seen the like." He handed her a glass of lukewarm lemonade. "And I assure you, no one at Gunter's has a copy."

⚜

ABRAHAM LANDSDOWNE, EARL OF TORRINGTON REMINDED himself again, as he looked down at Miss Richardson, that his life would be so much *easier* had he just not attended that bloody house party. Bram might never forgive Margarite. He wanted to strangle his sister for bringing Miss Richardson to his attention.

I know just the girl. One you can wed quickly and with little effort should Stanwell expire.

Blithe words uttered by Margarite. His sister had heard him remark in more than one instance that an obstacle to wedding again was the tedium of a courtship. He'd endured two and didn't care to have to suffer through a third because it would inevitably lead to marriage. Thus, the necessity of Stanwell, a distant, mildly disgusting relation who had been Bram's heir for the last five years.

But then, Stanwell had, in fact, expired. In the arms of his mistress, as it were, after an attack brought on by an excess of alcohol and rich food.

The idiot.

Just go have a look at her. Granby's house party is the perfect setting. No one else has piqued your interest.

Because Bram *wasn't* interested. Certainly not in marriage. Two wives had been enough, *thank you*. His second marriage in particular, which had been more armed combat than union, had cured him of ever wanting a wife again.

Bram had strayed. *Often*. And though it had earned him something of a reputation, it was only partially deserved.

Both marriages had been so brief, neither had produced the requisite heir.

She's polite. Unassuming. Possesses a robust constitution. Best of all, convenient. In her third season. She would be grateful should you offer for her.

Bram took in the girl before him. Polite? Miss Richardson had insinuated he wore a bloody corset, for God's sake. A robust constitution was Margarite's way of inferring Miss Richardson was full-figured, which didn't put Bram off in the least.

His cock stirred as a brush of arousal slid around his waist.

Claiming Miss Richardson to be unassuming was ridiculous, at best. The lowered eyes and soft way of speaking were more tools so she would not draw male attention. An excellent strategy if you were avoiding an overbearing mother who was determined you marry. Miss Richardson couldn't wed if no one offered for her. Grateful? Highly doubtful.

What traits Miss Richardson did possess consisted of a wide, almost sinful mouth. Better suited to a courtesan than a well-bred young lady. And an uninhibited, sensual nature as implied by the fact that she'd surrendered immediately when he'd kissed her and hadn't slapped Bram afterward. She'd been clinging to his coat. He'd very nearly compromised her in a duke's garden.

"A cookbook of desserts? In French?" Lovely dark eyes, the sheen of melted chocolate, looked back at him, the steely determination to pretend boredom in his presence fading away at the mention of a cookbook.

Oh, and Miss Richardson apparently had a passion for pastry, which Bram, for some unknown reason, found *highly* arousing.

"Yes." He plucked a nonexistent piece of lint off his coat. Miss Richardson wasn't the only one who could pretend boredom.

She gripped the lemonade tightly, staring at him with a calculating look on her pretty face.

The girl before him planned on going into trade, at least from what he'd gathered from the conversation he'd overheard between her and her cousin. It was a brave, clever, and scandalous thing to do. He admired her for it. Maybe that was what had made Bram mention the cookbook his mother had brought from France.

Unfortunately, Miss Richardson had also called him repulsive and ancient and implied he wore a wig along with a corset. His ego was still stinging. So, yes, it was a *little* petty of him to mention *Cuisiner pour les Rois* to Miss Richardson because he didn't mean to tell her anything else about the cookbook. At least not at present. Maybe if she apologized for insulting him. Or he figured out what to do with this stinging attraction he had for her.

She stood, barely breathing—though that could be because she was laced too tightly—and waited for him to say more.

Bram's cock throbbed steadily in her direction. It had for the remainder of his stay at Granby's, whenever he'd caught sight of her. The moment he'd seen her tonight, his trousers had tightened in an instant. He'd foolishly assumed his desire for her would fade after the damned house party. It hadn't.

Her luscious mouth pursed. "This cookbook. What is it, exactly? What makes it so special? I need to know more, my lord."

Yes, well, Bram needed his cock to stop twitching whenever she was in the general vicinity. It seemed they would both be disappointed.

He leaned in. "Another time, perhaps. I'm afraid, Miss Richardson, my memory fails me at the moment. A result of my advanced years." The words were heavy with sarcasm.

Frustration gleamed in her eyes at his dismissal. "I think

your corset is laced too tight, my lord. Perhaps you should speak to your valet." A tiny smile crossed her plump ruby lips.

Delicious termagant.

Bram's fingers pressed into his thighs, if only to keep from kissing her again, something he dearly longed to do. The doors leading to the dimly lit terrace were far too close, tempting Bram to simply lead her outside and ravish her, which would be unwise at present. Far better for him to retreat in the direction of the room set up for cards and save them both from ruination.

"I bid you good evening, Miss Richardson. Enjoy your lemonade."

A smile crossed his lips as he heard another puff of pure exasperation as he walked away.

2

"What is it we are looking for again at Thrumbadge's?" Lady Theodosia Barrington blinked at Rosalind before squinting down the street. "I was quite comfortable having tea and those delicious scones. They were nearly as good as the ones you make, Ros."

"A cookbook." Rosalind looked over at her cousin. "A rather marvelous one. Entirely made of pastry recipes and the like." *Torrington's cookbook*. He hadn't made up the existence of *Cuisiner pour les Rois*. No, cad that he was, he'd merely declined to tell her where she might find a copy.

Maybe I shouldn't have asked him if his corset was laced too tight.

"You've dozens of cookbooks. Does our visit to the booksellers have anything to do with Mr. Pennyfoil?" Theodosia's astute gaze took in Rosalind. "He greeted you personally when we sat in his small establishment and had our tea. You seem well acquainted."

Rosalind cursed the spurt of madness which had led her to taking Theodosia to Mr. Pennyfoil's small establishment.

But she'd needed to ascertain how well the tiny cakes she'd made were selling. It was an old recipe, one she'd found stuck in a forgotten drawer. As she often did, Rosalind had added some of her own ingredients, tinkering with the recipe until she was pleased. When she'd asked for one of the cakes, Pennyfoil had informed her, while glancing at Theodosia, that he had sold the last one merely an hour ago.

Rosalind had nearly swooned with excitement at her small success.

"Don't say his name so loudly," she instructed Theodosia in a whisper, sneaking a look at the maid and footman trailing them. "I don't want you to be overheard."

"You mean to enter trade with him, don't you?" she whispered back. "As Romy did with Madame Dupree. I think it a marvelous idea." Theodosia looked over her shoulder. "Something to rival Gunter's, I expect. That makes the most sense."

"Yes. A bakery or merely a café isn't nearly grand enough. I want to be a destination." Rosalind wished, not for the first time, that Romy was here to advise her on how best to enter trade and avoid scandal, though her cousin hadn't completely succeeded in the latter. But Romy was in Italy, on a grand tour with the block of ice most of London knew as the Duke of Granby, her new husband. Rosalind had written to her, of course, but it wasn't the same as being able to speak in person. It could take weeks or even months before a response was received.

And time was of the essence.

"You've always wanted to be in the kitchen, baking away. I loved when you practiced making roses, daisies, and swirls while you were decorating cakes."

"Because you were the recipient of my mistakes."

"So delicious." Theodosia gave a sigh. "You do have a way with icing. You're much better at making tiny marzipan trees than you are at playing the harp." She shot Rosalind an apologetic glance. "My mother's doing, I'm afraid. She convinced Cousin Winnie you must be musical. And you aren't."

Not in the least. Even Rosalind's singing voice left much to be desired. "How did you gain exemption from learning an instrument?"

"I'm an artist. I paint. You are an artist as well, Ros. Only your palette is dough upon which you use jellies, frostings, candied fruit, and the like." She squeezed Rosalind's arm. "You see, I do understand."

Rosalind smiled.

"And I'll be grateful if you never pluck the strings of a harp again. Gave me a headache when you were forced into a recital. As to learning an instrument, Mama says we must all find our passion, something which feeds our own hearts. She wrongly assumed yours might be a harp. But I suppose your true passion feeds all of us, does it not?"

Rosalind's smile broadened. "I like to think so. Nothing brings me greater pleasure than creating a special dessert and watching the pure enjoyment of those who taste it, all while knowing I was responsible."

"Very much like what I do upon canvas, I think," Theodosia said. "Where does Cousin Winnie think you are today?"

"I told Mother I'm posing for one of your little paintings."

Theodosia primarily painted portraits. All miniatures. The sort one might carry about as a keepsake. Lately, she'd been experimenting with creating landscapes the size of a book, excited to be expanding to art of a much larger size. Rosalind thought there was little difference between a miniature and a tiny landscape, but she knew little about art. "It was the only excuse I could come up with that might take hours. You can say if she asks that you couldn't get my hair quite right."

"Yes, we can't have her know you're visiting a man who owns a bakery. She might suspect you of doing more than kneading dough with Mr. Pennyfoil. As would anyone else who becomes aware of your friendship with him. Honestly, Rosalind, Cousin Winnie might make you wed Pennyfoil if she finds out. I don't think she'll even care that he's beneath you."

"Then I cannot allow her to find out. Mr. Pennyfoil is only a friend. He is *my* Madame Dupree."

"It hasn't been so long since there was talk about Romy and her dresses. I'm not sure anyone quite believes she isn't a modiste, though no one dares say a word now that she's the Duchess of Granby."

"But I'm much less important than the daughter of a duke," Rosalind said. "I doubt anyone is interested in me enough to bother to talk."

"I fear you underestimate the gossips in general." Her cousin nearly ran into a passing gentleman, his hands full of packages. She sidestepped, nearly pushing Rosalind into the street.

"Why on earth aren't you wearing your spectacles?" she hissed at Theodosia, pulling her skirts away from a puddle of water.

"You know why. Blythe could appear at any moment."

"He's unlikely to be at Thrumbadge's. He doesn't strike me as the sort to read." The Earl of Blythe was the object of her cousin's affections, a golden-haired god of a gentleman. Every young lady this season had set her cap for Blythe, though he didn't show a marked preference for any of them, including Theodosia, who had hopes Blythe would one day offer for her.

Rosalind thought her cousin would wait forever.

Blythe enjoyed the wealth of feminine attention far too much to marry. Another rake among the hundreds littering London society. Romy was terrified Theodosia would ruin herself over Blythe because she had made a complete cake of herself over him at Granby's house party, practically begging to be compromised.

Rosalind had promised her cousin she would watch out for Theodosia and keep her from doing anything stupid. A monumental task.

"He reads." A wistful look entered Theodosia's eyes. "Blythe *adores* poetry. He spent an entire hour reading to me once. He's very romantic."

Ugh.

Rosalind refrained from rolling her eyes. At this distance, Theodosia would have no trouble seeing her expression. "Is that why you agreed to accompany me today? So you could purchase him a book of poetry for his birthday?"

A small, secretive smile crossed her cousin's lips. "No, I've something else in mind as a gift. Far better than a book of poetry."

"You realize, Theo, how improper it is to give Blythe a gift. *Any* gift."

Theodosia shrugged. "I think your negative mood toward Blythe is reflective of your attitude toward Lord Torrington."

Rosalind slowed her steps. She spent quite a bit of time trying not to think of Torrington though it was because of him she was headed to Thrumbadge's. "What would Torrington have to do with Blythe? Or anything else?"

"Just an assumption."

"Well, it is an incorrect one. Mother arranged for our introduction at Granby's party. Our complete lack of interest in each other was readily apparent. We are barely acquainted." A warming sensation spread across her breasts and midsection as she remembered the feel of his mouth on hers. That ridiculous curl laced with silver falling over his cheek as he looked down at her. How badly she wanted to twist the curl around her finger. "We've had a total of two conversations, and both were equally unpleasant."

Theodosia shot her a dubious look. "Romy saw you together at the Ralston ball."

"Torrington was merely being polite. Mother asked him to escort me to the refreshment table, and neither of us could refuse without causing a scene." He'd thrust a glass of lemonade into Rosalind's hand while simultaneously teasing her with the existence of a rare and highly sought-after French cookbook. Then Torrington and his broad *unpadded* shoulders had disappeared in the crowd without another word. Rosalind had spent the time since the Ralston ball looking for the blasted cookbook, unable to think of anything else.

"Torrington merely handed me a lemonade and went on with his evening." The lie to her cousin came easily to her lips. "Even if he were interested in finding a wife—"

"How do you know he isn't?" Theodosia interjected.

"Because Torrington told me so himself. As I was saying, even if he desired a match with me, the feeling is not reciprocated. I find him far too old to be appealing. Much like every other gentleman my mother tries to match me with."

"Your cheeks are red, Ros."

"We're walking very fast, and I'm laced tightly. You'll be fortunate if I don't faint. Your poor footman would have to carry me back to the carriage. Think of the scene we'd cause."

"So, Torrington only handed you a lemonade? Nothing more? Romy says you were gone for some time."

"He left me at the refreshment table. I had to make my own way back to everyone through the horrible crush of guests without getting trampled."

"How very ungentlemanly of him."

"He has a sarcastic wit I don't care for, so conversing with him further wasn't warranted. We don't get on at all. I've not spoken to him since."

She and Torrington had been in attendance at a handful of

events since the Ralston ball, but he had not sought her out. Rosalind had wanted to question him further about the cookbook but had no idea how to approach him. They weren't exactly friends.

I've already surmised you would rather be fondling dough.

Something coiled rather deliciously in Rosalind's stomach at Torrington's remembered comment. A proper young lady would have been offended at his language.

Yes, but a proper young lady would also not have read a collection of erotic books. Several times. But that was entirely beside the point.

"The fact remains that Torrington never had any interest in me at all. His appearance at the house party was the result of a scheme hatched between my mother and Lady Hertfort."

"Lady Hertfort?"

"Torrington's sister." Rosalind waved a hand. "I suppose she finds me suitable. Sturdy."

"You're comparing yourself to a well-made table, Rosalind."

"There isn't any other reason why Torrington or any man like him weds a girl such as myself. The need for a wife. One that is convenient. Easy to wed. A desperate girl in her third season." She took in Theodosia, stunning even though she was squinting and feeling her way about like a blind mouse. "You couldn't possibly understand. In any case, I find him repulsive due to his age and his rakish past."

"Hmm." Theodosia gave her a thoughtful glance. "I admit, I'm relieved. Torrington will likely be at Blythe's party this evening, and I can't have you mooning at him over the punch. Thank goodness you aren't suited to each other."

"Not in the least. I told you. I don't intend to wed at all." Rosalind's heart pounded a little harder, and it wasn't because of their pace or her corset.

Torrington would be at Blythe's.

Rosalind and her mother, along with Theodosia, were attending Blythe's party tonight. She straightened her shoulders, pressing her fingers over her heart which refused to regain its normal rhythm. What would it matter if he were in attendance?

The only positive aspect of her brief acquaintance with Torrington had been learning of the existence of the French cookbook, as it might very well make her fortune. And Pennyfoil's. She found Torrington unacceptable. There was absolutely no reason for her heart to leap from her chest every time she caught sight of his silver-tinged head.

She really wished that would stop. The heart-leaping.

"So you think you might find this magical cookbook at Thrumbadge's?" Theodosia wisely changed the subject from Torrington.

"I must offer something unique if I am to become popular. Exquisite desserts that can't be found anywhere else. I must stand out from the dozens of bakeries and cafes in London. This cookbook contains such recipes."

"I agree you must stand out." Theodosia nodded. "But you've dozens of recipes tucked away, some you've been collecting for years. I've seen the little box where you keep them. Can you really improve upon your blancmange? Or that divine cake you made for my birthday? The trifle you presented at Christmas dinner was spectacular, but even so—"

"It's a *very* rare cookbook," Rosalind interrupted. "The recipes are uncommon. Different. It was Mr. Pennyfoil who first brought the cookbook to my attention." Another small lie, but she didn't want Theodosia becoming fixated on Torrington again. Besides, Torrington had only mentioned the *name* of the collection of recipes. He'd given Rosalind not one lick of information about what it contained or where she could find it. It had been Pennyfoil who'd told Rosalind the importance of *Cuisiner pour les Rois* when she'd asked. He'd agreed that obtaining a copy, though unlikely due to the book's rarity, would indeed make their establishment famous. "He's been seeking a copy for years. The original was written in French—"

"Your French is horrific, Ros."

"But there is a translation in English." She frowned. "Or at least Pennyfoil believes there might be."

Theodosia banged her shin as Rosalind opened the door of Thrumbadge's. "Blast, that hurts. How does Pennyfoil know of such a book?"

"Mr. Pennyfoil's mother once worked in the kitchens of the Earl of Ismere, whose French chef often consulted a cookbook when making some of his more spectacular desserts. The chef was so possessive of the cookbook, he let no one else look at it even though none of the staff spoke or read French."

"Very much like you cannot."

Rosalind nudged her with an elbow. "I know enough to read a recipe."

"Sounds incredibly mysterious, Ros. A secret cookbook in French. But how many ways could there possibly be to make a custard? Or a torte?"

Theodosia knew nothing about the creation of pastries and cakes. Her forte was paints. Brushes. Pastels. Pennyfoil called baking an alchemy of sorts. Knowing the exact measurement of each ingredient and how the slightest change could alter the entire taste and texture required great mastery.

"When he was a child, Pennyfoil was fortunate enough to sample some of those desserts. The chef always made extra for the staff." Pennyfoil had told Rosalind he would stay awake nearly half the night during one of Ismere's dinners, waiting patiently for his mother to bring him a small square of cake or a tart. The perfection of such pastries was what had compelled Pennyfoil to have his own bakery one day. "There is a custard which is so exquisite, so decadent, it is only made once a year." Rosalind's voice rose in her excitement, recalling Pennyfoil's worshipful account of the custard. "Can you imagine?"

"No, I cannot." Theodosia peered into the dim, enormous space of Thrumbadge's. "What if Pennyfoil is wrong?"

"He isn't." Torrington knew about the cookbook, so Rosalind knew it existed. And Pennyfoil's awe when Rosalind had claimed she might know where to find *Cuisiner pour les Rois* had been real. "An invitation to Ismere's dinner parties was highly sought after because of the desserts his chef produced. Pennyfoil told me a fight broke out once because one of Ismere's neighbors appeared, though he hadn't been invited. The dessert being served that night is said to have been *the tart*."

Theodosia stopped. "A tart?"

"Keep your voice down." Rosalind glanced around them to make sure no one was listening.

"Really, Ros. I doubt anyone cares about a tart," Theo whispered back.

"The tart was reputed to be the favorite of Louis XIV himself. The entire cookbook is filled with such exquisite desserts. A tart known to be the favorite of a king could turn a bakery into an establishment known all over London," Rosalind said. "Perhaps even all of *England*."

"So, a tart is going to make you and Pennyfoil wealthy?" Theodosia snorted in disbelief. "A tart."

"I'm sure of it. Don't you see? I'll have something unique, something that cannot be found anywhere else. And best of all, I won't have to wed. No husband."

"I suppose that's the point, isn't it?" Theodosia muttered under her breath.

"But first, I must find the cookbook." She'd searched all over London since the Ralston ball and had nearly resigned herself to approaching Torrington to demand he tell her where she could get a copy of *Cuisiner pour les Rois*, when she'd accidentally overheard one of the clerks at Thrumbadge's mention the bookseller had purchased the library of the Earl of Ismere. Rosalind was sure it was fate.

She and Theodosia strode about the cavernous space that was Thrumbadge's, their heels clicking on the wooden floor. Patrons wandered about the shelves that stretched floor to ceiling and were filled with neat rows of books. "Poetry is to your left." Rosalind pointed. "Try not to trip and knock over a bookcase while I consult with Mr. Manfred."

Theodosia's lips pursed at the admonishment before she peered in the direction indicated and floated away.

Rosalind marched smartly to the clerk manning the desk, instructing the maid and footman to stay put by the door.

Since Torrington's mention of the cookbook, Rosalind had made a practice of digging through obscure crates of books at every bookseller in London in hopes of finding *Cuisiner pour les Rois*. Today, she hoped her patience would prove fruitful. Excitement had her heart pounding. This could be it. Her success was at hand.

"Miss Richardson," Mr. Manfred, the Thrumbadge's clerk who had been assisting her, came forward. "I will assume your appearance today means you received my note that the contents from the Earl of Ismere's library have arrived?"

"Indeed, Mr. Manfred. Thank you so much for alerting me. I'm hopeful I'll be able to find what I'm looking for."

"I opened the crates myself and pulled out everything that seemed to apply to cookery. There are dozens of such books. Many are in French," he warned her. "I believe Ismere had a French chef."

Rosalind bounced on her feet in anticipation, anxious to

dig through the stack of books. *Cuisiner pour les Rois* was waiting for her.

"Do you speak French, Miss Richardson?"

"Of course," she lied. Pennyfoil knew a bit more. Rosalind knew enough. They would muddle through together.

"Good. I apologize that nothing has been cataloged yet. And should you not find what you are looking for, Thrumbadge's is expecting a shipment from France within the month. Would you like me to send word when the crates arrive?"

"That would be wonderful, Mr. Manfred. Thank you."

"This book must be important to you." He gave her a curious look, leading her in the direction of a small room set apart from the main floor of Thrumbadge's.

"Important? No. I merely have an interest in French cookery." Rosalind was determined to remain vague about *Cuisiner pour les Rois* and her purpose in wanting to find it. While she doubted Mr. Manfred would care about a collection of pastry recipes, he might well become more interested if he knew the book contained the recipe for a cherry tart so breathtaking, it became a favorite of Louis XIV's.

One careless whisper and every pastry chef and baker in London would want the recipe.

The clerk nodded and waved her forward. "Well, here you are, Miss Richardson. Again, my apologies that things aren't better organized."

Rosalind held a gloved finger to her nose to keep from sneezing at the dust in the air. She could see bits of it floating through the sunlight streaming through the small window above her. "Not at all. Thank you, Mr. Manfred."

Once the clerk left her to her task and returned to the counter, Rosalind ran her fingers down a stack of tomes atop the table. She picked one up and flipped it open. A guide on how to be a proper wife and the running of a household.

"No, thank you." Rosalind shook her head and put the book aside.

The next leather-bound tome was on the preparation of game, rabbits, pheasants, wild boar, and the like. Though it wasn't what she was looking for, Rosalind still found the book fascinating. The French terms used for braising, baking, poaching, she was familiar with, along with various spices. There was an entire paragraph on venison, for instance, most of which she couldn't quite make out because the writing had faded. She turned a page and another plume of dust floated from the pages.

A sneeze escaped her.

"Bless you."

Rosalind jumped, so startled she nearly tripped over the crate behind her. Her mouth popped open in surprise before she firmly clamped her lips shut.

What on earth was *he* doing here?

"Don't drop your book, Miss Richardson." The slightly mocking half-smile was fixed firmly on his perfect mouth. Sunlight struck his head and shoulders, making the silver in his hair gleam in the dim, dusty room.

Rosalind lifted her chin. Could he see the way her pulse jumped beneath the skin of her throat at his appearance? She willed it to stop. "Lord Torrington."

3

It never failed to amaze Bram the sorts of things one could find when poking about Thrumbadge's. Rare books on obscure subjects. Scholars wandering about with ancient leather tomes. Giggling girls, the latest romance clasped to their chests. Interesting conversation.

A plump, slightly hostile young lady with a delicious mouth who wasn't the least happy to see him.

How I wish I wasn't the least happy to see her.

He blamed his sister, Lady Richardson, and even the Duke of Granby. It had been his bloody house party after all.

Bram's heart thudded harder at the sight of her, standing amongst a stack of moldering books, obviously looking for one in particular. He hadn't seen her in at least a fortnight, the last time being when he'd spied her walking in the park with one of her Barrington cousins. And they hadn't spoken since the Ralston ball. Absence did indeed make the heart, as well as other parts of his anatomy, much fonder of Miss Richardson.

"My lord, how unexpected to find you here."

"I believe I found *you*, Miss Richardson, not the other way around."

Her luscious mouth tightened at his flippant remark, drawing his eye. Everything about Miss Richardson demanded his attention. The pale green frock draping her generously curved figure brought out the creaminess of her skin and the deep walnut of her hair. There was a tiny, almost indiscernible sprinkle of freckles across the bridge of her nose, something Bram found adorable. A crumb dangled at the lace of her bodice, probably belonging to some sort of pastry. The molten chocolate of her eyes clashed with his.

His chest constricted sharply.

Bram found Miss Richardson to be a most fascinating, gorgeous creature. Since learning of her passion for dessert making, he often imagined her baking or decorating a cake. Naked.

"I meant at a bookseller," she replied in a tart tone. "I frequent Thrumbadge's on a regular basis and have never seen you here."

"I hadn't realized you were looking for me, Miss Richardson, else I would have made myself easier to find. However, even ancient, corset-wearing rogues enjoy a good book on occasion."

She bit her lip, eyes falling to the book she held. "I've apologized for my remarks."

Miss Richardson had done no such thing.

"I don't believe you have." Bram stepped closer.

"I'm sure I meant to." A gritty sort of resignation crossed her pretty face before her features smoothed out once more. "Very well, my lord. Please accept my most sincere apologies for any insult I may have dealt you."

Moving nearer to her well-rounded form, Bram ignored the strain of his cock in her direction. "Why do I doubt your sincerity?"

"I've no idea, my lord. Ours has been a brief acquaintance. Barely noteworthy." Her cheeks pinked just a tiny bit.

"I disagree. Our discussion in the Duke of Granby's garden was entirely memorable."

The pink deepened into patches of red, flowering over her forehead, cheeks, and chest. Bram had never seen anyone, let alone a young lady, blush in such an unusual manner. It was as if someone had taken a brush and splattered her unevenly with red paint.

"We've barely spoken since, my lord."

"Rubbish." Bram cast her a sideways glance, hearing the hint of annoyance in her tone. "Are you put out because I didn't ask you to dance at the Ralston ball?"

Miss Richardson's scent invaded his nostrils. Vanilla. Sugar. Cinnamon. Like the inside of a bloody bakery. He wondered if she'd been baking biscuits or eating them. "I handed you a lemonade, didn't I? And told you about *Cuisiner pour les Rois*."

"And little else but the name." Her eyes narrowed while her fingers tightened on the book clasped in her hand. "The lemonade was procured for me under duress, as was your escort to the refreshment table. You left me to find my own way back through the crowd."

"But you seem so capable, Miss Richardson. I didn't think you required my escort."

"I didn't. But returning me to my mother would have been the polite thing to do."

Bram looked down at the tome clasped tightly in her hands. "You aren't going to toss that book at me, are you, Miss Richardson?"

"Why would I?"

"You seem annoyed."

"I find you irritating."

"Fair enough." Bram thought it a quite bit more than irritation, or perhaps he was merely hopeful. Head tilting to the side, his eyes roamed over the spine of the book, brows raised. Deliberately, Bram reached one hand behind her, his arm almost making contact with her waist. He heard her breath catch, anticipating his touch. Their gazes locked together, Bram's nose mere inches from hers as he plucked a book off the table.

"*The Preparation of Chicken.*"

"You read French."

"I do." Bram shrugged. "My mother was from Chartres, just outside Paris, so I grew up speaking both English and French. You might wish to sit down so you don't collapse when I reveal the rest of my language skills. I also know a smattering of Italian and German."

That lovely mouth pursed. "I didn't realize your mother was French."

"An émigré. She fled while others lost their heads. Worked as a kitchen maid for a time, hiding her noble background and learning to cook. My grandfather was a *comte*. Taken to *Madame Guillotine* like so many others." Gently, Bram pulled at the book she held.

Miss Richardson tugged back. "I'm sorry."

"It was a long time ago." Bram intentionally skimmed his fingers over the top of hers, and she finally released the tome with a small sound. "Ah, *How to Cook Wild Game*. Very nice, Miss Richardson."

"Don't look surprised, my lord. I've often wondered at preparing wild boar."

"As most young ladies do, I'm sure. I had imagined you striding across the moors, rifle in hand, ready to shoot an unsuspecting grouse. Or an unfortunate rabbit. But I hadn't considered a boar." Bram had a sudden, glorious vision of Miss Richardson, skirts flying about in the wind, striding through the tall grass, her hair down and whipping about her cheeks.

"Spare yourself the trouble, my lord. I've never once walked across a moor, let alone used a firearm."

"What a pity. Perhaps I'll teach you one day. Though it would probably be a mistake to show you how to use a firearm given your temper and obvious dislike."

"I don't have a temper."

Bram noted she didn't deny her aversion to *him*. "I must disagree. And you would look striking against the heather, Miss Richardson, with all that lavender color popping behind you." He turned back to the table, seeing how the blotchiness of her skin intensified, like some terrible skin rash. A deep sigh left him. It didn't matter. He still wanted her. The mottling of her cheeks and neck didn't deter him, or his cock, in the least.

"Are you looking for something in particular?" he said.

Her brows arched. "You know that I am."

Bram made contact with her shoulder purposefully while reaching for another tome, inhaling the vanilla clinging to her skin. "I piqued your curiosity."

Defiance flashed back at him. "Against my better judgement."

Miss Richardson was so determined not to like him. Partly, he assumed, because her mother favored a match between them. There was the matter of his age and admittedly somewhat tattered past, but that hadn't deterred any other young lady in London from seeking him out. She *was* attracted to him, no matter her denials. Bram could tell by the way her body arched just slightly in his direction, the tiny sounds she made when he drew too near, and of course, that terrible blush.

"I was trying to be helpful, Miss Richardson. I won't mock you for your ambitions. On the contrary, I applaud your determination." She had a singular purpose. Some gentlemen might scoff at the well-bred daughter of a viscount attempting to become a successful woman of business, but Bram did not. He found that she aspired to something more than being a wife and bearing children to be worthy of respect, if nothing else.

"Extending the olive branch of friendship, so to speak." He inhaled her, unable to help himself. She smelled like a cinnamon bun. One he desired most desperately to take a bite of.

Miss Richardson gave him a suspicious look. "You don't find it odd I wish to spend so much of my time making desserts?"

"I think everyone should hone their skills in the kitchen. No point in starving if your cook suddenly expires." Bram's second wife, Lizabet, had proclaimed surprise at how a roasted chicken came to be at the table completely unaware that an entire staff dwelled in the kitchens. He had amused himself by telling her how chickens were plucked.

"Surely, the right husband would encourage your ambitions, Miss Richardson. Perhaps even assist you."

Her lovely features hardened at the mere mention of the word 'husband'. Bram couldn't blame her. He'd probably made the same face when someone said the word 'wife' to him. At least he had before *her*.

"You said the cookbook had recipes for pastries of a unique and challenging nature," she countered, declining to address his comment. "I've consulted with . . . an associate of mine who also has knowledge of such a collection."

So, she hadn't completely believed him. Bram was only shocked she'd found someone else with knowledge of *Cuisiner pour les Rois*. The way her eyes shifted away from him told Bram that her associate was most likely male. He'd heard the rumors about Lady Andromeda Barrington playing at being a modiste before her marriage to the Duke of Granby and assumed Miss Richardson meant to emulate her cousin.

Clever Miss Richardson. She was busy making biscuits and cakes with an unnamed gentleman. Bram made a mental note to find out the identity of this baker.

"My associate—" She stumbled over the word. "Claims to know the book and has even seen a copy. There is a recipe for a tart. Made famous by —"

"Louis XIV. The Sun King," Bram interjected. The cookbook in question was at this moment sitting on his bookshelf at home, a small bit of information he *could* have shared with Miss Richardson when he first told her about *Cuisiner pour les Rois*. But at the time, he hadn't yet decided what to *do* about the young lady before him, though this meeting was leaving little doubt. "A cherry tart made with brandy, slivered almonds, custard, and a few more ingredients I won't divulge."

Miss Richardson's eyes widened. "How do you know so much about *Cuisiner pour les Rois*? Or know about the tart at all?"

Bram stepped closer to her, closing the small space between them. Unable to help himself, he glanced down, considering, as he often did, all the plump, silken softness hidden from him. That he wanted Miss Richardson was not up for debate. He'd deliberately teased her with the cookbook because he'd known she'd want it, and it would give Bram a reason to seek her out again.

At some point.

Once he decided what to do about Miss Richardson.

Which he now had.

"My mother made it for me," he said casually, flipping through another book. "Usually on my birthday."

A small gasp came from her. "Your mother made you Louis XIV's tart?" Miss Richardson looked at Bram with

53

actual longing, unfortunately not for him but for the bloody cookbook.

"She did." Bram tried not to stare at her lips. He found them incredibly sensual. The top lip fuller than the bottom and bow shaped. "I adore cherries."

Cuisiner pour les Rois was rare. Bram only knew of one or two others, friends of his mother, also émigrés, who had once possessed a copy. He doubted even the esteemed Thrumbadge's could procure the book for Miss Richardson. When first published, there had been only a few hundred copies produced of *Cuisiner pour les Rois,* all given as gifts and only to the French nobility. The recipes contained within were considered too marvelous, too royal to be shared with commoners. Copies were burned, according to Bram's mother, on huge pyres along with everything else associated with the titled class being expunged from France. Had she been caught with the book, she might well have forfeited her life.

Another squeak left Miss Richardson as her lips drew together. "I understand the tart is exquisite."

"Your," he paused, "*associate* sounds as if they have tasted some of the pastries described in *Cuisiner pour les Rois* personally." He forced himself to look away from her mouth, pretending to study another one of the books scattered about the table. What on earth was wrong with him? Every woman had lips. A mouth. Yet hers aroused him to no end. This was why Miss Richardson wasn't the least convenient. Why he was about to upend his existence and go back on a promise he'd made to himself years ago. The decision had been made the moment Bram saw her standing in this dust-filled room paging through obscure French cookbooks.

"*Maman* could make most of the desserts in the cookbook from memory," he said. "Even the *baiser du ciel.*" He turned back to her. "It translates to '*kiss of heaven*'. It's the name of the cherry tart once favored by the Sun King."

Miss Richardson made a sound. Ecstasy.

A rush of blood went straight to Bram's cock. He had to bite his lip to keep from moaning out loud.

"I didn't realize the tart had a name." She took a step in his direction, so intoxicated by the idea of the *baiser du ciel,* he expected her to jump into his arms.

"The tart *is* marvelous," Bram said. "I can see why Louis adored it so much. But there are other confections I prefer more. There is a sponge cake, for instance, using fresh oranges that is positively decadent. Difficult to make, however, if you don't have access to an orangery."

"A sponge cake?"

Good grief. Miss Richardson was in danger of throwing herself at him. Part of Bram wished she would. It would speed things up nicely.

"Yes. There's a lemon torte . . ." He allowed the words to linger in the air, deliberately teasing her. Bram decided Miss Richardson needed to be teased. Often. "A toffee cake. A torte using persimmons."

"Persimmons?"

"Some of the ingredients are unusual. *Cuisiner pour les Rois* was one of my mother's most prized possessions. After all, she risked her life to smuggle it out of France. She had thought to earn her living as a cook when she arrived in England. Instead, she met my father. He didn't inherit the title for many years. I wasn't raised in luxury." Much like Stanwell, Bram's father had been a distant relation of another Earl of Torrington in desperate need of an heir. "My mother cooked for us because she liked to, and it pleased my father. Alas," Bram laughed thinking of long afternoons spent in the kitchens with his mother. "My sister never learned to make the custard correctly."

"The custard that is so rich, it is only made once a year?" Miss Richardson breathed softly as if she were in a lover's arms. "At Christmas?"

Bram's cock twitched again. Did she have any idea how tempting he found her? Age was supposed to bestow patience and the ability to control certain carnal urges.

"The very same."

He often made the custard. The dessert was one of his favorites. He nearly shared that fact with her, but Miss Richardson was already overstimulated. "It's wondrous," he said of the custard, looking away as if catching sight of something angelic. "Like a bit of heaven on one's tongue." A rather dramatic description for a custard but one he thought she'd appreciate.

"Did your mother, by chance—" She bit her lip. "Leave you a copy of the recipe?" She looked up at him with lust-filled eyes. For a custard recipe.

Oh, Miss Richardson. The things I will do to you.

"She left me the entire cookbook," Bram said, watching his blithe pronouncement sink in. Miss Richardson, eyes wide, took a shaky breath, the near spill of her generous bosom surging against the modest neckline of her gown. Her creamy skin pushed against the lace, dislodging the tiny crumb caught at the edge of her bodice.

Bram was transfixed. *Magnificent.*

All that softness promised an assortment of delights to a gentleman who appreciated such things, which Bram did. She reminded him of a painting by Reubens with her beautiful mouth and the supple cream of her skin. He wanted all that voluptuous glory spilling over his bed where he could explore her to his heart's content. Her nipples would be taut, peaking when Bram bent to put them in his mouth. The exact color of—

"Cherries," she said, interrupting his thoughts.

Bram coughed, turning to hide the sudden tenting of his trousers. He hadn't heard a word she'd said. "I beg your pardon?"

"I asked you about the cherries for the tart. Are they soaked in brandy first?"

He couldn't answer immediately, too busy imagining how heavy her breasts would sit in the palms of his hands. "Possibly."

A frown tugged at her lips. "What possible reason could you have for not telling me? And why would you neglect to tell me *you* had the cookbook?"

Bram had his reasons.

Miss Richardson, though she wouldn't care for the comparison, reminded Bram of one of those tiny crabs he'd chased along the sand as a child, whenever his family visited the seashore. You couldn't catch the crabs by approaching directly. They sidled back and forth, resisting all attempts to be trapped in Bram's net. But if he left a pail near the water with something tempting inside, like a bit of fish or chicken, the crabs crawled inside of their own accord.

In this case, he was using a cookbook instead of chicken.

Miss Richardson made no effort to hide her annoyance that Bram didn't immediately offer up the recipe for the tart or the custard. Or even tell her whether the damned cherries were soaked in brandy. "It is my understanding, my lord, that there is an English translation of the cookbook," she said stiffly.

"Wonderful. Then you should have no trouble finding your own copy." A translation of the cookbook was a fallacy, probably fostered by French émigrés. It had been a matter of national pride to keep the book in French, at least according to his mother. Outside of his mother's friends, who were all long dead, Bram had never heard of nor seen another copy of the cookbook in London. And he *had* searched, mostly for his own satisfaction, for far longer than Miss Richardson. He might well have the last copy of *Cuisiner pour les Rois* in England.

Miss Richardson's lips trembled before she forced a smile. "Are you being so difficult because I might have suggested you padded your shoulders?"

"Don't forget the corset wearing," he replied.

"There you are." A feminine voice came from the doorway.

Bram turned to see a stunning young woman blink at him from a pair of incandescent blue eyes, marking her as a Barrington. He recognized her immediately, as they'd been introduced at Granby's house party. She was the sister of the new Duchess of Granby and Miss Richardson's cousin. Lady Theodosia Barrington.

"Lady Theodosia." He bowed to her. "How lovely to see you again."

"Lord Torrington." She cast a look in Miss Richardson's direction. "How unexpected to see you here. Digging through dusty cookbooks." She narrowed her eyes slightly, whether to pretend shrewdness or because she couldn't see clearly, Bram wasn't sure. Lady Theodosia stumbled, bumped, and ran into a great many things. He suspected she was in need of spectacles, but vanity kept her from wearing them.

"Miss Richardson said much the same. I wonder at the opinion you two have formed of me," Bram said. "I think you'd both be surprised."

His quarry watched Bram from beneath her lashes with a calculating look, likely trying to ascertain how she might wrest the cookbook from him with as little effort as possible. Miss Richardson was quite desperate to get a hold of *Cuisiner pour les Rois*.

Coincidentally enough, Bram was quite eager to get his hands on *her*.

Lady Theodosia smiled back at him. She really was a lovely girl. Stunning, as all the Barringtons were. He'd never seen a family so blessed with such good looks and copious amounts of eccentricity. Miss Richardson wasn't so different from her cousins.

"I fear I've tarried long enough." Bram bowed politely. "Manfred likely has my order packaged and ready." He tossed Miss Richardson a pointed look. "A collection of dull stories sure to remind me of my distant youth."

Miss Richardson shot him an annoyed look. "No doubt, my lord. I bid you good afternoon."

Bram wanted to kiss her again. Right here in front of Lady Theodosia and the patrons of Thrumbadge's. Cause a horrible scandal. Force a marriage neither of them wanted.

Hadn't wanted, Bram corrected himself.

"Perhaps we'll see you this evening," Lady Theodosia said as Bram headed to the door. "At Lord Blythe's birthday celebration."

"I'm sure of it." Bram inclined his head, looking directly at Miss Richardson, and strolled away, trying not to smile.

4

Torrington had the cookbook.

Rosalind drummed her fingers against the refreshment table at Blythe's overblown birthday celebration, frustrated beyond belief.

There were dozens of earls in London. Hundreds of people of French descent. Many of the most titled had a French chef. And yet how was it that *only* Torrington had a bloody copy of *Cuisiner pour les Rois*?

A French émigré. The former Countess of Torrington had been French, and Rosalind's mother had never mentioned the fact. Lady Hertfort had called on Mother at least a handful of times since the Ralston ball and never once had she proclaimed her mother an émigré. There certainly hadn't been any talk of a decadent custard or a tart fit for a king.

Rosalind lifted the cup of punch she held to her lips, took a sip, and did her best not to make a face as the liquid slid down her throat. The punch was terrible. More water flavored with a hint of fruit, but somehow still so sweet it made her teeth ache. One would think, given Lady Blythe's constant bragging at her refinement and that of her family, she would provide better refreshments.

Rosalind tapped her finger against her lips, recalling the tepid assortment of refreshments at the Ralston ball. Seemed a recurring problem. Yet another solution she and Pennyfoil could provide.

She took a small sip of the punch.

A glass of wine would have been Rosalind's preferred beverage had Mother not been watching her from across the drawing room. Her mother's gaze slid from Rosalind to a group that included the Earl of Torrington before returning to her daughter, a militant look clouding her features.

Torrington had not arrived alone.

Mother started across the floor in the direction of Rosalind, no doubt to discuss the appearance of the gorgeous, voluptuous Lady Carrington hanging on Torrington's arm. There would likely also be a lecture on missed opportunities.

I should have followed Theodosia.

And not only to avoid her mother. Theodosia was about to do something disastrous.

Rosalind looked down the hall stretching behind her. There was no sign of her cousin.

Dread, the sort you feel when you know you can't save someone, especially from themselves, was forming a small, hard knot in the pit of Rosalind's stomach. Her cousin had promised she wasn't up to something, but the secretive smile Theodosia wore on the entire ride to Blythe's home told Rosalind something different.

Mother's progress across the room was halted by one of the other guests, a woman of advanced years and poor style choices as evidenced by the out-of-date gown she wore. Rosalind didn't know the older matron, but she was incredibly grateful to her. She had no desire to be pushed before Torrington tonight, especially with Lady Carrington clinging to the earl as if she were in danger of drowning in Blythe's drawing room.

Rosalind fluffed out her skirts. She'd felt beautiful. Earlier. Before seeing Lady Carrington in a stunning gown of peacock blue decorated with wide panels of green silk. Now Rosalind felt positively awkward in her peach confection and far too girlish next to such a gorgeous creature. She wasn't even sure why she cared. Lady Carrington was welcome to Torrington. It was only that the other woman's presence would make it that much more difficult to get him alone and convince Torrington to allow Rosalind access to the cookbook.

She'd spent the remainder of the day after returning home from Thrumbadge's coming up with various scenarios by which she could ask Torrington to lend her his copy of the cookbook. All of them were ridiculous.

A burst of throaty laughter came from Lady Carrington.

Ugh.

Rosalind turned away from the scene and placed a hand on her midsection at the sudden churning of her stomach. It was merely the worry of the disaster she knew awaited Theodosia. Not the sight of Lady Carrington attempting to climb inside Torrington's coat.

It wasn't as if Lady Carrington were some over-excited girl at her first gathering since making her debut. Clinging to the first gentleman who paid her the least attention.

Disgusting behavior for a woman of her age.

Silver sparkled in Torrington's dark curls as he laughed at something Lady Carrington whispered to him. Why had Romy ever referred to Torrington as splendid? Because now Rosalind couldn't help but notice. He was breathtaking in his dark formalwear.

Rosalind turned abruptly away.

Mother had not mentioned Torrington or the possibility of a match between them in quite some time, something for which Rosalind was grateful. But her mother hadn't given up entirely; she'd brandished a list of suitors to Rosalind the moment she'd returned from Thrumbadge's. Lord Enfield, the youngest on the list, was close to fifty. Two were afflicted with gout so fierce they required a cane to get around. Baron Cotwith, the eldest at sixty-five, was so debauched, he'd been denied membership at Elysium.

Her mother's assumption that Rosalind couldn't do better than the likes of Cotwith was painful and told her how desperate Lady Richardson had become. Yet another reason Torrington must be convinced to part with a recipe or two.

Laughter filled the air of the drawing room. Rosalind glanced at Lady Carrington, who was now exerting her well-honed charms on Lord Blythe. She couldn't see Torrington, though he must be somewhere close by. The drawing room had grown much more crowded in the last half hour or so, humming with the sound of those gathered to celebrate Lord Blythe. There was a gigantic three-tiered cake on a table in the far corner of the room. Chocolate, if Rosalind's nose wasn't mistaken.

She stole another glance down the hall. Still no sign of Theodosia. If her cousin didn't reappear soon, Rosalind would be forced to go in search of her.

The more urgent problem was *Cuisiner pour les Rois*. She couldn't bribe Torrington. He had no need of her pin money. She considered, if only briefly, asking her cousin Tony for his help, but the idea of the Duke of Averell threatening Torrington to hand over a cookbook seemed ludicrous. And she wasn't quite ready to tell the duke she'd decided to secretly go into trade with a baker. Tony might feel he had to speak to Rosalind's mother.

Rosalind caught another glimpse of Lady Carrington out of the corner of her eye. A woman as shrewd as the widow circling about the room would surmise that seducing

Torrington would be the easiest solution to getting what she wanted.

But Rosalind wasn't Lady Carrington. At best, she was convenient. And seduction required talent she didn't possess, no matter how many of her father's books she'd read.

"Your brow is wrinkled in concentration, Miss Richardson. I do wonder what you're plotting." Smoke brushed along the skin of her arms. "Why do I have a feeling it involves custard?"

"And a tart." Rosalind set down her punch. "Good evening, my lord."

Her fingers sank into the folds of her skirts, nerves tingling at the appearance of Torrington. A sort of breathless anticipation filled her.

"I suspect you are up to something, Miss Richardson. I'm uncertain whether to encourage you or not." Torrington leaned an inch in her direction, bringing with him the scent of cedar, clean linen, and a hint of a cheroot. He smelled so good, Rosalind wanted to roll around in his scent, like a dog in a puddle of mud.

"What is your opinion?" The sound of him tickled the edge of her ears, blotting out everything else.

That you kiss me again.

Rosalind tried to push the thought away, but it refused to leave. How many nights had she relived the press of his mouth against hers? "You are incorrect in your assumption, my lord. I am merely enjoying the punch."

Lady Carrington's laughter echoed once more in the drawing room.

Honestly, what on earth was so amusing about Blythe? Rosalind didn't find him the least entertaining.

Torrington glanced at the lady he'd escorted tonight, handsome features inscrutable.

"Do you need to . . ." Rosalind looked upward, searching for the right word. "*Attend* to something?"

The half-smile fixed on his mouth tilted up. "I don't believe so, Miss Richardson. Besides, I feel certain there is something you are dying to discuss with me. Shall we take a stroll through Blythe's portrait gallery?" His hand wrapped around her elbow before she could answer.

Blissful heat slid up Rosalind's arm to her shoulder.

"I'm told Blythe's gallery is filled with pears, not distinguished ancestors," Torrington informed her in a delicious tone. "Should be interesting if nothing else. I've never known anyone to devote an entire section of their home to fruit."

"Pears?" Rosalind strolled beside him, as Torrington discreetly led her across the edge of the drawing room. No one paid them the least attention.

"The gallery." One brow raised. "I'm told it is covered with portraits of pears. That sounds odd, doesn't it? Perhaps a symphony of still life. At any rate, I'm *desperate* to experience them."

Rosalind bit her lip to keep from laughing. She rather enjoyed his sarcasm when it wasn't all directed at her. "I thought you preferred cherries, my lord. At least in regard to fruit."

Torrington's eyes lingered over the rise of her bosom far longer than was polite. "I adore cherries," he said in a husky tone.

Warmth stirred deep inside her. The way he spoke made it sound as if—well as if they weren't actually speaking of cherries at all but her—

Rosalind attempted to take a deep breath and push aside such erotic thoughts.

"Don't faint on me, Miss Richardson," Torrington murmured along the curve of her ear. "At least not before we've reached what I understand is an endless supply of pears in a darkened hallway."

"I won't faint." She *did* feel a bit light-headed, however. The cut of her dress required most of Rosalind be . . . contained. But her breathlessness was more likely the result of being alone with Torrington. If he had been one of her other suitors, Rosalind might be concerned she was at risk of being compromised, but Torrington wasn't looking for a wife. He would be unlikely to do anything remotely improper despite his flirtatious manner.

"You will faint if you don't cease having yourself laced so tightly," Torrington murmured under his breath. "No gown, in my opinion, is worth such efforts."

"My corset," she whispered, horrified their voices would carry to the other guests even as they skimmed the edge of the drawing room, "is none of *your* affair. Though I'm sure with your many years of experience, you find yourself qualified to give your opinion."

"Well, you have referred to me as an aging rogue."

"I'm not certain I used that exact phrase to describe you."

"Ancient rake. Elderly lecher. Feeble fornicator."

A bubble of laughter escaped her lips. "I don't recall saying any of those things."

Torrington shrugged. "I don't have any smelling salts on me tonight, Miss Richardson. If you collapse in my arms, I'll be forced to drag you into Lady Blythe's parlor, lay you on a settee"—his voice lowered to a smooth purr—"and do my best to revive you." He steered her around the corner and toward a wall lined with framed pictures lit by the muted light of a half-dozen sconces.

"You're very good at this."

"What is that?" His brows raised in confusion. "Ascertaining the lack of talent required to produce this atrocity?" Torrington stopped before an immense still life covering half the wall. A white bowl, cracked down one side, overflowed with unripe pears. "Just look at those exquisite brush strokes," he said in a serious tone. "Amazing detail work. If you look closely, I believe you'll see a worm just peeking out from one pear. Do you see the worm, Miss Richardson?"

"Your eyesight is rather good, considering," she said, shooting him an amused glance. Torrington was very charming, his sardonic wit notwithstanding. There wasn't another soul in the hall, and they were no longer in view of the drawing room.

"Frankly, one of my nieces could have painted these and none would be the wiser. I wonder that I shouldn't have Cora, that's the youngest who is all of three, create an entire portfolio of pears for Lady Blythe. I could sell them to her. Say the artist is an old acquaintance of my mother's from France." He turned to face her. "Cora's interpretation of a pear would be far better than the artist Lady Blythe seems to favor. What do you think is behind this obsession with pears?"

"Perhaps the artist is Lady Blythe herself," Rosalind answered, staring at a smaller painting of a lone pear sliced in half. Torrington's arm brushed against hers, lighting a spark up her shoulder.

"Hadn't considered Lady Blythe could be a secret painter of pears. I'm trying to picture her in a studio, surrounded by fruit, skirts fluffed up around her as she sits atop a stool, holding a paintbrush." He turned to her and smiled.

Another warm sensation coiled around Rosalind's midsection and up her chest, though she willed it to stop. "My lord—"

"I suppose I could understand cherries," he mused, his gaze once more lingering over her bosom with intent. "As I've mentioned, a personal favorite of mine."

Rosalind's nipples, of their own accord and beneath the

layers of silk and corset covering them, tightened under his perusal.

"Possibly apples due to the various hues. But *pears*? I find, even in the best instances, pears are bland," he continued, as if he hadn't just rather blatantly compared her nipples to cherries. At least she thought he had. Her experiences with Torrington had all left Rosalind feeling a bit unbalanced.

"Pears are best with cinnamon and a bit of ginger," Rosalind answered, unsure how else to respond. The entire conversation was absurd.

"Agreed. But only tolerable at best, Miss Richardson. There are other things I'd rather sprinkle with cinnamon and taste."

A quaking sensation slid all the way down Rosalind's spine.

Not once had Rosalind ever considered the eating of fruit to be erotic. Not until Torrington. Cherries would no longer seem so innocent. She took in Torrington's handsome profile, the slash of his nose and bits of silver sprinkled along his jaw.

He gave her a cheeky wink. "I confess, Miss Richardson, you are most bold, enticing me down this hallway under the guise of admiring pear portraits."

"But I didn't entice you," she protested. "Nor bring you in this direction at all. You led *me* here."

Torrington shook his head. "You could only have brought me down this dark hall—"

"It's lit by sconces. Not a score of blazing lamps, but it certainly is not dark." She held out her hand. "I can see quite clearly."

"—for one of two reasons," he continued, ignoring her interruption. "My first assumption would be that you wish to take liberties with me."

"Perish the thought, my lord. I would never take advantage of someone so elderly. It would be poor of me, don't you

68

think?" She was more amused than angered by his audacity in suggesting she might attempt to grope him. "Any other assumptions you've made, my lord, are the result of your inflated ego."

"My ego isn't the least inflated, Miss Richardson," he said with mock outrage.

"I disagree. I have a firsthand account."

"My past experience, decades of it, has told me what to expect when a young lady asks for escort to view portraits." He inclined his head and a curl of dark hair fell over one eye, giving him a rakish look. Well, more rakish than usual.

"I didn't ask—you're incorrigible, as I'm sure you're aware." Rosalind had trouble remaining stern when Torrington was so intent on being playful.

I like him. The thought settled inside her chest. *Very much.* She hadn't expected to, when they'd first met at Granby's house party. Or even when they'd spoken at the Ralston ball.

The knowledge worried her. Physical attraction was one thing. Liking someone, quite another.

"So that only leaves one other reason for luring me under the pretense of pears, Miss Richardson." His eyes widened as if he were an actor emoting on stage.

"Luring is a rather strong word, my lord."

The amber in his dark eyes sparked at her. Small creases radiated from the corner of his eyes when he smiled. A sign of his age. Or of a man who laughed often.

There was a tugging sensation in her chest. Her heart. Rosalind immediately pressed a finger to the spot, willing it away.

"Ask me, Miss Richardson."

"A gentleman would offer."

"Alas, I am merely a corseted, elderly rogue, not a gentleman. So, ask."

Rosalind looked up at him. "I should like to look at

Cuisiner pour les Rois. I don't expect you to merely hand it over to me as we barely know one another," she said in a rush. "And I assure you, promise you, I won't allow any harm to come to the book. I realize how rare it is. You can trust I will return it in good condition."

"I have no doubt, Miss Richardson. However, I can't lend it to you."

She'd hoped he would agree. "Why would you mention it to me if you didn't intend to allow me to read it?"

Torrington gave her a patient look. "What is your greatest achievement in the kitchen thus far? The creation of which you are most proud?"

Rosalind was taken aback. "Why do you want to know such a thing? It has nothing to do with the cookbook."

"Indulge me."

She had no idea why Torrington would care about what dessert she was most proud of. Or why he cared about a collection of recipes. It was a *cookbook*. She doubted he was sitting about reading *Cuisiner pour les Rois* in his free time. He was an *earl*.

"Miss Richardson?"

"I'm thinking." She thought back to all the different scones, cakes, tortes, and the like she'd made over the years, settling on one moment that meant more than all the others. Moisture immediately gathered at the corners of her eyes, and she blinked it away.

"A cake, my lord. Lemon with blackberry between the layers." The last cake she'd ever made for Marcus Barrington, the Duke of Averell might not have been her finest, but it was the one that stayed lodged in her heart. Cousin Marcus had requested Rosalind bake him something magnificent shortly before he'd left London. He would never return to the city for he fell ill shortly thereafter and died at his ducal estate, Cherry Hill. Cousin Marcus must have had a sense of the fate awaiting him, for he'd requested only Rosalind and the cake, neglecting to invite anyone else to tea. He'd eaten two slices, extolling Rosalind's talent with flour and sugar. He'd called it a gift. *Her* gift.

I love you dearly, Rosalind. Do not ever doubt the talent you possess or allow anyone else to do so. Wars are not won on empty stomachs.

Rosalind blinked at the portrait of tumbling pears directly in front of her, not wishing to burst into tears. Cousin Marcus had always been so kind to her. He'd often waved at his dining room table, crowded with Barrington women, proclaiming himself to be the luckiest of men to be surrounded by such beauty.

"A cake for the Duke of Averell. Not the current duke. The previous one." The wretched sadness of her words echoed in the empty hallway.

It was Cousin Marcus who'd saved both she and Mother when Lord Richardson had died and his heir had nearly tossed them out in the street. More than that, Cousin Marcus had believed in Rosalind.

"Lemon and blackberries." She cleared her throat, trying to swallow her grief.

Think how much worse it could be—would be—if she—

"Eight layers. The icing was an inch thick." The words trembled from her lips.

"You miss him." Torrington's voice was gentle.

"We all do."

A vision of Cousin Amanda, collapsed and weeping on the floor, merged with the memory of Rosalind's mother in similar circumstances. Rosalind had only been a child when Viscount Richardson had died. She barely remembered her father, but the agony surrounding his death had never dissipated. The sheer terror of him departing this world. It had been the same for Cousin Amanda when Marcus Barrington had died.

Rosalind had the sudden urge to bake something.

"Miss Richardson—"

She cut him off and pasted a polite smile on her lips. "His Grace often admired what I could accomplish with a bowl of flour, some sugar, and eggs." She forced her mind back to the cookbook. Her establishment would be the finest in London. "At any rate, if you will not part with the cookbook, perhaps you would allow me to simply look at it? I don't expect that you should call on me—"

"Good. I hate taking tea and discussing the weather. Utterly dull. How many ways can you express your displeasure at rain, for instance?"

Rosalind had to agree. And she couldn't very well have Torrington showing up at her home with a cookbook. "I don't wish my mother to know anything about . . ." She searched for the right way to phrase things. Torrington knew of her ambitions, but he didn't know the specifics, and Rosalind meant to keep it that way. Mother couldn't find out. At least not until she and Pennyfoil were successful.

He was watching her intently, but Rosalind found it difficult to discern his thoughts.

She cleared her throat. "I would appreciate your discretion, my lord. It would be best if Lady Richardson didn't know about my desire for the cookbook or . . . anything else."

"You find me to be an ancient, reformed rake who is morally bankrupt—"

"Your words, not mine, my lord."

"Yet you trust me to be discreet. Do you see the irony?" Torrington's hand settled near her skirts, the tip of one finger lightly caressing the fold of silk. The slight pressure had Rosalind's insides twisting pleasurably.

"I could call on you at your convenience," she said,

barely above a whisper, distracted by the intimate touch of his finger on her skirts. "You do not even have to be present—"

"Do I not? In my own home?"

"Perhaps your butler could oversee my visit. Or a housekeeper? I do not wish to put you out in any way."

"How *convenient* of you, Miss Richardson." He'd drawn closer, the warm cedar scent she associated with him embracing her as if they were lovers. "But then, you think of yourself as endlessly convenient, do you not?"

"It is a small thing I ask." She caught his gaze. A mistake. Those amber lights were mesmerizing.

I only want the custard recipe. Maybe the tart. Nothing more.

"Will you be coming to my home alone, Miss Richardson?" He leaned over her, his lips nearly brushing the curve of her ear.

"I can bring one of my cousins," she said in a halting tone, the sensation of his breath buffeting her hair, sliding down her neck. Rosalind remembered well this intoxicating feeling. It had been the same that day in the Duke of Granby's garden. "Or possibly a maid. Please?" She took a small step back and lifted her chin, studying the brush of beard along his jaw. "It's very important to me."

"I know." His eyes were soft on hers.

Warmth spilled from Torrington, all of it falling over Rosalind in a wave that made it difficult for her to remember why she'd ever found him unappealing. Or claimed him to be repulsive. She might well faint. Torrington was far too close. She couldn't breathe properly. "I think I am laced too tightly," she blurted.

"Of course you are." His thumb skimmed lightly along the curve of her cheek. "You've a cluster of freckles across your nose, Miss Richardson."

"My mother claims them to be unsightly." Why couldn't

he smell terrible? Like pomade? Or onions? Why must Torrington be so bloody splendid?

The cookbook. Focus on the cookbook.

"I disagree with Lady Richardson's assessment." The tip of one finger trailed down the slope of her nose before retreating. His usual half-smile appeared on his lips once more. "I will call on you, Miss Richardson, and bring a copy of the custard recipe."

"A copy?"

"It will have to be translated. Unless you've suddenly become fluent in French."

Rosalind nodded. She hadn't thought of that. How kind of Torrington.

"Lady Richardson will not hear of your pursuits from me. You must send word when it is convenient for me to call."

"I appreciate that you would make the time, my lord."

"I'm not so busy, Miss Richardson." Torrington's gaze dropped to Rosalind's mouth. His jaw lowered a fraction in her direction. She found herself wishing he would kiss her again, no matter his reason for doing so.

Her head tilted back, eyes fluttering closed, baring the line of her neck and anticipating the feel of his mouth. "Is this the price for the custard recipe?" she whispered in what she assumed to be a seductive manner.

Several beats passed. Nothing happened. No kiss. No press of his chest against hers. When Rosalind opened her eyes, it was to see him watching her with that irritating half-smile fixed firmly on his lips.

Rosalind's mortification slowly bled up her cheeks. She was moments away from blotchy patches of red mottling her skin. Saying a silent prayer of thanks that the lighting was muted, she struggled to find something witty to say to cover her embarrassment.

A scream of outrage and offended sensibilities erupted,

the sound coming from further down the hall and echoing toward them.

Rosalind's stomach tightened. *Theodosia.*

It only took a moment to discern what had occurred.

The shrill, strident sound which pierced the ear and startled one's nerves had come from Lady Blythe and left no doubt as to the ruination of Lady Theodosia Barrington.

5

W *hat an evening.*
Bram tossed his cloak to a waiting footman and proceeded directly to his study and his well-stocked sideboard, relieved to finally be home. Not only had he had to contend with Lady Carrington, who he'd agreed to escort weeks ago and instantly regretted the offer, but he'd very nearly kissed Miss Richardson against a poorly painted still life of pears.

She'd been so utterly delicious, standing there in the muted light of the hall, chin lifted, gorgeous mouth slightly parted. Her disappointment at not being kissed had been so evident, Bram had nearly capitulated. Then a horrified scream had filled the hallway.

The party, from that point forward, had all the makings of a Shakespearean tragedy.

Miss Richardson had gasped, covered her mouth, and gazed with determined panic down the hall from whence the scream had come. Worry had transformed her lovely features.

"Theodosia," she'd whispered.

His lovely, plump little baker had pushed away from him

without another thought, marching back to the drawing room to find Lady Richardson. Miss Richardson had whispered in her mother's ear, causing Lady Richardson to tilt slightly before nodding with resignation. A short time later, Lady Blythe, like an enormous, blustering canary, had burst into the drawing room, whispering of ruination and the bold behavior of Theodosia Barrington with a shocking lack of discretion.

Lady Richardson had been sent for, her daughter trailing in her wake. When the Duke of Averell had appeared, strolling into Blythe's home, grim-faced and shooting an icy glance to the remaining guests, Bram had thought it best to take his leave.

LADY THEODOSIA BARRINGTON, BEAUTIFUL HALF-BLIND young lady, had been ruined in Blythe's study, but *not* by Lord Blythe. The Marquess of Haven was the culprit, eliciting a round of shocked murmurs from Lady Blythe's guests.

Bram wasn't surprised because he'd been at the Duke of Granby's house party. Theodosia had been so enamored of Blythe, she'd never noticed the large, slightly predatory male stalking her like a giant housecat following behind a mouse. Or possibly she couldn't see Haven. Theodosia really needed to wear spectacles.

Oddly enough, Miss Richardson could also be accused of not seeing what was in front of her, namely Bram. Lady Carrington, for all her pouting and batting of eyes, had noticed to whom Bram's attention had wandered. She had asked Lord Rivercrest, a recent widower, for a ride home with Bram's blessing.

Is this the price for the custard recipe?

It wasn't Lady Blythe's scream that had stopped Bram from kissing Miss Richardson, but her question. Did she *really* think Bram was the sort of man who would require a kiss in return for a custard recipe?

He really must remedy her opinion of him.

Pouring himself a brandy, Bram flopped down in a chair before the fire. Watkins, his butler, ever attentive, appeared at the door. Taking a careful sip of the brandy, he let the warmth sink into his bones before craning his neck over the edge of the chair.

"Retire for the evening, Watkins."

A disgruntled noise came from the butler.

"I insist. I've no need of anything further." Bram rarely needed anything further. A houseful of servants for only one person, even if that person was an earl, often seemed extravagant to him. Privacy, the sort accorded to eccentrics and the like, Bram found much more desirable. The same had not been true for his second wife, Lizabet. She had adored being waited on hand and foot as if she were the queen or some other member of royalty.

His sister reminded Bram often that he was a titled lord and not some hermit living on a distant estate in the countryside. If it made him feel better, Margarite said, he was providing employment to those who needed it. Watkins, for example, was older than Bram and unlikely to find another position should he be dismissed. Margarite made a valid point, but Bram still missed the simplicity of his life before his father became the Earl of Torrington.

Bram's eyes flickered over the thick packet from his solicitor. A detailed report on the search for an heir to replace Stanwell, a search which now stretched across the ocean to America. He doubted the team of men his solicitor had looking under every rock and tree would uncover another distant relation. The search was futile and a grand waste of money.

The other papers contained in the packet were far more important.

Another sip of brandy slid between his lips.

Bram hadn't been a husband for a long time. Neither of his marriages had been satisfying, to either party, only brief. His first marriage had been over before it had actually begun, his wife dying of a fever barely three months after they'd wed. But it was his second marriage, to Lizabet, which had truly soured him on taking another wife. His union with Lizabet had been fraught with lies, disappointment, horrible arguments, and poor behavior. Bram had been madly in lust, though he'd mistaken it for love. Lizabet had demanded Bram dance attendance on her, and foolishly, he had. She'd been the most sought-after young lady that season, lauded for her beauty, her wit, and her intelligence. Bram had courted her with extravagant gifts. Carriage rides. He'd become the best patron of every flower vendor in London. When he'd realized Lizabet wasn't a virgin on their wedding night, Bram had been surprised but accepting. But when she'd told him casually over a glass of sherry that she was with child barely a month after they'd wed, their relationship had become openly hostile, mainly because Bram had known it was too soon for the child to be his.

After that, Lizabet made no effort to hide her lovers from Bram or to justify her behavior. She left London shortly after their discussion for a holiday in the country. Lizabet, always dramatic, had claimed that Bram was nothing more than a rake who had tossed her aside once she became with child. A convenient tale which added to his mildly tattered reputation.

When the news reached him that Lizabet had died, her lover at her side, or at least one of them, Bram had felt nothing but immense relief that the marriage was over. He promised himself he would never, ever wed or go to such lengths for a woman again.

The memory of Lizabet no longer stung the way it once had, but the echo of their brief relationship had colored Bram's existence for many years.

Bram's gaze landed on the papers from his solicitor once more. His grip tightened on his brandy. And here he was, about to be foolish again.

A cold nose pressed into his hand followed by a small whimper.

"Ah, I wondered where you were, Bijou. You're usually waiting up for me." His hand fell to the dog's head, sinking his fingers into the thick comfort of her fur. Bijou was of no discernable breed, just a large, black shaggy dog who preferred chicken over any other treat he gave her. She had been a puppy when he found her, ribs sticking out, limping along the side of the street as he left his club. Something in Bram's heart had ached at the sight of the half-starved animal. He couldn't leave her to die or be hit by a carriage.

Bijou put her paw on his thigh and rubbed the side of her head against his leg.

She was old now. Her muzzle nearly white. There were times Bram or one of the footmen had to carry her up and down the stairs because her back legs pained her. But Bram never minded. Bijou was the only female companionship he needed most nights. There had been no reason to welcome another woman into his life.

Until now.

"I'm sorry to say, Bijou, but another lady has enticed me with her charms." He scratched the dog behind one ear. "I'm as surprised as you are, trust me. I thought I would soon forget her, but I haven't. And now it appears I must take a wife because Stanwell is gone." He paused. "Well, not *only* because Stanwell has died, I must admit."

Bijou cocked her head. She was a very good listener.

"I didn't—" Bram paused and looked down into Bijou's face. "Think I would want to marry again, and I'm not completely sure it's wise."

A bark came from Bijou.

"I know, but this young lady is different. I think you would like her. But I will have to be very patient with her. She is not fond of marriage either. I must convince her to want me. I've never had to do that with a woman before."

Bijou barked again.

"I know. Very arrogant of me. But true. You were enticed into my carriage for a chicken leg. I think Miss Richardson will require much more than that. I'm starting with a custard recipe. But don't be distressed. No one, not even Miss Richardson, can replace you in my heart, Bijou."

He glanced once more at the packet sitting on his desk, mulling over the wisdom of actions, before turning back to Bijou. "I promise."

❧ 6 ❧

Rosalind stepped into the foyer and handed her cloak to their butler, Jacobson, who stood patiently hovering nearby. She'd had a simply wonderful afternoon. Kneading dough always put her in a good frame of mind. Something about the stickiness between her fingers. The smell of spices and sugar lingering in the air. Oddly enough, cherries had been involved.

Which, of course, had made Rosalind think of Torrington.

Glancing down at the flowered muslin of her dress, she was relieved to find out there wasn't so much as a crumb on her skirts to signal she'd spent the day pitting cherries and making pastry crust. Pennyfoil and she had made at least three dozen pies while discussing their plans.

When the first batch of pies had been placed in the oven, and Rosalind had a cup of tea at her elbow, she told Pennyfoil that she had located a copy of *Cuisiner pour les Rois*. But she'd hastily added, as Pennyfoil jumped up, spilling his own tea in excitement, the cookbook was not in her possession.

Pennyfoil had sat back down with a disappointed flop.

The owner of the cookbook was possessive, she'd explained. But she would be receiving a translated version of the custard recipe very soon. The remainder of the recipes would follow.

At least, Rosalind hoped they would.

The rest of the afternoon consisted of checking on the pies, icing teacakes, keeping herself hidden in the back of Pennyfoil's shop, and assuring Pennyfoil that the Duke of Averell wasn't going to burst through his doors and take him to task for dragging Rosalind into trade.

A decadent custard, Rosalind decided, would go a long way toward keeping Pennyfoil calm and launching their business partnership. Even if Pennyfoil was having second thoughts, he wasn't about to walk away from the recipes in *Cuisiner pour les Rois*.

Now all she needed was for Torrington to appear, as he'd promised, with the custard recipe.

Rosalind fretted over that. She'd sent him a note shortly after their discussion at Blythe's— a night all the Barringtons wanted to forget. Theodosia had ruined herself, with, of all people, the Marquess of Haven—informing Torrington that on Tuesdays and Thursdays, Lady Richardson paid calls and was absent the better part of the afternoon. He was free to stop by at any time. Thus far, he had not. She doubted his need to give her the custard recipe was as urgent as her desire to receive it. Perhaps she should pay a call on Torrington herself. Granted, she could hardly force him to allow her access to the cookbook but—

"Jacobson, have you ever heard of a collection of recipes containing a dessert which was Louis XIV's favorite? *Cuisiner pour les Rois*."

"Cusine per—"

Rosalind waved away his terrible mispronunciation. "A cookbook from France."

"I have not, miss. But I can check with Mrs. Hudley if you like."

Mrs. Hudley was their cook. "Yes, thank you." If Torrington didn't appear soon or he neglected to be home when she eventually called on him, Rosalind would have to accept failure or find another copy of *Cuisiner pour les Rois*. She was getting desperate. Last week, she'd even approached her cousin to ask if he'd ever dined on a special custard made only at Christmas. Tony was the Duke of Averell. Surely, if someone were to make the bloody custard, they would serve it to *him*.

Tony had rolled his eyes and asked Rosalind if she was taking nips of the scotch he kept in his study.

The butler, still holding her cloak, stared at her expectantly.

"Is there something else, Jacobson?" Honestly, sometimes gleaning information from their butler was an exhausting process. Mother said he would have made a brilliant spy.

"You have a caller, miss," Jacobson finally said, shooting her a look of concern. "A gentleman. I informed him you were out, but he insisted on waiting." He held out a card to her.

Rosalind's pulse jumped as she read the card. *Torrington.* Finally.

"I've put Lord Torrington in the drawing room. He declined tea." A frown crossed Jacobson's tight lips. "Although he did avail himself of the sideboard."

Of course he had. "Very good, Jacobson."

"Should I summon your maid?"

For propriety's sake, Rosalind knew her maid, at the very least, should be present to act as chaperone. But quite honestly, she was at the end of her third season, inching toward being on the shelf. Mother would be gone for hours yet. Their servants wouldn't dare gossip. There really wasn't anyone who would care if Torrington called on Rosalind except possibly Jacobson and his sensibilities.

"I don't think that's necessary, Jacobson. Lord Torrington is merely delivering a recipe to me." She lowered her voice. "I wish to surprise Lady Richardson. I'm making a custard, a special one." The staff knew of Rosalind's passion for making desserts as they were often the recipients of her experimentation.

Jacobson frowned again but merely bowed. If he wondered why the Earl of Torrington was delivering a custard recipe, he was too well-trained to ask. "Very good, miss. The staff won't breathe a word to Lady Richardson. I do not want to risk ruining her surprise."

"Thank you, Jacobson." Taking a deep breath, Rosalind made her way to the drawing room, reasonably assured Mother would not find out about Torrington's visit. Smoothing her skirts, she stepped through the open door, careful not to allow her excitement at his appearance to show on her face.

Torrington, a glass of what looked to be brandy in his hand, stood at the window, staring out at the small garden behind the house. He didn't turn when she entered. Instead, his gaze stayed fixed on something outside.

Rosalind couldn't fathom what held his interest. There wasn't much of a garden to look at. Her mother wasn't enamored of nature. Hated flowers until they were cut and artfully arranged in a vase. Didn't care for birds, saying the sound of their warbling gave her a headache. Claimed to be absolutely terrified of bees, or any winged insect, really. One of the reasons Mother decided on this house when they'd left their previous home was the absolute *lack* of greenery.

The garden consisted of a standard row of hedges, trimmed expertly so that not one leaf stuck out. Rose bushes sat in a circle, all perfectly pink. A small weeping willow kept lonely guard at the far corner along with a somewhat diseased maple tree which, even under the best circumstances, rarely sprouted a profusion of leaves. A stone bench sat beneath the maple's nearly bare branches, a bench Rosalind rarely sat on because it was so uncomfortable.

"Lord Torrington." Rosalind came forward, hands clasped before her. "My apologies you've been kept waiting." Her gaze slid down his lean, muscled form garbed in riding breeches and boots. She knew now those broad shoulders weren't padded. The bunched muscles of his thighs, visible beneath the tight leather, weren't an illusion either.

A rush of warmth settled inside her. She pressed a palm to her midsection to still the feeling.

"The maple needs to be trimmed." He gestured with his brandy. "I see a rotted branch. Several, in fact."

Rosalind came forward. "I'll inform the gardener." Her heart pounded harder with every step she took in his direction. The anticipation, she guessed, was over the fact he had finally brought her the custard recipe. Or maybe it was Torrington's masculinity, on full display in his riding clothes, with his curls wind-tossed and the sun sparking the bits of gray to silver.

Something stirred at her core, nearly halting her steps.

He finally turned, the slightly mocking half-smile she was coming to like a great deal on his lips. "Come here, Rosalind." The husky command brushed over her shoulders. "I've brought you something."

Rosalind's breath hitched at the intimate use of her name, but she kept walking, drawn to Torrington as if he were pulling her toward him with a length of string.

He inhaled slowly at her approach. "You smell like cherries, Rosalind. Vanilla. Sugar. Why is that?" The tiny lines at the corners of his eyes deepened.

He's pleased to see me.

The knowledge sent a spike of pleasure through her, unstoppable and entirely blissful. She tried to focus on getting the recipe, but the only thing she could think of was the tight fit of Torrington's riding breeches. "I don't think I gave you leave to address me by my given name, my lord."

"Oh, you didn't." The grin on his beautiful mouth stretched wider, taking Rosalind's breath away. "But I like Rosalind better. And we're friends, are we not?"

"Are we? I don't recall deciding we were. But I suppose we are." She wasn't sure how else to refer to her furthered acquaintance with Torrington. They were either arguing or he was being flirtatious, which then left her wanting him to take liberties. And now she liked him. Which was making things that much worse.

Focus, Rosalind.

"Oh, good." He cocked his head, eye on her bosom. "Then allow me." Torrington's hand reached out and carefully plucked a small bit of pink frosting from the neckline of her bodice. He'd discarded his gloves, and Torrington's hands were . . . *large*. Graceful. Warm where they briefly touched her skin.

She wanted them on her body.

Dear Lord, where had that come from?

"You had a bit of pink frosting just there." One finger traced the piping along her neckline while Rosalind watched in fascination. "What have you been up to, Rosalind? I'd venture you weren't walking in the park or sifting through old books at Thrumbadge's. Not smelling of cherries with frosting on your"—his eyes flicked to the rise and fall of her bosom—"person."

Torrington's fingers were elegant. Long. The nails neatly trimmed. A gentleman's hands. Except for the tiny cuts on two of his knuckles. Those looked as if he'd been in a fist-fight. His thumb had a purplish tint beneath the nail. It was possible Torrington didn't spend all his time being charming.

"Rosalind?" His hand dropped. "You're frowning. Are you angry? Or puzzled? I can't tell which."

"A teacake." She looked away from his hand. Several *dozen* teacakes. Pennyfoil had been decorating the small rounds when she'd arrived, and Rosalind had decided to help. She'd been so careful with the dough and the cherries for the pies, worried over crumbs from the crust, but there hadn't been a thought given to the pink icing for the teacakes getting on her clothes. "I was—having tea with a friend."

"You've also got a bit in your hair." He nodded toward her left ear but made no move to pluck out the bit of pink as he had on her bodice. "Were you tossing the cakes at each other?"

"No. Of course not." Her eyes fell back to his fingers now lightly curled against his thighs, wondering about the cuts. And how those hands might feel trailing between her breasts. A tiny sound escaped her.

"Rosalind? Are you well?"

"Quite," she said firmly, ignoring the increased coiling sensation in her stomach. "Have you brought me the custard recipe?"

"I have." A curl hung next to his cheek, tempting her to wind the strands around her fingertip. Cedar floated into her nostrils along with the scent of wind and the outdoors. Torrington was more tempting than a hundred cookbooks.

"May I have it?" Rosalind stretched out her hand. "Please."

"I translated and copied it myself. Didn't use my secretary."

"Good for you, my lord," she shot back, frustrated at his delay. "I'm sure you have perfect penmanship."

"*Years* of experience."

Rosalind was growing weary of the constant reminders about his age. When had she stopped thinking of him as an aging rake and begun thinking of him as just Torrington? Every reference made Rosalind feel foolish, especially when faced with his magnificence. And those overly tight riding breeches.

"I've apologized for my insults, but to be fair, my lord, you would never know of them if you hadn't been eavesdropping."

"Insincerely apologized." His smile never faltered. "The recipe." He patted the space over his heart.

Rosalind's hand wavered in the air as she waited for Torrington to take the recipe out of his pocket and place the paper in her fingers. Nothing happened. Not very different from when she'd been convinced he meant to kiss her at Blythe's but hadn't. She tapped her foot impatiently, mainly as a way to distract herself from the fact she was enjoying herself. Immensely.

"Very well." Torrington made a sound of resignation and moved to set his brandy down on the table. Turning back to her, he took hold of his coat and pulled the sides open. "Do you see the slip of paper? In my pocket. Go ahead and take it." There was a challenge hovering in his eyes.

She took a deep breath, *thankfully*, because she wasn't laced too tight today. It was difficult to properly roll out pastry dough when she couldn't even bend. "Why—" Rosalind blushed furiously and pulled back her hand. "Why can you not just hand it to me?"

"I'm afraid that's impossible." Torrington gave her a pained look. "Tremors in my fingers. Happens to we elderly gentlemen. I'm always dropping things. Very tragic."

Rosalind narrowed her eyes at him. "Yet you held on to your glass of brandy with no problem whatsoever. And I must ask, my lord. Can we not allow the matter of your age to rest? I grow weary of defending my actions."

He leaned forward, enough so that one of those delectable curls dangled before one eye. "Care to give it a tug?"

Rosalind coughed. Sputtered. Tried not to laugh at his antics. "You, my lord, are a fine example of an earl in his declining years—"

"Rosalind." He made a tsking sound. "You were doing so well."

Her heart squeezed, very softly. "A paragon of ancient masculinity."

Torrington snorted. Then laughed outright, a rich decadent sound that did nothing to dispel the ever-growing hum along her skin. "Ancient masculinity?"

Rosalind shrugged, knowing she'd won whatever game it was they were playing. Torrington nodded toward the piece of paper. "You only need take it from my pocket, my brazen baker. Custard making awaits."

My brazen baker. She was unbelievably pleased at the title.

"Open your coat wider." Rosalind flapped her arms open. "Much wider." Her entire hand and part of her arm would brush against Torrington's chest if Rosalind dared reach for the recipe at present. "You're making this oddly difficult, my lord. I thought we were friends."

"*I* never said we were friends. I merely asked if *you* thought that the case." He winked.

"You are splitting hairs." Rosalind's legs wobbled slightly as she took a step toward him, reaching for his pocket. The motion sent her breasts crashing into the warm, muscled wall of his chest. She thought of his thighs, encased in leather, only inches and several layers of skirts from hers.

As she closed her fingers around the scrap of paper sticking from his pocket, Torrington pulled the edges of his coat together abruptly, trapping her into an unexpected embrace. He was so incredibly warm and smelled . . .

wonderful. Rosalind had to stifle the sudden urge to nuzzle her nose into his neck. Possibly pull at that mischievous curl hanging over one of his eyebrows.

"Do you have the paper between your fingers?" His nose sifted gently through her hair.

"Yes." Her body flared sharply, like an ember being stoked to a flame.

"I'm not sure if I've mentioned this, Rosalind. But you smell of cherries. Which I adore."

"You've said as much." The air in her lungs was shaky. "Often." Her body throbbed delicately next to his larger form, trapped unbelievably against his chest. Her free hand trailed over his ribs, palms heating from the muscle hidden from her.

Torrington jerked at her touch. She looked up, surprised, to find him—*wincing*? At her touch?

Horrified, Rosalind immediately stepped back, paper in her hands. She looked down at the rug beneath their feet, then out the window, anywhere but at Torrington. It was not the first time she'd mistaken his intent. Torrington merely liked to flirt with her and keep her off balance. "My apologies, my lord."

"Not at all. I am a little sensitive in that spot." He turned from her and back to the window.

Rosalind couldn't imagine what was so fascinating about the blasted maple tree aside from the rotten branches.

"Do not sit on the bench outside, Rosalind. Not until you've had the tree trimmed else you might well be injured," Torrington said with mild concern. The sort any friend would share with another.

Friends. Like Pennyfoil.

Pennyfoil *was* her friend. And her partner. Torrington was —something different.

Rosalind's gaze ran over Torrington. Very unlike Pennyfoil

who most closely resembled a stork with ginger hair. "Thank you for bringing me the recipe."

Torrington said nothing for a moment, before his lips twitched, ever so slightly. "Make the custard, Miss Richardson. There is a secret to ensuring it is fluffy. Light. Airy like a cloud. I realize that is a strange way to describe a custard. I'm certain you'll figure out what I mean once you read the instructions. Make sure that the eggs you use are of normal size else there will be too much yolk and—well, you'd be surprised at how such a simple thing alters the consistency."

Rosalind's eyes widened at his instructions. "My lord, you sound as if you've—"

"Made the custard? I have, Rosalind. And I make it far more often than just at Christmas." He bowed over her hand, brushing his lips over the ridge of her knuckles. "I'll see myself out."

7

"**A**re you certain, miss?"

"Positive," Rosalind answered. "When Lord Torrington arrives, Jacobson, you are to send him here to me, in the dining room. Do not put him in the drawing room." Her hand went out, adjusting the bowl holding the custard. It was perfect. Perhaps Torrington's opinion of Rosalind's version of the custard shouldn't matter, but he'd admitted to making the dessert.

The thought of him whipping eggs with his graceful hands did something to Rosalind.

She pushed aside such blatantly carnal thoughts. Pennyfoil had beaten eggs, rolled dough, and iced tea cakes and not once had the sight of him doing so turned her legs to jelly or twisted her insides pleasurably. It was merely because she and Torrington had once shared a kiss.

Something she had no intention of doing with Rudolph Pennyfoil.

At any rate, Torrington's opinion of the custard could be important to the success of Pennyfoil's.

Her hand gripped the edge of the bowl of custard. *Penny-*

foil's. Yes, it sounded elegant. Sophisticated. And absolutely no one would guess at Rosalind's involvement. Which was exactly the point.

She straightened the spoon beside the bowl.

Though it was the wisest course, Rosalind couldn't help the slight pang at the knowledge no one would ever know that she was responsible for so many of the magnificent creations that would soon grace Pennyfoil's display cases. But there was no other way. Whether the establishment was named Pennyfoil's or not, the fact remained that Rosalind would have her independence. There would be no reason or need for her to marry. Even her mother would be forced to admit it.

Rosalind had sent a note to Torrington earlier, and he'd promised to arrive promptly. She once more smoothed down her skirts, taking in the dining room table. She'd had fresh flowers brought in. The plates were set just so, along with napkins. The custard would be scooped out in a perfect portion along with a bit of the cherries she'd prepared. Presentation was often as important as the actual dessert.

"Lady Richardson—" Jacobson started to object.

What was Jacobson still doing hovering about? She'd forgotten he was even here.

"Is out shopping with the duchess," Rosalind finished for the butler. In a stroke of true good luck, Mother had gone shopping with Cousin Amanda and would be gone most of the day. Theodosia, stuck at Haven's run-down estate, had sent an entire list of items she needed her mother to procure for her. "She won't return for hours. And not a word to Lady Richardson when she does." Rosalind gave the butler a pointed look. "I mean it, Jacobson."

"Miss—" The butler's face had grown stern, almost fatherly in disapproval.

The very last thing Rosalind required was to have her

butler deciding what was best for her. Mother was quite enough. "I know about you and Gert," Rosalind said calmly, lifting her chin.

A gasp, then a gurgle came from the butler. Like a gutted fish.

Rosalind pressed her lips together, holding back a smile.

Jacobson, stiff and proper man that he was, had formed a surprising attachment to Rosalind's maid, a slightly bawdy girl with bright red hair.

"I won't say a word if you don't." She wouldn't normally engage in such tactics, but Rosalind wasn't about to be dictated to by the butler. Besides, Torrington had already called on her once. It would hardly matter if he did so again. The worst that could possibly happen would be Mother assuming she could restart her campaign to make a match between Rosalind and Torrington.

Jacobson paled. He opened his mouth. Closed it. Finally, the butler nodded, mouth drawn into a thin line. With a bow, he stepped away as the arrival of a carriage sounded outside.

Rosalind peered down at the custard, admiring the rich color. Some of the ingredients for the custard were unusual but not too strange. Nutmeg, for instance, was fairly standard. But not the pinch of cardamom. She often tinkered with recipes, convinced she could improve upon the original. In the case of the custard, Rosalind had added a minuscule amount of anise. She'd prepared some stewed cherries which sat in another, smaller bowl off to the side. A last-minute choice on Rosalind's part to pair with the custard because the tartness of the cherries mixed well with the hint of anise.

It had absolutely nothing to do with the fact that Torrington adored cherries.

Pennyfoil had nearly wept when she'd made the original version of the custard for him yesterday. Taking a spoonful, he'd sighed as if in the midst of a religious epiphany. Between spoonfuls, he'd told Rosalind that all the pies and teacakes had sold out within hours. While Rosalind went over the ledger, double-checking Pennyfoil's entries, her partner went to work on making more of the custard under her watchful eye. She'd have to tell him about adding the anise when she visited next. Their partnership was already showing signs of success. They'd made a small profit in a short time. Now that they had the custard recipe, Rosalind expected their business to do even better.

A knock sounded on the dining room door before Jacobson swung it open to reveal Torrington, curls falling over one cheek, mouth tilted in his usual half-smile. His gaze fell on the table, taking in the two plates, spoons, custard, and cherries. He waited until Jacobson departed before greeting her.

"Hello, Rosalind," he drawled.

The smoky rumble settled pleasurably inside her. "Miss Richardson," she reminded him.

"I don't think so." One side of his mouth tilted higher. "I prefer Rosalind."

"Do you merely ignore what you don't agree with? Does no one deny you?"

Cedar and clean linen filled her nostrils as he came closer. Rosalind had always claimed the smell of a freshly baked batch of scones to be her favorite scent, but now she thought it might be Torrington.

His mouth stretched into a brilliant smile, stealing what little breath was left in her lungs. "Not usually. Only you, Rosalind." A graceful hand waved over the table. "What have we here?"

"I've made the custard." She lifted her chin proudly. Next to the custard sat the stewed cherries, crushed, and sprinkled with sugar. "With an accompaniment."

"So I see." The amber in his eyes sparkled as they lowered

to the tops of her breasts. "I adore cherries." One elegant finger traced the outline of a plate.

Rosalind stared at his hand, thinking of his fingers circling a—cherry. "I remembered."

Their eyes caught for a moment, his so intent on her, Rosalind finally had to look away. Torrington had the ability, with merely a look and a few thinly veiled innuendos, to raise all sorts of wicked thoughts and feelings in her. She'd dreamt of Torrington last night and afterward had spent a great deal of the night thinking about the nature of arousal. Specifically, *her* arousal.

She turned to the custard, but upon looking at it, she immediately had another rush of sinful thoughts.

Good lord. It's only custard.

Putting a scoop of the custard on each of the two plates, she placed a spoonful of the cherries beside it.

"Shall we sit?" He pulled a chair out for her, his breath fanning across her shoulder as a hum started beneath her skin.

"Yes." She took her seat, heart hammering in her chest, and smoothed down her skirts.

"You look lovely, by the way." The words caressed the air around her neck.

Rosalind wore one of her favorite dresses, a pale rose frock edged with a tiny row of lace at the bodice and sleeves. The dress wasn't extravagant and not cut so sharply it required her to be tightly laced. The last thing she wished to do was become breathless with Torrington in the room.

"Thank you."

Torrington pulled out his own chair, angling it so that he faced her instead of the table. Pulling off his gloves, he laid them carefully aside.

Rosalind swallowed, her eyes following the movements of his hands. "I'm rather eager for you to taste the custard.

97

I made a few small changes. I hope you'll approve, my lord."

"I'm certain I will. I suspect I would adore anything you placed before me."

Rosalind inhaled softly as their eyes caught and held once more. "Why does everything you say sound slightly improper? I'm never sure if you are serious or not."

"I'm always serious about being improper. That is something I don't joke about." Torrington picked up a spoon. "As I mentioned when I gave you the recipe, I've made the custard many times myself. Secretly, of course." He shot her a glance. "I expect your discretion, Rosalind, in return for my own."

"You have it." A smile tugged at her lips. His presence overwhelmed her senses. Intoxicated her. As if she'd drunk an entire bottle of champagne.

"Earls are expected to have a variety of skills," he continued. "Most completely useless. How to play whist. How to find a proper valet. The study of Greek."

"Greek?"

"Possibly interesting but not useful. How many people in London speak Greek?" Torrington rolled his eyes. "Learning to cook *is* useful but definitely not taught at Eton or Harrow."

"Which did you attend?"

"Eton. And before you ask, I excelled in history and mathematics."

"An interesting combination." Rosalind found it hard to look away from Torrington. She noticed everything. How one side of his closely shorn beard held more gray than the other. The brackets around his mouth when he smiled, which was often. The lone curl that no matter how often he pushed it back seemed to fall against his cheek.

"My sister once hosted a grand dinner party. The guest list contained some of London's most influential titles. The Marquess of Hertfort is very well connected."

Rosalind knew that to be true because her mother had once remarked that Lady Hertfort seemed to know everyone.

"Margarite's cook, though skilled at roasting a leg of lamb, hadn't created anything special for the dessert course, or at least nothing Margarite felt would impress her guests, especially the Duke of Castlemaine. He couldn't have merely a chocolate toffee cake. Not as the guest of honor. I'm not sure why. I happen to like chocolate toffee cake very much."

She smiled at that. "Lady Hertfort wanted to impress Castlemaine."

"Indeed, she did. So, Margarite swore her kitchen staff to secrecy, threatening to sack them all if they said so much as a word, and sent a note to me. She begged me to arrive that morning, insisting I prepare something worthy of a duke."

Her heart skipped ever so softly at his words.

"*Maman* had taught me to make the custard. I possessed an aptitude for such things. Margarite did not."

Rosalind tried to picture this elegant, handsome man with a riot of curls hanging about his cheeks, descending into his sister's kitchens, scattering the staff, and making a decadent custard in secret. "You like to cook."

Torrington smiled at her. "I shared my mother's love of being in the kitchen, something my father allowed as long as I kept up my other studies. She and I spent a great deal of time up to our elbows in flour or chopping vegetables for a stew." He held up one pinky finger to her. The tip was missing. "Sliced off the end while cutting up a potato. My mother nearly fainted at the sight of all the blood." He laughed softly, his face unguarded so that Rosalind could see the boy he once was, lost in his memory of a day spent in the warm confines of his mother's kitchen.

"I am often comforted by the scent of vanilla and sugar." He leaned close to Rosalind for a moment and inhaled slowly before leaning back.

She had to stop herself from following.

"Margarite's cook was scandalized at seeing me in her kitchen. One of the scullery maids, shocked at my appearance, dropped an armful of plates." He cocked his head at her. "I kept her from getting sacked. It was my fault for stepping into the kitchens unannounced."

"That was kind of you." Rosalind had the inclination to cup Torrington's face and brush her mouth against his. All because he'd been kind to a kitchen maid. Many fine, titled lords wouldn't have cared.

Good lord, what was wrong with her?

"Imagine, an earl whipping up a dessert for a duke." He gave a soft laugh. "His Grace heaped rapturous praise upon Margarite's cook and even insisted on meeting the poor woman, who blushed and stammered. Poor Cradditch. I worried she'd expire on the spot."

"You allowed her to take credit."

"I did. What else should I have done? Admit the truth? Cradditch was a wonderful cook and served my sister well for many years. She retired a year or so later and now lives in Cornwall with her daughter."

Were all reformed rakes so kind? Or so capable in the kitchen? Bore so much affection for their sister they would risk their reputation by making a custard for a dinner party?

Oh. Her heart squeezed gently once more.

Rosalind insisted it stop.

Torrington took a spoonful of the custard and scooped up some of the cherry mixture, placing both in his mouth as Rosalind watched in rapt attention. The only thing better than watching his hands, she mused, was the movement of his equally beautiful mouth.

An appreciative sound came from his chest as the spoon left his lips, his tongue licking a bit of cherry off the side.

She swayed in her seat, nearly overcome with . . . *lust.*

Rosalind knew full well what she was feeling. Her father's books had been very descriptive. She may also have experimented on herself in an attempt to satisfy her curiosity. So far, she'd had only mild success. Nothing at all like the delicate, pulsing heat between her thighs that Torrington invoked.

I may not survive if he runs his tongue along the spoon again in such a way.

"The Duke of Castlemaine was so enamored of the custard, he insisted on being given the recipe, which Margarite declined to do. He retaliated by trying to hire her cook, but Mrs. Cradditch declined for obvious reasons. This custard is still a bone of contention between the duke and Margarite."

"Didn't Lord Hertfort insist she give the duke the recipe?"

"One does not 'insist' with Margarite. Hertfort learned that fact early in their marriage. Hertfort doesn't press Margarite and thus does not need to sleep with one eye open." Torrington took another bite and sucked on the spoon, watching her the entire time. "This is very good."

The throbbing between her thighs became more insistent. Rosalind shifted in her seat, squeezing her legs together.

"Do you also cook?" His eyes were alight with some undefinable emotion. "Or is it only making custards and cakes which thrills you?"

You thrill me.

The thought unsettled her. Rosalind tore her eyes from Torrington's lips and fingers, struggling to maintain what little decorum she had left. "I do enjoy cooking, but my passion is the making of pastry. Desserts. Confections. As you can imagine, Lady Richardson finds that my time icing cakes is less important than paying calls."

"I don't doubt it."

"But I believe there is artistry in creating a cake," she said.

"Determining the exact position where I'll place the delicate roses made of marzipan. Or deciding how I should alternate the layers so that when the cake is cut and one piece lifted out, the appearance causes everyone to gasp in pleasure. It is difficult to explain the feeling I have when someone tastes a nibble of one of my tarts, for instance, and I see the pleasure it brings them." She gave him an embarrassed smile. "I tend to ramble, my lord. I know it is only making a cake. Not at all like being a true artist such as my cousin, Theodosia, who paints miniatures. Not of pears, of course, but people."

"I disagree, Rosalind. There is art in creating something so beautiful and delicious. Food is one of the greatest pleasures life has to offer." He paused, and the timbre of his voice lowered. "Among other things."

Rosalind drew in a long breath, her entire body feeling as if she were being licked by flames. "I like to think so."

"You'll find no judgement from me over your ability to make a pie or a scone. But you'll have to keep it secret that I enjoy doing so as well. And a good roasted chicken. The secret to the chicken is what you stuff inside the cavity to flavor the meat."

Even stuffing a chicken sounded sensual coming from Torrington.

"Oh." Dear Lord. Rosalind was about to swoon for the first time in her life. Torrington and all his . . . gloriousness combined with his love for her beloved pastries and the way he sampled custard had become . . . a seduction of sorts. She wanted very much to be in the kitchen with Torrington. Watching him move about. Whipping eggs or . . . something.

Exactly as she did with Pennyfoil.

It would be nothing like my time with Pennyfoil.

"I could easily have opened my own establishment or perhaps found myself in the kitchens of the Duke of Castlemaine. My French is excellent. No one would suspect I wasn't from Paris. Every duke wants a French chef in his employ." He rolled his shoulders. "But instead, I'm an earl."

Rosalind sensed he'd rather be a chef with a kitchen to command. "So you don't find my ambitions to be outlandish?"

"No. We must all do things which feed our souls, Rosalind. But the structure of London society means that discretion must be practiced. My sister's plea for me to make custard is a perfect example. Friendly advice, Rosalind. Should you choose to take it."

She very nearly told him of Pennyfoil, sensing he would understand, but Rosalind kept silent. It was enough he didn't condemn her for her ambitions. "Do not keep me in suspense any longer, my lord. I must have your opinion of the custard."

Torrington dipped an elegant finger into the bowl of custard and held a dab to her lips. "Close your eyes, Rosalind. Let the custard sit on your tongue. What is it you taste?"

Rosalind's heart nearly beat out of her chest at the intimate gesture. Tentatively, she wrapped her mouth around his finger, forcing herself to focus on the taste of the custard and not the warm finger in her mouth.

"The anise." Rosalind sucked gently at the remaining custard on his finger.

A hungry look entered Torrington's eyes. "The flavor is not as strong or noticeable when you also take a scoop of the cherries." A seductive purr came from his chest. "Here. Try a bit more." Dabbing his finger into the custard again, Torrington added a bit of the cherry mixture.

Rosalind parted her lips, her gaze locked with Torrington's. As the custard-covered digit slid into her mouth, she flicked her tongue along the length of his finger before sucking gently at the tip.

A sound came from Torrington. Blatantly sexual and male. His eyes dropped to her mouth. Pulling out his finger, he rubbed it along her lower lip, growling when she grazed his finger with her teeth.

The space between her thighs gave an insistent pulse. The air fairly swarmed with her impending ruination. It hadn't been how she'd planned to end Torrington's visit today, but the custard. The cherries. The firm, muscled form only inches from hers.

She'd always planned to take a lover. Eventually.

According to her father's books, there was an act a woman could perform on a man involving a certain male appendage that was very much like tasting the custard from Torrington's finger.

"You must consider"—his smoky tone turned rough as it slid over her breasts—"how it will taste without the cherries."

The edge of her skirts tugged, ever so gently, in Torrington's direction.

"Why—" Rosalind sounded quite breathless—"do you like to pull at my skirts? You've done so before." Her senses had become muted to everything else but Torrington and the taste of the custard on her tongue. Including the fact that they were seated in the dining room with the doors open and a small army of servants milling about the hall.

"Because I want to touch you," he whispered, hunger stamped plainly on his handsome features. "And I should not."

She drew in a long shaky breath and glanced in the direction of the door. Jacobson wasn't stationed directly outside, or at the very least, he didn't seem to be observing them from the shadows. Rosalind's eyes returned to Torrington. She lowered her hand, boldly pulling her skirts up until her ankles and calves were exposed.

A low moan left her as the heat of his fingers wrapped around one silk-clad ankle.

Watching her, Torrington dipped his finger in the custard once more. "Open your mouth, Rosalind."

His words vibrated over the length of her body. She obeyed him instantly, grazing her teeth along his finger. Rosalind sucked and licked at the custard on Torrington's finger as his other hand trailed further up her leg, heating the skin beneath her silk stockings. His thumb teased at the hollow of her knee.

A thread of moisture made its way between her thighs. The pulse of the blood beneath her skin sped up along with the beat of her heart. Rosalind bit her lip. Her legs splayed open in invitation.

Torrington's eyes fluttered shut. His palm stretched over the top of her thigh, fingers pressing into her skin. "I'm not"—the rasp of his voice was barely above a whisper —"going to ruin you in your mother's dining room." His eyes flew open, the amber more pronounced, giving him a predatory, almost feral look. "But it isn't because I don't want you." He flipped aside the edge of his coat. It was impossible to miss the tenting of his trousers. "Do not attempt to convince yourself otherwise."

He sounded angry. *Ravenous.*

Torrington's hand ran back down the length of her leg, pausing to draw his finger around the curve of her ankle once more before removing his hand completely. Then he sat back in his chair as if nothing untoward had occurred and took another spoonful of the custard.

Rosalind loosened the grip on her skirts, smoothing the muslin back into place. She felt dizzy. Warm. Aroused. Disappointed. Mildly horrified she'd been so bold with Torrington to the point he had to inform her he wasn't going to ruin her.

A throat clearing sounded from the door.

"Excuse me for the interruption, miss," Jacobson intoned. "But Mrs. Hadley has a problem in the kitchen which requires your attention. It cannot wait until Lady Richardson's return but must be dealt with immediately."

Rosalind nodded, knowing there was no issue which would require her presence in the kitchen. She hadn't realized Jacobson would be so concerned for her virtue, although he probably hadn't had a reason to worry before now. Thank goodness he hadn't decided to make an appearance when Torrington's finger had been in her mouth. "A moment, Jacobson."

I would have been compromised and forced to wed Torrington.

An unpleasant, bitter knot drew tight inside her chest at the thought of marriage.

The butler bowed, shooting Torrington a look of warning before retreating.

Torrington gave a soft chuckle. "Your butler has impeccable timing, Miss Richardson. You've done a fine job on the custard. And while I appreciate the addition of the cherries, you may wish to reconsider the anise."

"I will, my lord. Thank you," she replied in a clipped, precise tone, knowing Jacobson had only retreated a few steps. Once Torrington departed, Rosalind planned to return to her room, possibly with the remainder of the custard, and contemplate whether she could be seduced by the earl without it resulting in a more permanent attachment.

He pulled a piece of paper from his coat pocket and held it out. "Orange sponge cake."

"Sponge cake?"

The half-smile appeared on his lips and the lovely creases, the ones at the corners of his eyes, appeared. "Yes." He leaned over, pretending to push away his plate of custard. "And when you present it to me, Rosalind," Torrington's breath tickled over her ear, "do not wear a corset or I will cut it off you."

Rosalind's lips parted in surprise. A pulse of pure longing shot between her thighs. "I see."

His voice was low. "I certainly hope so." Torrington stood and pulled on his gloves. He bowed and took her fingers, his mouth hovering along her knuckles, tongue flicking between her middle and ring fingers.

Her knees buckled. She reached out with her free hand to take hold of the table for support.

Torrington's eyes glinted at Rosalind. "I bid you good afternoon, Miss Richardson," he said in a loud voice for Jacobson's benefit. Releasing her hand, he strode out, his steps echoing as the butler showed him out.

Rosalind kept perfectly still, holding her breath and the table, not trusting herself to move until the sound of Torrington's carriage departing met her ears. Taking a seat, her limbs continued to tingle. Lifting the spoon, she took another mouthful of the custard without the cherries.

She frowned. He was right about the anise. It only made sense with the cherries added. Looking down at the slip of paper he'd given her, she saw the recipe for an orange sponge cake written out carefully in a masculine hand.

Torrington *did* have excellent penmanship.

There were comments along the edge of the recipe from him on preparation. The proper way to extract the juice from the fruit to maintain some of the pulp. A tiny orange was scribbled in the corner. Her fingers traced the shape of his letters as she remembered the feel of his hand on her thigh.

Torrington wanted to seduce her. Rosalind intended to allow him to do so.

Neither of those things would be at odds with her ambitions, Pennyfoil's, or escaping whatever older gentleman her mother deemed suitable for her. Logically, men and women had physical relations all the time. Marriage and affection weren't requirements. The fact that she liked Torrington would only make the experience more pleasurable.

She scooped the remaining cherries into the bowl with the custard and took up her spoon. It was possible the custard tasted different when eaten off the finger of a splendid, amber-eyed gentleman with silver in his hair.

Rosalind smiled to herself and made her way to her room.

There was only one way to find out.

❧ 8 ❧

Bram sat back against the fine leather squabs of his carriage as it pulled away from Lady Richardson's home. Aroused. Frustrated. Annoyed. Rosalind was incredibly fortunate he hadn't locked them both in the dining room and compromised her. Loudly. With witnesses.

Patience.

But Bram wanted so much more than to simply ruin her.

He pinched the bridge of his nose, willing the hardened length of his cock to stand down. Rosalind wanted him to seduce her—which Bram would gladly do—but *not* wed her. She was a stubborn, confounding woman. And her opinion of him, as a man dishonorable enough to bed her and not marry her along with him being far too old and having had a past, obviously hadn't improved much with his generous offer of the custard recipe.

Bram slammed his palm down on the leather.

There had once been a time when he would have been *thrilled* at the knowledge that a young lady, one he desired as much as Rosalind, wanted nothing from him other than to be seduced and properly ravished with no further expectations. She thought of him as a friend, and nothing else.

Friends. Bram snorted in derision.

Friends did not speak of food in erotic terms, unknowingly or otherwise. Or pretend to adore cherries when they both knew it was Rosalind's nipples Bram was actually considering. Nor would a mere *friend* lick custard off his damned fingers while mimicking having his cock in her mouth.

Where had Rosalind learned about such a thing? Because it was clear, after watching her nibble the cherry off his finger—

A grunt of frustration left him, compounded by the insistent, unrelenting throb of his cock.

The entire direction of his otherwise peaceful existence had been altered by one plump, pastry-making young lady. One he hadn't wanted originally but who now consumed his thoughts. Had he not attended Granby's party, Bram might have missed Rosalind entirely and settled for a more convenient, less bold young woman who didn't have such a luscious mouth. One who he could have forgotten after begetting an heir. A girl whom Bram wouldn't have wished to be his companion as well as his lover.

He'd never wanted a woman to be his companion. Not even Lizabet.

That's why he'd gotten a dog.

Bram's desire for Lizabet, up until he'd realized she enjoyed bedding every man in London but him, paled in comparison to the way his entire body seemed to curl in arousal at the mere sight of Rosalind.

Dear God. Rosalind inspired the most erotic visions. He often imagined dribbling chocolate over her naked form, which he would then lick off every inch of her skin. Now he had the image of her sucking on his finger to add to it.

Today, when Bram had seen her standing at the dining room table, proudly displaying the custard for his approval, he'd found himself . . . *longing* for her. It had caused a physical ache. And not just in his cock.

Bram slapped his palm against the seat in frustration once more. He was in a trap of his own making. One built of patience and not only for Rosalind's sake, but his own. He didn't care for the subterfuge being practiced, but neither did he want Rosalind to end up hating him. Another union as he'd had with Lizabet would be untenable for Bram. But *forcing* Rosalind to do anything would be a mistake. She would be resentful of having her choice taken from her.

Yes, but you've already taken her choice.

His fingers drummed on the leather.

He had. He'd probably regret doing so.

But Bram *couldn't* allow Lady Richardson to continue to toss Rosalind at a series of unsuitable gentlemen, not when he meant to have her. Not only was it humiliating for Rosalind, but the idea of another man even taking her arm made Bram long to punch something. None of them appreciated her as he did. Lady Richardson didn't understand, but she had agreed Bram could handle things as he saw fit.

His chest tightened right over the area of his heart. Now that organ throbbed in tandem with his cock, and Bram willed it to stop. He would need to make arrangements for a box of oranges to be sent to Rosalind later today so she could make the sponge cake. Bram prayed, as he rarely did, she would perfect the damned cake sooner than she had the custard.

In the meantime, Bram meant to pay a visit to Mr. Rudolph Pennyfoil.

It hadn't been difficult to find the identity of Rosalind's business partner. Taking a hack from her home and allowing the driver to drop her a block away from Pennyfoil's establishment, then walking down the alley to enter a back door wasn't incredibly secretive. Rosalind hadn't so much as looked over her shoulder as she'd knocked on the door for entry.

Careless of Rosalind. Reckless. Much like licking the custard from his fingers in Lady Richardson's dining room. Or raising her skirts so Bram could trail his hand along the curve of her knee.

A groan left him at the memory.

Bloody hell.

Bram rapped on the top of the carriage. "Take me to Hagerty's," he instructed his driver.

A few rounds in the boxing ring were sure to take his mind off Rosalind. It was difficult to stay aroused when you were being pummeled. If he were lucky, Bram would return home in a few hours, a little worse for the wear but with a head clear of amorous thoughts.

He'd be bruised. Sore. But nothing that a snifter of brandy and a hot bath wouldn't fix. And his mind blissfully not on Rosalind.

9

Two weeks after she'd nearly been ruined in the dining room, Rosalind was once more contemplating seduction. She'd thought of little else while perfecting the orange sponge cake since Torrington's last visit. It was a daring, scandalous thing she meant to do. It was possible that most young ladies of good family didn't think overmuch about physical relations. But thanks to Lord Richardson's extensive, obscene collection of books, her opinion on the subject was far different from that of her contemporaries. Also, there was the matter of Cousin Amanda, the dowager duchess. She believed all young ladies needed to be forewarned about what their futures held and not be led blindly into the marital bed. The dowager duchess had been quite thorough in her descriptions.

The point being, Rosalind was fairly knowledgeable but still innocent, which made her vastly curious and not the least afraid. A dangerous combination.

Since she intended to remain unwed and free of the encumbrance of a relationship so she could devote all her energies to her craft, Rosalind saw no reason to not satisfy that curiosity. Remaining unwed didn't necessarily mean she must remain a virgin or deny herself the benefits of physical pleasure.

Rosalind stood before the mirror in her bedroom, turning back and forth in one of her oldest dresses, slightly out of fashion, but one cut loosely enough that it didn't require the wearing of a corset. She thought the absence of the corset much more important to today's mission than the style of her dress.

Tugging at the bodice, she fluffed the lace at the neckline, making sure not too much flesh revealed itself. Her bosom hadn't been nearly so large when she'd been fitted for this dress, and she didn't want bits of her poking out in the wrong places. Torrington seemed to like her more generous form— or at the very least, didn't seem to want to seduce her less because of it.

Do not wear a corset when you present me with the sponge cake.

Nothing in the world could make her wear a corset today after hearing such a declaration.

Arriving at Torrington's home, alone, with no chaperone, stretched the very bounds of what was proper. Even Viscount Richardson, who undoubtedly had seduced a great number of young ladies, Rosalind's mother included, wouldn't have approved his daughter's course of action.

Actually, Lord Richardson would likely have been far more scandalized at the knowledge his daughter had entered trade.

Yesterday, Rosalind had spent the entire day in Pennyfoil's company, preparing the orange sponge cake and discussing their future. They were in agreement that the current space housing Pennyfoil's would not be large enough for their future plans. The small bakery was already overflowing with customers. Word had spread about the custard. Largely due to Rosalind convincing Pennyfoil to allow their patrons to sample it. She'd had him set out several small plates, offering a taste to anyone who came in to purchase another pastry. One of those customers had been the valet of Baron Rothwell. After tasting the custard, he'd immediately asked for a full order, which he'd then taken back to his employer in Mayfair.

The very next day, Rothwell's cook had arrived to place a rather large order of the custard for a dinner party Lord Rothwell was giving the following evening. The day after Rothwell's dinner party, the small bakery was inundated with requests for the custard. Pennyfoil had even had to hire a girl for the front counter.

The orange sponge cake, now perfected, was spectacular and would likely produce the same results.

Pennyfoil was overjoyed.

He had found them the perfect location for their new establishment near Berkeley Square, but the expense was great. Mr. Ledbean, the owner of the building, wanted far more than Rosalind and Pennyfoil could afford at present. Yes, they were making a profit, but not so much that they could spend all of it on their new establishment. Rosalind, footman trailing her, had walked past the building earlier, knowing in her heart the location would be perfect.

Pennyfoil told her he would visit Ledbean again the following day and see if there was any movement on the price. If not, there were other buildings in London.

She gave herself one last glance in the mirror and, satisfied with her appearance, made her way down the stairs. Rosalind had prepared an entire tale to explain her absence today should her mother inquire after her whereabouts.

The butler awaited her downstairs. "Miss Richardson."

"Jacobson." Rosalind gave him a small nod. "I'm off to see my cousin." She didn't bother to specify which one. If Mother thought she was visiting the Averell mansion, she wouldn't ask for details.

"Yes, miss." He nodded. "Another box of oranges has been delivered to the kitchens."

"Wonderful." Oranges had appeared the day after the custard tasting, and a new box had arrived every few days. Torrington had access to an orangery, either his own or someone else's. There had been no note on the box of fruit when it was delivered, but the oranges couldn't possibly have been from anyone else.

Rosalind claimed to the kitchen staff she'd ordered them to experiment with a new recipe. Not a complete lie. She held out her hand. "My basket, please."

Jacobson handed her the small basket Rosalind had packed earlier containing the orange sponge cake. After pulling back the napkin to ensure the cake was tucked safely inside, Rosalind tilted her head in the direction of the drawing room, hearing the muted voice of her mother. "Do we have a caller?"

"Lady Hertfort, miss. She arrived a short time ago. Lady Richardson asked not to be disturbed."

"Very good. I might be gone for some time. A walk around the park will likely be in order after cake." She patted the basket. Rosalind had no idea how long seduction might take but thought it best to be prepared.

"I'll inform Lady Richardson, miss."

Rosalind hopped into the carriage, secured the sponge cake, and clasped her hands in her lap. Nervous energy had her toe tapping against the floor of the carriage as the vehicle lurched forward. She hoped Pennyfoil could negotiate the price down with Ledbean. Rosalind wanted to do it herself but had been sternly reminded by Pennyfoil that she was a silent, *discreet* partner.

She firmly pushed aside her irritation. Pennyfoil was right.

What did it matter that she couldn't speak to Ledbean directly? Rosalind's final season was at an end. Pennyfoil's was well on its way to becoming a success. Mother would be forced to accept the inevitable.

Add to all that the fact that Rosalind wasn't wearing a corset or underthings and would likely return home with another magnificent recipe but not her virginity? It was quite a lot to contemplate.

🦋 10 🦋

A short time later, Rosalind was ushered into the foyer of Torrington's home, her eyes moving over the tasteful, elegant décor. She'd never been to an unmarried gentleman's home without a proper chaperone.

Her expectations of Torrington's home were based on the house she'd lived in until her father's death. Rosalind had been expecting thick burgundy velvet covering every surface. Plush, expensive rugs. Lots of gold tassels. Gilt gracing every surface. Statues of cherubs engaged in questionable activities. Poorly painted art, also of a questionable nature. Mother had not redecorated, for some reason, only managing to force most of the more dubious furnishings out of view of visitors.

Torrington's home was far different than Rosalind had imagined.

The interior was warm. Comfortable. Smelling, oddly enough, of chocolate and not stale cheroot and dust. The furnishings, though masculine, weren't overly heavy or intimidating. No cherubs dotted the tops of his tables or were hidden in an alcove. Rosalind didn't have an appreciation for art—that was her cousin Theodosia—but even she could see that the paintings hanging in Torrington's foyer were likely done by a master artist.

"Lord Torrington is expecting me," she crisply informed Torrington's butler, a tall, faintly disapproving older gentleman. "I am Miss Richardson."

Rosalind had sent Torrington a note late yesterday asking if she could call. He'd responded that he would be at home but said little else. A brief rush of panic filled her at the thought that perhaps he'd forgotten. About inviting her. Telling her not to wear a corset. All of it.

She clasped her fingers tighter around the basket.

"I am Watkins, Lord Torrington's butler." He looked behind Rosalind to her carriage, in expectation of someone else popping out. When no one appeared, the butler gave a sigh and shut the door. "Shall I take that, miss?" He nodded at the basket in her hand.

"No, thank you. This"—she held up the basket—"is for Lord Torrington."

"Very good. This way, Miss Richardson."

She'd expected to be led to the drawing room and offered tea while she waited for Torrington, but the butler passed by what Rosalind took to be the drawing room. Instead, he led her down a long hall to a set of stairs at the back of the house.

Watkins waved her forward.

"The kitchens?" While Rosalind was more comfortable in a kitchen than most, she didn't find it a particularly good spot for seduction. She bit her lip. He had forgotten. Or he'd been teasing her and nothing more.

Rosalind willed such mortifying thoughts away before her skin could redden. She'd no desire for Torrington to see her looking like a moldy cherry.

"Not to worry, miss. There isn't anyone about."

"There isn't?" She took a step forward.

"The staff has the day off, except for myself. And Bijou, of course. She's down there with his lordship."

Bijou. Was she a kitchen maid? Or the cook?

"I see. Thank you, Watkins." Rosalind held on to her basket and descended the steps, her nose immediately assailed with the chocolate she'd caught a whiff of earlier in the foyer. The space wasn't overly large, but it was well lit. Light streamed in from a series of windows set up high along one wall. Neat rows of pots and pans were stacked on shelves beneath the windows along with bowls, ladles, spoons, and the like. Strewn across an immense, pitted worktable was a large pad of chilled butter on a plate, a tin of flour, and two large bowls. The scent of chocolate hung heavy in the air.

Torrington stood before a small pot, stirring something. Chocolate, she supposed, given the aroma lingering in the air. The spoon moved rather ferociously before Torrington paused and took a taste from the spoon. He hummed while he worked, a low sensual tune that set Rosalind's pulse to beating harder.

Her legs trembled, the basket tilting to one side.

The space was warm, so Torrington wore no coat. The sleeves of his shirt had been rolled back, and Rosalind caught a glimpse of muscular forearms dusted with dark hair. He turned and looked over at her, the lone curl, a bit longer than the others, dancing against one flour-stained cheek. There was a tiny bit of what looked like dough caught at the edge of his jaw, stuck to his beard. He licked the side of his mouth where a drop of chocolate had landed.

Rosalind had never seen anything more beautiful in her entire life.

A pile of what she thought were rags moved just to the left of Torrington. The rags formed into the shape of a shaggy dog with coal-black fur. A bark erupted from the animal along with the thump of a tail as it looked at Rosalind in expectation.

A small hall led to what was probably the scullery and the larder, but no sound came from that direction. It seemed she and Torrington were truly alone.

"Hello, Rosalind."

"My lord." She bent down and held out her hand to the dog. "Bijou, I presume."

Bijou sniffed her hand, then her skirts before thumping her tail again. She pushed her head against Rosalind for a scratch behind the ears and then retreated once more to her spot near Torrington.

"Very polite, Bijou." Torrington tossed what looked like a bit of chicken into the air and the dog caught it. "Good girl." He turned and smiled at Rosalind.

Oh, he's splendid.

"I didn't realize you had a dog."

"Every ancient lecher needs a pet, don't you agree?" Torrington gave her a roguish wink.

"Not once did I refer to you as a lecher." Honestly, she might have. Once. Her opinion of the man before her was now far different.

"Hmmm." A doubtful look was tossed in her direction. "I know titled lords are supposed to have a dog useful for hunting. Or perhaps one of those tiny animals which are carried around on pillows—"

"A Pomeranian?" Her mother had once had a friend, Lady Crestwell, who'd had a Pomeranian.

"Yes, my wife owned one of those little dogs. The second wife. I can't remember the animal's name, but she had a pink silken pillow for it. Nasty thing. Bit me on the ankle once. Bijou is much better behaved."

"You've been wed twice, haven't you?" she said before she could stop herself.

"Yes. The first time when I was very young. Barely twenty. We were married three months when she perished from a fever. Anna didn't care for dogs. The Pomeranian belonged to my second wife."

When he didn't elaborate or tell her anything more, she said, "How long have you had Bijou?"

"A very long time. The longest relationship I've ever had with a female." Torrington was back to stirring the pot before him, his face turned away so Rosalind couldn't guess at his expression. His hips swayed as he moved back and forth, stirring the chocolate and tossing little bits of cold chicken from a plate by his elbow to Bijou.

Warmth spread across Rosalind's chest. Torrington was so much more than she'd expected.

"I brought the sponge cake for you to try and to thank you for the oranges." She cringed at her overly polite tone. Torrington knew she wasn't here to thank him for the oranges and have him try a bloody sponge cake. At least, she assumed he did.

He paused in his stirring. "No corset, I hope."

Rosalind's pulse picked up. "No." Or any underthings. A bold decision, made impulsively, only moments before she'd left her home.

He turned and held up the spoon he'd been using. "Come here, Rosalind," he coaxed, the timbre of his voice lowering just slightly.

Rosalind stepped in his direction and opened her mouth.

"Try this." Torrington held the spoon to her lips.

Her tongue flicked out before her mouth closed over the tip of the spoon while Torrington's eyes followed the movement of her lips. "Chocolate." A sound of pure pleasure came from her. "With a touch of hazelnut. Maybe some cinnamon."

"Ah, Rosalind," he purred. "I so love the sounds you make."

"I didn't realize I made sounds."

"When you tasted the custard, the most intriguing little noises came from you." Torrington watched her with a mischievous glint in his eyes. "I enjoyed every one. I hope to hear you make them again."

Rosalind's cheeks heated. She hadn't thought she'd made any sound while licking custard off his fingers. "What are you making?"

"I'm making *pain au chocolat* or a *chocolatine*." One side of his mouth tipped in his usual half-smile. "It isn't from the cookbook, just something delicious I tasted once while in Paris last year. Depending on what part of France you are visiting, this pastry might have a different name. I'm honestly not sure *pain au chocolat* is entirely a French invention. But it doesn't matter. I find them delicious no matter who is responsible."

Another pastry not well known in London would be a feather in her cap and go well toward Pennyfoil's further success. Rosalind returned his smile, her heart threatening to fly out of her chest. But not because of Pennyfoil's and *pain au chocolat*.

"I adore chocolate." She patted her hip, suddenly feeling self-conscious. "As you can probably tell."

"You seem overly concerned with such things, Rosalind. I am not." Torrington leaned over her, his mouth inches from hers. "I find you perfect as you are."

Please kiss me.

"I made this to accompany the sponge cake." He held up another spoon, this one layered with fluffy cream. "Part of me wondered if you would bring not only the cake but one of your cousins. Or a maid."

"With no corset? Perish the thought." She closed her lips over the edge of the spoon, moaning softly as the taste exploded on her tongue.

"Have I whipped the cream properly?"

The ache returned between her thighs. There shouldn't be anything remotely wicked about whipping cream, chocolate, or tasting anything from a spoon except that when Torrington was involved, everything became sinful.

"I—" Her fingers gripped the edge of the worktable, nails biting into the wood to steady herself. Rosalind had the urge to fling herself at him and never let go. A knot tightened inside her at the thought, the fear so absolute it momentarily banished the sheer joy of being with Torrington. She had the fleeting notion to run up the stairs and never return.

"—Didn't expect to meet you in the kitchen." She looked down at Bijou who had closed her eyes.

"What *did* you expect?" He set down the spoon, leaning toward her once again, his nose gliding along her temple, gently forcing her back until Rosalind felt the press of the worktable against her upper thighs.

"That you'd give me an opinion on the sponge cake," she said, reaching inside the basket to brandish a bit of the cake at him. "Would you like a taste?"

"Yes, Rosalind." The teasing glint disappeared from his eyes. "I most certainly want a taste. Of *you*. I think of little else." His hands shot out, taking hold of Rosalind's hips.

"Oh." The cake in her fingers fell to the floor with a plop as he half-lifted, half-pulled her to sit atop the table.

"Spread your legs, Rosalind."

"I—yes." She took a shaky breath, the blood pulsing ferociously beneath her skin, and inched her legs apart.

Torrington's hand hooked beneath the hem of her skirts, drawing them up to her knees before wedging himself into the space between her thighs.

Rosalind's skin warmed all over with anticipation and a small bit of mortification at her own actions. There was the matter of her boldness, which she kept regretting on and off. For instance, the absence of—

"You're not wearing any undergarments, Rosalind." Torrington was looking at her, his shocked gaze shot full of amber lights.

"No," she said in a shaky voice. "I am not." Rosalind tried to control her breathing as she reached for another piece of the orange sponge cake. "Will you try some?" she whispered, holding out a small slice.

Torrington's hand slid up her stockinged legs to her thigh. He traced a circle with his forefinger before parting his mouth and taking a bite of the cake, his eyes never once leaving hers. Eating the cake from her hands, he licked up every last crumb, tongue gliding along the side of each finger —an unexpectedly, erotic experience—before pressing a kiss to the center of her palm.

"I might swoon," she said in a rush. "I don't, usually. But—"

"Breathe, Rosalind." He brushed his lips gently over hers, claiming her mouth with exquisite care until she was grasping at the collar of his shirt. His mouth moved to trail along the slope of her neck, whispering in French against her skin.

I should have learned how to speak French.

The warmth of his fingers glided through her already damp flesh, teasing at her slit, circling the sensitive nub hidden in her folds. The very same part of herself Rosalind had fumbled over with her own fingers. Her experimentation had never felt like this.

"What about the *pain au chocolat?*" She choked at the feel of his thumb circling her entrance. "Won't it be ruined?"

"The fact that you came to me without wearing any underthings is far more important." His lips fell on hers once more, hungry, and urgent, licking at her mouth, while his fingers—

A whimper left her. "Please. More of that." Hips tilting forward, Rosalind plucked at his shirt. He wasn't wearing a cravat, and her fingertips made contact with the heat of his skin. Her hands ran over his chest to his ribs, hesitating at the edge of his trousers.

Torrington's mouth pulled away. He rested his forehead against hers.

Her hand trailed down from his waist, feeling the hardness beneath the fabric. Curious, Rosalind traced the outline, fascinated at the way he pulsed and twitched beneath her fingers. She wanted to see him. Touch him. She—

Torrington gently pushed her down until her back was against the table, her legs dangling haphazardly off the edge. His free hand trailed down to her breast, toying with the lace at her bodice before running one finger back and forth until her nipple peaked beneath his touch.

Her legs kicked against his. "Please don't stop," she moaned.

When he pushed her skirts all the way up her thighs, Rosalind's eyes fluttered shut. Silence stretched between them. She could feel her arousal, the wetness growing between her thighs intensifying the longer he looked. Embarrassed, she tried to squeeze her legs together, but he stopped her.

"No." He pressed a kiss to her thigh. "You're beautiful, my brazen baker. Perfect, in fact. Don't move. Don't open your eyes yet."

The heat of his body disappeared for a moment before returning. She gasped as something warm was dribbled over her skin. The scent of chocolate filled her nostrils.

He's poured chocolate on me. Another rush of wetness slid between her thighs.

Torrington dribbled a bit more chocolate along her naked hip. His finger painted something there.

"B for Bram," he growled possessively. Then his mouth fell to her hip, licking and nipping at the chocolate.

Bram. Torrington's given name.

"Short for Abraham?" She stuttered as his nose nuzzled into the soft hair of her mound.

"Yes." His reply hummed into her flesh, his tongue flicking out to taste her.

A low sound left her throat, one Rosalind didn't even know she could make.

He painted more chocolate over her thighs, licking and nipping as he did so, but came no closer to the one part of Rosalind which required his attention. The illustrations in her father's books had been highly educational, but their descriptions of this act and her imaginings paled in comparison to the reality. Her eyes opened, peeking down at the dark streaks painting her thighs and stomach.

For one thing, no chocolate whatsoever had been mentioned.

Torrington's dark curls, laced with silver, tumbled over his cheeks as he licked at her skin. "I adore cherries, Rosalind," he whispered against one plump thigh.

"So you've claimed many times." Her fingers tangled in the silk of his hair.

"They often"—his tongue sank into her wetness—"top the finest desserts." Torrington's mouth closed over the tiny aching bud hidden in her folds. The edge of his beard chafed pleasurably along the inside of her thighs.

Rosalind's back arched off the table, her mind nearly incoherent with pleasure. *And all this time I thought it was my nipples he meant when he spoke of cherries.*

Curls twisted against her fingers as her hips pushed up. He had such beautiful hair. As marvelous as the rest of him.

Torrington paused and looked up at her. "Go ahead and

give it a tug, Rosalind. Just so you can assure yourself it isn't a wig."

"I've apologized—" The word ended on a whimper as he sucked her back into his mouth, his tongue making the most divine circles. She pulled at his hair, urging his mouth to give her the release she so desperately needed. The sensation only hinted at those nights when she'd been alone in her bed.

Torrington flung one of her legs over his shoulder and Rosalind dug her heel into the muscles of his back. What an idiot she'd been to assume he'd worn an ounce of padding.

"I want to see you naked," she whimpered. "No clothing."

A satisfied grunt came from him. His tongue swirled and sucked, driving Rosalind into a near frenzy. His palm settled on her stomach, stretching possessively to hold her in place.

Another moan left her.

Torrington is my spark.

She cried out, startling poor Bijou, as her pleasure peaked sharply, bursting before her eyes like dozens of tiny stars all flaring at once. It was far more marvelous than she'd ever imagined. "Bram."

Her hips writhed on the table, thrusting herself more firmly into his mouth as his tongue coaxed every bit of bliss from her trembling, bucking form. Just as it retreated, he forced another wave upon her, pulling so much pleasure from her throbbing body, Rosalind was sure her heart had stopped. She knew nothing but him in that moment, wanted nothing else but Torrington, as dangerous and unwelcome as that thought would become. Once the last of the waves receded, leaving her spent and panting, Rosalind glanced down her body, unsurprised to see herself stretched across the kitchen worktable as if she were being prepared for a feast.

"Spectacular." He nipped the inside of her thigh.

"Yes, it certainly was." She sat up on her elbows and

looked down at him. He'd let go of her legs and propped his chin up on top of her stomach, watching her.

"Ruin me further," Rosalind choked out. She might never allow herself to be so close to him again once her body had calmed and her mind became less muddled. "This isn't my mother's dining room."

"No. It's my kitchen." Curls danced against his cheeks. Torrington looked so solemn. Conflicted.

"Bram." Rosalind sat up as he reluctantly stood. Her hands slid across his stomach, but his hand circled her wrist before she could go further.

He shook his head, looking far more pensive than Rosalind expected. She reached for him again, but he took a step back.

"There are things we should discuss, Rosalind," Torrington said quietly. "Important things. I won't take your virtue in my kitchen."

How bloody disappointing.

"But why? I won't cry ruination," she pleaded. "My opinion of marriage hasn't changed, I promise." Torrington didn't want to wed. He'd told her so before he kissed her at Granby's house party. "I wouldn't expect you to do the honorable thing, if that concerns you."

The line of his jaw sharpened. "How progressive of you."

She bit her lip. Shouldn't Torrington be pleased Rosalind wouldn't expect him to wed her? That she wouldn't tell anyone she'd been compromised? "I thought—"

"What did you think, Rosalind?" he shot back in a rough, almost angry tone.

"That you don't want to marry. That you would be happy I expect only friendship." She couldn't bear to think of Torrington as anything other than a friend. "You've been so kind to share the recipes with me and I appreciate—"

KATHLEEN AYERS

Rosalind's hand hovered in the air between them before she drew it back once more. "I wanted—"

It was exactly the wrong thing to say. A snarl came from Torrington as he looked down at her, his handsome features clouded with anger, mouth drawing into a thin line. One of the spoons fell from the table with a clatter, spraying whipped cream all over the floor.

"Is that what you think this is, Rosalind? An exchange of *favors*?" His voice was low and full of menace. "I'm surprised you would invite me to fuck you without first securing the recipe for *baiser du ciel*."

The crudity of his language, the assumption he'd drawn, had Rosalind falling back to grab at the worktable. "Bram."

"Stop talking. Now." He turned from her, placing both his hands on the edge of the stove. The set of his shoulders became rigid. Unmovable. "You should go, Rosalind," he said without turning to look at her. "This instant. It was foolish for you to come here alone. If you're seen, you will be as good as ruined. Forced to wed an elderly rogue who would doubt-less breed you like a prize mare." He flung her own words back at her. "You need to work on the cake. Much too dry. The candied orange rind is unnecessary."

Her heart twisted painfully. "You can't possibly think— Bram, I didn't mean to imply—"

"Yes, you did, Rosalind. Why else would you be here?" He reached into his shirt pocket and without looking at her, extended his arm, the paper clasped in his fingers. "Oh, yes. You came for this. It's a lemon torte. No need to have me taste it. Or offer yourself up again. It isn't necessary."

"That isn't—" She stopped. He wasn't going to listen to her or even look at her.

Fine. Though it really wasn't.

Carefully she took the paper from his fingers before bending to pick up the basket, still heavy with the remains of the sponge cake. She could feel the stickiness of the chocolate between her thighs. It had never occurred to her that he would draw such a conclusion or that he might wish something more from her than merely to become lovers.

"Watkins will show you out. Good day, Miss Richardson."

Torrington didn't move or turn in her direction as she made her way up the stairs and out of the kitchen. Resolutely, she straightened her shoulders, fingers biting into the handle of the basket. This was for the best. It really was. Happiness. Affection. An excess of feeling. She wanted none of those things. Not from Torrington or anyone else. Her judgement, as evidenced by coming here today, was already clouded. Better her relationship with Torrington come to an end now before any true damage could be done.

It was best to put her efforts, her *soul*, into her pastries.

⚜ 11 ⚜

Bram was a fool.

Desire had a way of making idiots out of the most intelligent of men. He'd tried to keep it from happening, yet here he was, allowing himself to be beaten senseless as a way of banishing Rosalind from his thoughts. It hadn't worked over the last week since Rosalind's visit. Still, he kept trying.

The punch from his opponent, an enormous man built like an ox, hit him square in the jaw, making Bram's head snap around.

Christ, that hurt.

"You might wish to pay attention, my lord." Hagerty, the owner of this fine establishment, stood at the edge of the ropes, watching Bram take his beating with great interest.

Bram wiped the blood from his lip and put his fists back up. This was his fourth time in the ring today, the second with the Irish butcher named O'Leary, who was now circling him with a nasty grin on his thin lips. O'Leary had taken it easy on Bram during their first go-around. Not so, this time.

When Rosalind had arrived at his house, with no corset and lacking her underthings—

So brazen. I adore that about her.

—Bram had thought things would soon be settled between them. Whatever objections she'd been harboring against Bram and marriage had been set aside. Because coming to his house, alone, with no underthings, meant she wished to be seduced. Ruining her would result in a marriage. She *knew* that.

A left jab from O'Leary caught Bram along his left side, and he staggered back.

Instead, Rosalind had thought him an unprincipled bastard. She'd expected them to be lovers, and only that, while he continued to toss obscure French dessert recipes at her. The only thing worse was Bram's own stupidity in thinking Rosalind wanted something else.

Him.

"Milord, perhaps you should call it a day."

"I'm fine," Bram snarled, staggering just slightly.

Actually, he wasn't fine. There was a terrible pain in his chest. But it wasn't due to O'Leary and his meaty fists. No, the insistent ache which never seemed to fade was because of Rosalind and the fact she wanted a tart recipe more than Bram. He'd thought—

Another brutal blow caught him in the ribs, pushing all the air out of his lungs. Bram fell back against the ropes and Hagerty started toward him, but he waved the man away.

Obtuse. A perfect description of Rosalind. Couldn't she see how *incredibly suitable* they were for each other? Not only sexually but in every other way that mattered?

He danced away from O'Leary, who was strong but lacked agility.

No underthings. No corset. Friends who understood each other.

Bram threw a right hook at O'Leary, who stumbled back and snarled.

Rosalind was fully prepared to take him as a lover, but nothing more. He'd as much as told her that a husband could support her ambitions. Encourage them. Who the hell had she thought he was speaking of if not himself? He'd be a much better partner than Pennyfoil, in and out of the bakery. How could Rosalind not see that?

Well, even if she didn't, Bram wasn't about to allow her to go about kneading bread and baking pastries with fucking Pennyfoil.

O'Leary hit him again, sending Bram to his knees.

"Hold," Hagerty yelled from the edge of the ring.

"Just need to catch my breath," Bram mumbled through a mouthful of blood.

He'd lost his temper, a rare occurrence. He'd said terrible things to Rosalind to get her to leave. After she was gone, Bram had sat on the floor with a spoon and eaten the bowl of whipped cream with Bijou at his side. The *pain au chocolat* had burned. He'd nearly sent a note to Lady Richardson that he'd changed his mind about her inconvenient daughter.

"I probably should have," he said, standing.

Bram's ribs ached. His physician, Dr. Graw, would prescribe bed rest if he suspected more than a bruise. It hadn't been required after his bout a few weeks ago when his entire side had been one long welt of purple, but today might prove worse. He'd brought Rosalind the custard recipe shortly after that first injury. Her slender fingers had slid up his ribs—a bloody marvelous feeling but one which would be much more appreciated if they were both naked—and inadvertently touched a painful spot. He'd winced and pulled away from her without thinking. It had been amusing, at the time, the idea that Rosalind didn't think he desired her. Especially because Bram had spent most of his visit that day making sure the length of his coat had hidden his mounting erection.

Perhaps it was time to end this. No other gentleman would have been so patient with Rosalind. She was bound to be angry no matter what he did.

Bram managed to get another solid shot at the butcher's chin. This time, O'Leary didn't so much as wobble.

Lady Richardson had called on Bram yesterday, wringing her hands. The more he delayed making an announcement, the more anxious she became. Wasn't the whole purpose of choosing Rosalind so that he *didn't* have to court her?

"Haven't you had enough yet, Torrington?" Hagerty said over the ropes. "I'd rather O'Leary here not be tried for the murder of an earl."

Unlike most of the finer gentlemen's boxing establishments in London, where dandies pranced around each other and threw punches no more painful than a slap, Hagerty's served a different sort of clientele. The sort that hit hard and drank hard. The first time Bram had entered Hagerty's, he'd been barely ten and his father had not yet inherited the title. He'd learned the proper way to not only box but to protect himself with his fists. Boxing was also excellent exercise if one didn't have to be pulled out of the ring unconscious.

It had only happened to Bram once.

O'Leary, whose fists resembled the slabs of beef he cut with a cleaver at his shop, grinned at Bram, showing several missing teeth. Bram wasn't a slight man. He was above average in height and kept himself fit. But the Irishman had three inches and about fifty pounds on him.

What the hell am I doing?

Bram lowered his fists. His head was already starting to ache, and one of his teeth felt loose. Wonderful. He'd be a toothless elderly rogue now.

He held up a hand to O'Leary. "I accept defeat, Mr.

O'Leary." Bram bowed and tried not to fall over. His eye was already starting to swell.

The butcher grunted in response.

"Wise, my lord," Hagerty said from just outside the ropes. "You're bleeding all over your fancy cravat. You'll never get the blood out. And I saw the blow you took." He nodded to Bram's side. "Best have that looked at. You aren't as young as you once were."

"Neither are you." Bram glared at Hagerty before shaking O'Leary's hand. "Thanks for the match."

The butcher pounded his massive fists together. Bram could well imagine his head between them. "Next time, milord."

Groaning, Bram crawled between the ropes and stepped out of the ring, taking a towel from Hagerty. His visits to this fine establishment were fairly regular, at least once a week. But he'd been here almost daily since Rosalind's visit.

"Drink, milord?" Hagerty pulled a cork out of a bottle with his teeth and brought out two glasses which appeared to be clean. Didn't mean they were, of course. Hagerty wasn't running a gentleman's club.

Bram nodded. "I think that's in order." His entire left side throbbed. He may have to send for Dr. Graw. The whisky stung the cut on his lip but helped numb the pain radiating out from his ribs. He and Hagerty drank in silence for a time, watching O'Leary take on a young man whose lean build belied the strength of his fists. The butcher fell to the mat several times.

"Dunlock," Hagerty said, nodding at the young man. "Fast, isn't he? Only man to be able to hold his own with O'Leary. Well, him and one other."

"Me?" Bram gave him a smile, wincing at his split lip.

"Nah. American fellow who was visiting London a while back. Laid O'Leary out flat. Brutal with his fists. Can't recall his name." He shrugged. "Never returned, at any rate. O'Leary was looking for a rematch."

Bram drained his glass, trying not to wheeze as he took a breath. "Thanks for the drink."

"I'm at your service, milord." Hagerty gave him a bow. "If you want a bit of advice—"

"I don't."

Hagerty ignored him. "Whoever she is, you need to either forget her or bed her. Having yourself beat to a pulp by the likes of O'Leary ain't fixing things."

"Sod off, Hagerty." Bram grabbed ahold of the wall to keep from falling down as he made his way to the bench where he'd left his coat. His head was finally clear. He could think of Rosalind and what he'd done to her in the kitchen without even so much as a twitch from his cock, which was as exhausted as the rest of him.

Good.

Bram slowly made his way to his waiting carriage, one hand pressed to his side. *Damn.* The stab in his side made his eyes water.

His driver came around the vehicle, took one look at Bram, and flung open the door.

"My lord—"

"Not one bloody word, Carson. Don't even grunt in my direction. I had a wonderful mother. I don't need another."

"Yes, my lord." Carson tried to take his arm to assist him.

He jerked away, feeling old for the first time. "And I don't need to be lifted into the carriage as if I'm an invalid." Bram took his seat, gritting his teeth at the pain streaking across his side. Every turn and lurch of the carriage had him groaning.

I may have overdone things.

When Bram finally arrived home, he tripped out of the

carriage, not even chastising Carson when the man caught him.

Watkins, eyebrows raised in disapproval, hurried down the steps. He took one look at Bram and yelled for a footman to fetch Dr. Graw. The butler helped Bram inside, half-carrying him as they started up the stairs, sending for Bram's valet and a hot bath.

"I'll have a scotch brought to you, my lord," Watkins said as they reached the landing.

Bram patted his butler on the shoulder. "Bring the whole damned bottle, Watkins. I don't even need a glass."

❧ 12 ❧

"Everything, Miss Richardson, is settled with Ledbean."

Pennyfoil barely looked up at her as he relayed the news, intent on the plate of scones he arranged for an elderly gentleman and his wife seated at one of the small tables near the counter. He stepped away to place a pot of tea on the tray.

"How is that possible?" She stood and rearranged the scones while his back was turned. Presentation wasn't exactly Pennyfoil's forte. The work area, where Rosalind stood, preparing her pastries and the like, was well hidden from the front room where the patrons enjoyed their tea. None of the customers seated at the tables or those placing their orders with Olive, the shopgirl Pennyfoil had hired to manage the counter, could see her. Nor would they. Rosalind would leave by the same method she'd entered Pennyfoil's, through a storeroom and out a back door leading to an alley behind the building.

Pennyfoil placed napkins and silverware on the tray, along

with a small pot of honey. "I've received a small inheritance," he said avoiding Rosalind's eyes. "My uncle."

"Your uncle?"

"Actually," Pennyfoil's voice wavered slightly. "My great-uncle. He was a baker as well. In Surrey. Once his shop was sold, my father thought I should have the proceeds for my own venture." He picked up the tray. "I used the sum to secure the property with Mr. Ledbean. We can start moving in next month."

Before Rosalind could ask him anything else, Pennyfoil rushed out to the front with the tray, a smile on his face as he faced the busy shop filled with customers.

She frowned at the batter in the bowl before her. Pennyfoil had never mentioned a great-uncle who was a baker, but then, they didn't share everything with each other. Or very much at all, beyond their mutual adoration of pastry and the establishment they hoped to create. Certainly nothing of a personal nature. Rosalind sensed Pennyfoil didn't want to know too much about her on the off chance the Duke of Averell came waltzing in.

Wiping her hands on a towel, Rosalind picked up the small piece of paper beside the bowl. The recipe for the lemon torte, written out for her in Torrington's elegant scrawl. He really did have lovely penmanship.

Rosalind pressed a hand to her midsection, at the hollowness that lingered there because she missed Torrington. A great deal. An unexpected, most unwelcome complication.

Torrington had made several notes in the margin for Rosalind, just as he had for the orange sponge cake. Charming little notations which brought him to mind no matter how Rosalind tried to push him away.

Roll the lemons across a table to bring out their juice.
Be careful not to use too much milk.

In the corner of the recipe, Torrington had drawn a small lemon with a smiling face.

A few days ago, Rosalind had sent a note to his home, informing Torrington she'd successfully managed the torte and to thank him for sending her a box of lemons. Apparently, in addition to an orangery, Torrington also had access to lemons. Rosalind had asked if she could call and bring a sample of the lemon torte. It seemed the polite thing to do.

When Torrington had finally replied, he'd claimed to be indisposed and unable to receive callers.

Undeterred and against her better judgement, Rosalind had arrived at Torrington's doorstep, basket in hand, lemon torte tucked neatly inside. She'd considered not wearing a corset or underthings, but given the way they'd parted previously, Rosalind wasn't certain such boldness would be appreciated.

Watkins, Torrington's butler, had denied her entrance. Lord Torrington was not receiving callers at present. Not even Miss Richardson. His lordship was under the weather. Watkins had taken the basket from her hands and shut the door.

Rosalind's gaze fell on the worktable as a flurry of panic struck her. She'd sent Torrington another note, wishing him a speedy recovery, but there had been no reply. Could he be so ill he was incapable of holding a pen? What if Torrington were in danger of—

The knot which liked to twist about in her stomach whenever she examined her feelings for Torrington moved to take up space in her chest until Rosalind could barely breathe. She pummeled the lemons she'd been rolling across the wooden surface before her, bruising the fruit.

"How can I be expected to survive without him? I won't. I can't."

Rosalind heard her mother's wail of anguish so clearly, she might have been standing right beside her. Her fingers lost their grip on the spoon, spilling the batter all over the table. Two lemons rolled to the floor.

Pennyfoil, red-faced and smiling, burst back into the kitchen. "The samples of the lemon torte were gobbled up in moments. I've ten orders for the torte." The smile on his lips faded abruptly as he took in Rosalind and bent to pick up one of the escaping lemons.

"Miss Richardson, you're quite pale." Lemon in hand, he led her to the stool and gently urged her to sit. "Are you unwell?"

"Just a bit warm," she lied. The opposite was true. Rosalind was chilled to the bone. "I think I've lost another lemon." She peered beneath the table and, spying the other yellow fruit, bent to retrieve the lemon, returning it to the worktable. "I think a cup of tea will set me to rights. Not to worry. What were you saying about the torte?"

"Ten orders, Miss Richardson. What a stroke of brilliance to offer a sample of each one of our signature recipes."

She nodded as he bustled over to the stove to fix her a cup of tea. Pennyfoil rambled on as he worked, telling Rosalind how they would likely need to hire more help for the back room once they moved into their new building. Did she have any idea of the renovations she wished to make? The color scheme and the like?

Rosalind barely listened. She was thinking of spice cake. In particular, the first cake she'd ever made. The recipe was one she knew by heart. Mrs. Norris, her mother's cook when Rosalind was a child, had taught her how to make the cake. The day had been perfectly ordinary. Rosalind had been playing with her dolls after a visit to the park when Lord Richardson had just fallen to his knees, collapsing onto the floor while sharing a brandy with Mother. The screams filling the drawing room had driven Rosalind to the kitchen, where it was warm and safe and she didn't have to see her father's twitching body.

Pennyfoil lightly touched her hand. "Are you sure you're well, Miss Richardson? I can finish this batch." He nodded at the bowl.

"No. You've the custard orders to get ready. Whenever Rothwell hosts a dinner party, we end up with dozens of new customers. We can't afford to disappoint them. I never imagined we would come so far so quickly."

"It's the recipes from *Cuisiner pour les Rois,* Miss Richardson. I told you they were unique. Exquisite. Like nothing else in London. Rothwell claims he's never in his life tasted a custard quite like ours. I suppose it doesn't hurt to mention the recipes were once only served to kings and the nobility. Now all we need is the tart and our fortunes will be made."

Pennyfoil had been gently nudging her for the recipe for *baiser du ciel* the entire week, and Rosalind didn't have the heart to tell him that there was a real possibility the recipe might never be in her possession. "I'll have the tart recipe soon, Pennyfoil. I promise."

"Wonderful, Miss Richardson. But I must ask why we are limiting ourselves. Wouldn't it be better—"

"No, not at all." Rosalind had neglected to inform her partner that she didn't have complete access to *Cuisiner pour les Rois.* He assumed she could consult the cookbook whenever she wished. "I think only presenting one new pastry or dessert at a time creates excitement. You told me that Lord Manville's cook comes by every morning hoping for something new. We must keep London guessing, Mr. Pennyfoil."

"True, true." Pennyfoil ran a hand through his thick ginger hair. "And it is wise to limit our quantities thereby driving demand for specific desserts."

"Exactly. We have the custard, the sponge cake, and now the torte."

"Rothwell adores the sponge cake. I've sent word to him that we now have a lemon torte and he'd best order his before they're all gone."

"Very wise, Mr. Pennyfoil." Rosalind's hand snaked out, grabbing Torrington's recipe for the torte and putting it in her pocket. She'd recopied the recipes for Pennyfoil. It didn't feel right to allow her partner to have the ones Torrington had done specifically for Rosalind with his special notes and drawings.

Another pang of longing for Torrington stung Rosalind, sharper than the first.

Her fingers brushed over the paper, thinking of how beautiful Torrington had been with flour on his cheek, stirring chocolate sauce. She should be grateful he'd had the sense to stop before completely taking her virtue. Becoming lovers would not have been a wise decision, Rosalind could see that now. She could well have found herself married to Torrington, or worse, her emotions might have led her to do something far more stupid.

Like fall in love with him.

"Lady Richardson is in the drawing room, miss. She is taking tea with Lady Hertfort."

Rosalind's fingers stilled on the banister. She'd snuck into the house about an hour ago, exhausted and covered with flour and bits of icing after her afternoon at Pennyfoil's, quietly avoiding Jacobson and the other servants who might wonder at her appearance. The day had stretched far longer than she'd expected, and she'd rushed to make it home for tea. An order for Lady Derby had been placed which had required a great deal of time to fulfill. Lady Derby wanted not only the orange sponge cake, but the lemon torte and an assortment of smaller biscuits and other pastries.

The order was the largest yet for Pennyfoil's. The price Rosalind had named for Lady Derby had been far higher than the sum they needed because she'd expected to negotiate. But Lady Derby's butler hadn't blinked at the price.

Pennyfoil had squealed with delight.

She'd hated to leave Pennyfoil today, but he'd waved her away. He knew Rosalind couldn't be caught icing cakes with him until the wee hours of the morning. Mother had expected her home for tea. Hopefully, Lady Hertfort's presence today would be brief. Rosalind wanted to avoid anything that reminded her of Torrington, and that included his sister.

He'd never acknowledged the lemon torte she'd left for him. Not until yesterday when a note had arrived. Well, not exactly a note. Only a recipe. And not one from *Cuisiner pour les Rois*.

Pain au chocolat.

Did he know that even the smell of chocolate reminded her of that afternoon? There had been no special instructions on this recipe. Nothing which would lead anyone to think she and Torrington had any sort of connection to each other.

Because we do not have a connection. Not even friendship, any longer.

Which was entirely for the best.

Rosalind smoothed down her skirts. Checked her hands to make sure there wasn't any dough stuck beneath her nails. "I can see myself in, Jacobson. Thank you."

The butler gave a resigned sigh and turned back in the direction he'd come.

Reaching the drawing room door, Rosalind placed her hand on the knob, faltering when she heard Lady Hertfort's voice echo through the door.

"Torrington finds her acceptable." The snobbish tone of Torrington's sister met her ears. "He won't rescind his offer. You worry needlessly."

"Then why hasn't he made a formal announcement? Or allowed me to do so? I've been so concerned he would tear up the contracts, I even mentioned to Lord Cheshire that my daughter had not yet made a suitable match. Just in case."

"Heavens, Winifred. I wish you hadn't done so. Cheshire?" Lady Hertfort made a sound. "Torrington would never go back on his word. He's far too honorable. Everything has been signed. Witnessed. Agreed upon. You needn't concern yourself further."

Rosalind pulled her fingers back as if the metal had scorched her palm.

Oh, God.

Her breathing halted, paused momentarily by shock and sheer panic at Lady Hertfort's words.

"I worried that he'd found someone to replace Stanwell," Mother said. "And was no longer in need of a wife."

"The search continues, of course, but it is highly unlikely Torrington's solicitor will find another Stanwell. Thankfully." Lady Hertfort made a derogatory sound. "I never approved of Stanwell to begin with. How stupid must you be to secure a title and then be foolish enough not to keep it? He didn't even expire"—she lowered her tone—"with any sort of taste or dignity."

"So I'm given to understand," Mother replied.

"There isn't any hope of finding another distant relation, Winifred. Please, put your fears aside."

Rosalind fell back a step, thinking of how close she'd been to being seduced in Torrington's kitchen. Had he succeeded, would he have merely done the honorable thing, with Rosalind never knowing—that he and her mother had already agreed—

"I'm sure you're right. I only grew concerned, Margarite. I told Cheshire I was hoping to have Rosalind wed by the end of the season, which is, for all intents and purposes, at an end. I wish my daughter to have a home and a family. A husband. Not become some withered spinster with nothing to recommend her but a delicious plate of scones."

Mother had *never* understood.

Rosalind had to press her hand against her mouth to keep from screaming.

No. No. No.

Panic bubbled in her chest. Her first inclination was to escape to the kitchens and mix up a batch of muffins. A good way to soothe her nerves—but muffins would not solve the problem at hand. Instead, Rosalind turned the knob and opened the door to see her traitorous mother and Lady Hertfort calmly sipping tea. You'd never know the two of them had been deciding Rosalind's future for her.

Regarding her mother with a cool look, Rosalind reminded herself to stay calm. At least until Lady Hertfort had vacated the premises. "Good afternoon, Mother. Lady Hertfort."

"Ah, Rosalind. There you are. I was growing concerned." Mother waved her forward. "Lady Hertfort and I were just enjoying a little bit of gossip. Lady Huft is about to marry again, for the fourth time. Can you imagine? Come join us."

Torrington's sister inclined her head and gave Rosalind a beaming smile, one far too welcoming.

Suitable. I'm suitable for her beloved brother. A convenient brood mare.

A surge of anger in Torrington's direction had Rosalind wobbling. How could he have done this and not told her? He had given her the recipes. Encouraged her. Admired her skill.

Licked chocolate off my thighs.

"How nice to see you, Miss Richardson. You look lovely," Lady Hertfort said.

"Thank you, Lady Hertfort."

"As lovely as our time has been, I must take my leave, Winifred." She waved her hand as Mother started to protest. "The girls will be wondering where I have gotten off to. I dare not have Hertfort suffer a moment longer. He took them to the park so that I could enjoy a pot of tea with you." She looked at Rosalind. "You must enjoy the park as well, Miss Richardson. Your mother says you walk daily, often for hours at a time." Lady Hertfort's eyes ran down Rosalind's form, probably wondering how Rosalind remained so plump with all the walking.

Or possibly she was trying to determine what Torrington found so *suitable* about her.

"I do walk, my lady," Rosalind answered in a wooden tone, perching carefully at the edge of one chair. She willed Lady Hertfort to speed up her exit. There were things that needed to be said to her mother, the first of which was that Rosalind wasn't marrying anyone because there was no compelling reason for her to do so.

Especially Torrington.

Lady Hertfort took Mother's hand. "I'll see you soon, Winifred." Torrington's sister took her leave with an incline of her regal head, the silk of her skirts whispering in the quiet of the room as Jacobson escorted her to the door.

Once Lady Hertfort was gone, Mother turned to Rosalind with a smile. "The tea is still warm, I believe, but if it is not, dearest, I'll have a fresh pot brought. Mrs. Hadley made biscuits, but they aren't nearly as good as the ones you make. Perhaps you'd have a word with her?"

It was never a good sign when Mother acknowledged Rosalind's skill in the kitchen.

"What have you done?" Rosalind's fingers twisted together.

Her mother sat back against the cushions of the sofa, one brow raised, and brought the cup of tea she held to her lips. Small curls, once the color of winter wheat but now faded to nearly white, dangled from her temples. "I've had tea with Lady Hertfort." The curls trembled dramatically as she spoke. "And I asked that Mrs. Hadley not prepare a dessert tonight. I think we should go without in the future." Her eyes took in Rosalind's waistline. "All that walking," she said in a far too casual tone, "doesn't seem to be working."

Rosalind's gaze narrowed on her mother, her stomach

pitching in the most unfortunate way. "I suppose not. But it doesn't matter, does it? I've been found suitable *as is*."

"You seem upset, dearest. Your mouth is puckered as if you've bitten into a lemon."

"I'm trying to keep from screaming, Mother. How could you?" Rosalind's fingers tore at her skirts with agitation. "How *dare* you?"

Mother took another sip of her tea. "I've told you more than once, Rosalind, that eavesdropping rarely turns out well for anyone involved. It appears you haven't taken my advice."

Rosalind loved her mother. Truly. But at the moment, she could have cheerfully strangled her. "You've sold me to Torrington. Without my knowledge."

"Sold? I find that dramatic even for you, Rosalind."

"I know that you seem to think a mature gentleman is preferable as a husband for me, but I do not. Unlike you, I find elderly men to be repulsive."

Her mother choked on her tea. "Repulsive. You find the Earl of Torrington repulsive?" A derisive snort came from her. "That must be why you received Lord Torrington, *twice*, without my being present."

Rosalind swallowed. "You were out. Would you have preferred I turn him away?"

She would kill Jacobson for this breach of privacy. They could make do without a butler. They had half a dozen footmen. "Lord Torrington was kind enough to provide me with his family's recipe for custard. Which I greatly appreciated. Nothing more."

"Hmmm. What about when you called on Lord Torrington, at his *home,* without benefit of a chaperone? Was that an expression of your disgust?"

"His butler was present during the entire visit as well as another member of his staff. Nothing improper occurred. We were merely exchanging recipes." Bijou could be counted as a kitchen maid, couldn't she? "The fact remains, Torrington is twice my age and a former rake, which I don't find the least appealing. You must undo this. I won't marry him."

"I see." Mother sipped her tea and gave her a bland look. "Nonetheless, you *will* wed Torrington."

"I won't." Rosalind lifted her chin. "I'll speak to him. We are friends—"

Another derisive snort from her mother.

"And ask him to beg off," she finished. "I'm sure he will have no trouble finding another suitable young lady." Rosalind could practically feel the press of her mother's heel on her neck.

Mother set down her cup before regarding Rosalind with steely determination. "I will not undo this, Rosalind. Be thankful it was Torrington who offered for you when I found out about Rudolph Pennyfoil."

Rosalind blinked, her fingers digging into her thighs. Mother knew of Pennyfoil.

"Else you would find yourself wed to Cheshire," her mother continued. "Walking in the park every day. For hours. How addled do you think I am?"

"You"—she paused and took a breath—"told me you didn't wish me in the kitchens, Mother. I was forced to find another place to practice my talents."

"So this is my fault?" Mother shook her head in resignation before her voice grew steely. "You've entered *trade* with a baker, Rosalind. You, the daughter of a viscount. Once I found out, there was little else I could do but get you wed as soon as possible before a scandal could erupt. Because it will."

"Romy—"

"Destroyed her reputation by playing at being a modiste. You wish to do so with dough stuck between your fingers. I should have known you would attempt to emulate her. You've some notion you're going to become London's most famous pastry chef. Did you think your visits to Pennyfoil would go unnoticed?"

"Who would possibly care, Mother? I am at the end of my third season. I plan to remain unwed. What difference could it make where I go or with whom I spend my days?"

"I can't believe I raised such a foolish girl." Mother leaned in. "You are the cousin of the Duke of Averell. A Barrington by blood if not by name. London will gleefully look in your direction to see what gossip erupts around you, Rosalind."

"Now who is being dramatic?"

"Let me ask, do you think that anyone will patronize your establishment once word circulates that you are in trade with Pennyfoil? Because word *will* get out. If Granby hadn't made Andromeda a duchess, there isn't any telling what her prospects would have been like considering the trouble Theodosia got herself into. The fact remains, an unwed girl of good family, a viscount's daughter, cannot spend hours with a baker without someone taking note." Mother shot her a pointed look. "Servants are prone to gossip, Rosalind. Someone is always watching."

"Our desserts are magnificent," Rosalind whispered, feeling her dreams slip through her fingers.

"I'm sure they are. But no one will buy a bloody tart from a pariah, Rosalind." Her mother's tone softened. "Not even Averell will be able to salvage you then. You need to marry. Especially since I don't know who might have seen you call on Torrington. Or witnessed you making cakes at Pennyfoil's."

Rosalind refused to give up. Years had been spent on avoiding marriage. She and Pennyfoil were successful. And Torrington—something pinched at her chest in thinking of him.

"Then send me away. I'll go to the Continent. I can join Andromeda in Italy. Or apprentice myself to a baker in Paris."

"You don't even speak French, Rosalind. You'll marry Torrington."

"I will not." She stood, fists clenched. "I am not you, Mother. I have no desire to be some *brood mare* for an aging rogue."

A weak gray mass of wrinkles inside soiled sheets and the sound of her mother weeping.

"One to whom I must read and feed broth, all while he flirts with the nurse while my back is turned."

Her mother paled so dramatically, Rosalind could see the delicate blue of her veins beneath her skin. "Don't you dare," Mother said in a threatening hiss, "speak about your father in that manner. Not in my presence. *Ever again.*"

"Why not?" Rosalind trembled. "It's the truth. You are trying to force me into the same situation you were once in. Married to a much older rake. Destined to play nursemaid. Well, I won't have it. I won't." An angry tear ran down her cheek.

"I won't survive this. I want to go with him."

The sound of her mother's long ago anguish still lingered in her mind, the pain of that horrible day never fading. Rosalind forced away the image and replaced it with one of a warm kitchen and spice cake.

"You've no idea what my marriage to Viscount Richardson entailed. You were a child when he—" Her mother's words grew thick. "Left us. You may think me blind to Lord Richardson's faults." She plucked at her skirts. "But I was not."

"I won't marry Torrington," Rosalind whispered. She couldn't.

Mother slapped a hand down on the sofa, startling her. "You *will*. You'll be a countess. At the very least since Torrington is older, you can look forward to being a young widow. A widow who can then spend her days baking to the exclusion of all else." Her mother smacked the sofa once more to make her point.

Rosalind shied from the anger in her mother's voice. Her fingers drew back into the folds of her skirts. Panic flooded her throat. Her mouth. She would drown in it. The knot in her stomach grew and tightened, retying itself. A widow was the very last thing she wished to be. *Ever*. And definitely not Torrington's, because that would mean—Rosalind's hands went to her stomach.

Mother cocked her head. "Rosalind?" Her expression softened. She leaned forward and took Rosalind's hand, worry etched in her features. "Dearest, is that what worries you? Is this about your father? I should not have said—Torrington is a great deal younger than Richardson was when I married him."

Rosalind jerked her hand from her mother's. "Enough, Mother," she choked. "You've made your point."

"Torrington is a brilliant match for you." Her mother sat back against the cushions, watching her carefully. "I doubt he would deny you anything. Even your partnership with that baker, if you are discreet."

"You don't know that."

Her mother gave a deep sigh, clearly frustrated by their conversation. "He allowed you to lick custard off his fingers, Rosalind. I'm fairly certain he'll allow you to keep baking tarts."

Rosalind's eyes widened in absolute horror. She couldn't even find the words to refute her mother's claim.

"Jacobson," Mother said, standing and brushing a stray crumb off her skirt, "cannot keep a secret from *me* to save his life. Eventually, he tells me everything. Sometimes it takes a great number of threats on my part, but this time he was motivated by genuine concern for your reputation. The rest of the staff will be unable to keep from gossiping about you entertaining the Earl of Torrington in the dining room. It is only luck the news of Torrington and your custard-making abilities isn't already making the rounds. Good lord, you're as bad as your cousins."

Rosalind looked out the window to the garden where the rotted branches of the maple tree still hovered over the stone bench. She'd forgotten Torrington's suggestion to have the gardener cut them off. Forgotten everything, even the damned recipes, because of him. There was a small bit of joy struggling to fill her heart at the knowledge that Torrington wanted her.

"Why didn't you tell me?" she said to her mother. "That Torrington had offered for me? He told me at Granby's house party he wasn't looking for a wife. I believed him."

"Perhaps at the time, it wasn't a lie. His heir didn't expire until shortly before the Ralston ball. He and his solicitor called on me the day after Theodosia ruined herself at Blythe's. You were out, taking one of your many *walks*." Mother raised a brow. "One of Torrington's requirements was that you not be told he'd offered for you and that I make no formal announcement of your betrothal until what he deemed the appropriate time. I'm relieved to no longer carry on this charade. The worry that he would retract his offer has led to many sleepless nights."

Mother's inability to sleep was the least of Rosalind's concerns. "Perhaps you should try some chamomile tea," she snapped back. "What I want to know is why? Why didn't he want you to tell me?"

"Only Lord Torrington knows the reason. You'll have to ask him yourself if you wish to know." Her mother headed to the door.

Rosalind felt a push of anger toward Torrington.

"Don't worry, Mother. I plan to."

❧ 14 ❧

Rosalind marched down the path in the park, one of the few amusements she was permitted since Mother had put a stop to visiting Pennyfoil's. She'd sent him a note, of course, but had failed to disclose the reason for her absence.

Pennyfoil, in his reply, hadn't questioned her, only saying that he would keep things well in hand should she return.

Should she return.

It was almost as if he knew Rosalind's presence at Pennyfoil's might be limited in the future. Frustration had her stomping her feet, stirring up clods of dirt around her ankles. She would not give up Pennyfoil's. She would fight Torrington tooth and nail to keep her partnership with Pennyfoil.

She halted, turning to face the maid who dogged her every step. "Wait by the carriage."

"But miss—"

It was Gert who trailed behind Rosalind. The maid Jacobson was busy tupping. She wondered if her mother knew about *that*.

"Go." Rosalind pointed at the carriage. "You can report my behavior to Lady Richardson when we return."

Nodding, the red-haired girl ducked her chin and turned back.

Rosalind scanned the park. It was early. Most of society was still sleeping off the excesses of the night before. If anyone did happen to catch sight of her, it was doubtful they would care that Lady Richardson's plump, nearly on-the-shelf daughter was exploring the park by herself.

Yes, but now I'll never be on the bloody shelf.

Mother was already planning a wedding. She had wanted a lavish spectacle that all of London could admire, only moderately smaller than the ceremony that had united Romy and Granby. Mother had been rather disappointed when Torrington had declined.

Strolling toward a small copse of trees facing the Serpentine, Rosalind inhaled the muddy, wet scent of the river. The hem of her skirts grew damp from the dew still lingering on the grass.

Rosalind didn't care.

She stopped abruptly, one hand reaching out to grab hold of the wide tree trunk before her. Her fingers stretched over the gnarled bark, tracing the jagged lines with the edge of her glove as she stared at a pair of geese floating by on the water. A leaf blew by Rosalind, lifted by the wind. The air spiraled about the leaf, pulling it down toward the grass before tossing it into the pond where one of the geese nipped at it.

I'm that leaf.

Rosalind detested feeling powerless. She was upset with her mother, of course. But there was a great deal of annoyance reserved for Torrington. Not to mention her fear.

She was very sure that once wed to Torrington and in close proximity to his gloriousness every single day, she might —*become lost*. The very thought had Rosalind considering fleeing her mother's house and escaping to the Continent. Surely if she appeared in Italy, Romy would welcome her. Granby probably wouldn't.

In the midst of a crisis these last few days, and with both Romy and Theodosia gone from London and no one else to confide in, Rosalind had done what she always did. She'd retreated to the kitchen and started to bake. In the last few days, the staff had benefited from the decadent custard, a ginger spice cake with pears, and two cherry tarts. The tarts had only made her think of Torrington.

Feeling peevish, she made sure that Jacobson was served the tiniest slice of everything.

"Is this about your father?"

Rosalind's eyes closed.

Lord Richardson *had* been an elderly rake. Partially reformed at best. All she remembered about him was that he had been an older gentleman who giggled quite a bit and sometimes fondled the maids. He'd often said Rosalind was a 'sturdy little thing' while he hugged her. And always, Mother had floated in his wake, adoration on her face. He'd liked tickling Mother, which Rosalind could see now was likely more sexual in nature. They'd probably read his bawdy book collection together.

Rosalind frowned. It was rather cringeworthy to consider her parents reading those books. Worse to consider what Mother had become after Lord Richardson's death.

"I cannot survive this. My heart is shattered into a thousand pieces."

Not her mother's words. No, this time it was Cousin Amanda, prostrate with grief over the death of the Duke of Averell. Inconsolable. *Frozen* with such anguish she couldn't move from the sofa where she sat next to Rosalind's mother.

Rosalind hadn't needed another example that grief made

one powerless. Or that loss consumed you. But one had been received all the same.

She'd taken one look at the two women, both mourning, and run to the kitchens where she couldn't hear them weep. Her hands had flopped about, determined to bake something, do anything which would stave off her own grief at the death of Cousin Marcus.

Lemon blackberry cake. Proclaimed his favorite.

As if making a bloody cake would bring him back.

She'd been fine assembling the ingredients. Mixing the flour and eggs together. But once the cake had been put in the oven, Rosalind's head had fallen to the worktable. She'd grieved not only for herself but for Cousin Amanda, who was now alone without her duke. The cake had burned while Rosalind wept. When you lost yourself to grief, you were apt to burn a cake. Among other things.

"You shouldn't wander off by yourself. There could be vagrants in the park." The smoky voice curled around Rosalind's ankles and up her skirts as she stood, looking at the river. Her heart fluttered madly, as it often did when Torrington appeared.

She would do anything to make it stop.

Opening her eyes, she said, "It's not even nine yet, my lord. Hardly an hour for vagrants."

"Or elderly rakes?" Torrington said in a mocking tone, beautifully handsome with the silver in his curls sparkling in the early morning light. He didn't look as if he'd been ill, but healthy and vital as he always did.

Her heart beat wildly once more, reaching for him.

"Stop it," she whispered under her breath.

Torrington raised a brow. "Rosalind?"

"Why are you here?" All the terrified, confused feelings toward him crashed over Rosalind in a wave. *He* would be a source of incredible anguish if she allowed it. There would be no end to burnt cakes. Ever.

"You're angry, and you've every right to be," he murmured, one hand reaching out to tug, very gently, at her skirts.

Rosalind turned her gaze back to the water. "I am angry. And I will not marry you. I refuse." She'd repeated those words dozens of times. No one seemed to be listening. "Don't you care that you're forcing me into a marriage? I don't want you." The lie burned her tongue. "Beg off. Tell my mother you've changed your mind."

"Could you be any more direct?" His reply was thick with sarcasm. "I'm not sure I take your meaning. Perhaps you need to remind me once again how elderly and repulsive I am."

"I'll run away, perhaps."

Torrington gave a deep sigh. His forefinger trailed down her arm, circling her wrist. "It defeats the purpose of fleeing, Rosalind, if you tell me you intend to do so."

"You can't force me. Think of the scandal, of dragging me kicking and screaming before a vicar."

"I'll merely give you laudanum. Only enough to make you sluggish so you don't injure me or anyone else with your flailing about. Besides, for a large enough donation, the vicar will turn a blind eye to a nearly unconscious bride." A lopsided, amused smile crossed his lips.

"This isn't funny," she snapped.

"It is, a little. Given you were spread over the worktable in my kitchen with my head between your legs. You tasted better than the chocolate."

Rosalind sucked in a breath, shocked at how quickly her body responded to his words with a low, pulsing hum between her thighs. "Why didn't you just ruin me? What would it have mattered?"

Torrington didn't answer.

She tilted her chin, wishing he didn't look so bloody

marvelous. Cedar flitted into her nostrils, mixing with the smell of the Serpentine. Torrington's warmth, even from the distance that separated them, seeped into her skin, banishing the chill of the early morning. Rosalind had the sudden urge to wrap her arms about his waist and cling to him, like some pathetic vine. Her fingers dug into the trunk of the tree.

"Go find another *convenient* young lady, Torrington," she choked out. "My understanding is that Lady Mildred is available. She'd wed you in a trice."

"Yes, but Lady Mildred *wants* to marry. Where's the challenge in having a willing bride?" he said in a flippant tone. "You aren't in the least convenient. You never have been." Torrington looked out across the water. "I am ashamed to admit that when we were first introduced, I had little interest."

"Embrace that feeling, my lord. Return to it."

A laugh came from him. "I fear that is impossible." Sadness colored the words. He looked out over the river. "For both of us."

Rosalind's lips pulled tight. "You lied to me. You said you didn't need an heir. That you weren't looking for a wife."

Torrington tilted his chin, turning to gaze at her once more. "At the time, it wasn't a lie," he said, absently brushing at a curl when it fell against his cheek. "I merely changed my mind."

"Change it back."

"Your cousin, the duke, would be adamantly opposed to my doing so. I've ruined you. Not completely, of course. But certainly, with intention. He was relieved to know we were already betrothed."

Mortification filled her. Torrington had visited her cousin, the Duke of Averell. Told him Rosalind had allowed herself to be compromised in a kitchen. Tony had always praised

Rosalind for being the only level-headed member of their family. The one least likely to do something disastrous.

Yes, well, it seems I've lost that distinction.

"I didn't give the duke details, of course," Torrington continued. "I'm not one to carry tales. I didn't mention a word about how you visited me wearing no corset or underthings, though I'm certain he wouldn't have been completely surprised. He's surrounded by bold women. In case you're wondering, the duke and I are previously acquainted. I'm a member in good standing at Elysium."

"I'm not surprised," she snapped back. "Given your tendencies."

"By tendencies, if you mean I wish to lay you naked across my bed, Rosalind, and fuck you for hours, then you are correct. My tendencies may also lead me to touch every inch of your skin. With my mouth."

Her breasts pulsed and tightened, drawing more moisture between her thighs, no matter her upset. "No need to be crude, my lord."

"Why not? It arouses you."

A blush heated her cheeks, spreading out across her chest. He was right, damn him.

Rosalind tilted her chin up at him, furious that Torrington wielded such power. It wasn't fair. Any of it. She'd thought he was her friend. Hoped he could be her lover, one she could keep at arm's length. He knew of her aversion to marriage. Yet, he didn't care. Trampling her feelings, he'd committed the unpardonable sin of offering for her.

"Yes, but not arousal for *you*, my lord." The frustration boiled inside her. "Only for *Cuisiner pour les Rois.*" Her words were horrible. Ugly. Completely untrue. But she wanted to hurt him. Drive him away.

Torrington's jaw hardened as Rosalind's barb hit its mark.

"Tell me, my lord, what must I do to see the rest of the

cookbook? If I get on my knees and take you in my mouth, will that be worth the king's tart?"

The amber in his eyes glittered back at her. "You'll have to do much better than that, Rosalind, to secure the tart." Torrington took a step in her direction. "I'll have all of you."

Rosalind shrank back farther into the safety of the tree. "If you come any closer, I'll call out for my driver. He's a big man. He'll—"

"Do nothing." Torrington moved swiftly until he was merely inches from her. "I informed him of my presence and relationship to you while you were looking at the Serpentine and contemplating how best to drown me in it. Now bend down and pretend there is a pebble in your slipper or something."

"What?" She looked up at him in confusion. "Why would I do so? And I'm wearing half-boots."

"I don't care what's on your feet. Just do it. Fiddle around a bit. When you straighten"—his voice rolled over her in a low dangerous purr—"lift the hem of your skirts."

"You can't be serious." But she could see he was. "We're in the midst of an argument. I've just said the most horrible things to you." Rosalind trembled against the tree at her back but not from fear.

"You provoked me, deliberately, I might add, with a vision of you on your knees. Eventually, you'll have to tell me how you came to know about how a cock fits in a woman's mouth."

"My father," she whispered, feeling the way her body arched in his direction. "He had a collection of books." Her nipples throbbed against the confines of her corset while an insistent ache took up residence between her thighs. "I told you Lord Richardson was once a flagrant rake."

"Interesting. Now be a good girl and lift your skirts," he growled.

Another pulse shot straight down her legs, curling her toes. "I don't care to be ordered about." But she was already bending to grab at the hem of her skirts, her arousal stoked by their argument and the wicked thoughts he so effortlessly put in her mind. "Someone will see."

"Your back is to the path and the waiting carriage. You're against a tree. Your driver and maid won't come closer." The amber gaze flicked downward. "Higher."

She brought up her skirts further, wobbling slightly as her stocking-clad legs were exposed to the cooler air. Thank goodness for the tree. "We are barely speaking to each other."

Torrington removed the glove from one hand with his teeth. "Our discussion has been very illuminating. Your thighs are luscious, by the way. I failed to mention the fact to you earlier." His fingers disappeared beneath her raised skirts, finding the opening in her underthings with little effort. His finger ran along her slit, stroking lightly. Torrington swore under his breath.

"I'm so angry with you," she breathed, leaning further into his touch.

"So you keep saying, yet your arousal coats my finger. You're a terrible liar. You would desire me even if the recipe for a tart weren't involved," he murmured. "Wouldn't you?"

Two fingers thrust gently into her heat, impaling her against the tree.

"Tell me you don't want me." The words buffeted against her neck. "Say it."

She couldn't pretend or lie at this moment, not with every inch of her body craving his. A small sob left her throat, knowing she was doomed. She would never win this argument. Rosalind wasn't even sure she wanted to.

His thumb brushed against the sensitive nub hidden in her folds.

Goodness. She really adored his thumb. "You are merely

attempting to prove a point, as any elderly rogue would do."
The statement had little weight, considering she was moaning
as she voiced her opinion.

"Don't look away from me, Rosalind." Torrington's fingers
stopped moving until her eyes once more focused on his.
"Maybe flutter your free hand past the tree so your maid
thinks we are having a lively discussion." Another finger
thrust inside her and she arched against the sensation. "I've
such plans for your mouth, Rosalind."

"Oh." His *cock* in her mouth. The thought sent a ripple
over her skin. "This is unfair." Deliberately, she ran her
tongue along her bottom lip.

A predatory sound left Torrington. "You would have made
a splendid courtesan, Rosalind. The slightest touch from me
and you climax. I've never seen anything like it. Do you want
ours to be a marriage of convenience?"

A whimper left her as his fingers found a particularly
sensitive spot. "No," she stuttered. Her body felt honed to a
fine point. Sharp. Exact. The very idea of Torrington with
another woman was revolting. "I won't share you." The words
clawed out of her, her heart shying away from the admission.

Torrington's thumb pressed down, stealing her breath and
nearly every thought in her head. Bliss twisted up her spine,
so intense, her hips bucked. His other hand, palm splayed
against her stomach, held her in place as she climaxed, his
eyes never leaving hers.

Rosalind was lost. Completely.

"Bram." Soft, demanding lips claimed hers. She no longer
cared if anyone besides the birds above her head witnessed
what was happening. Her eyes fluttered closed as his fingers
coaxed the last bit of pleasure from her, leaving Rosalind
shaken and grabbing at the tree for support.

Gently, he pulled her skirts from her clenched fingers and
let them fall to the ground.

Rosalind turned from him, letting the trunk of the tree scrape against her cheek, still feeling the gentle throb of her body. The feel of his fingers inside her. How much more would she long for Torrington after they were wed?

Torrington tried to take her hand, and she jerked away.

A grunt of frustration came from him. "Look on the bright side, Rosalind," he said casually. "As you often remind me, I'm many years your senior. You'll likely be a young widow."

Stop. Stop. Stop. Rosalind's hand clawed at the tree.

"The males in my family are never long-lived. Take that to heart. Maybe it will make wedding me more palatable." The words were clipped. Chilly. So unlike Torrington's usual teasing.

"I thought we were friends—"

Torrington's lips twitched. "You never thought we were *only* friends. Nor is this about a tart recipe. Or your ambitions —which I would want you to have. This is about what we feel for each other, Rosalind. And nothing else."

She cleared her throat, refusing to acknowledge his statement, but neither could she deny it was true. "No, it is only I refuse to be a brood mare—"

"My God, Rosalind." His voice thundered in the quiet morning air. "Do you *hear* yourself? The same words over and over as if they were a bloody prayer to banish me. *This* is why I didn't tell you. Why I wouldn't allow your mother and my sister to inform everyone in London. Your objections are invalid. So completely untrue each time I hear them, I wonder if you've lost your mind. We are right for each other in every way that matters."

Rosalind bit her lip and looked down at her feet. "No, we are not."

"*Christ.*" The word thundered out of him, scattering the birds in the tree above them. "I'm not sure what it is you are afraid of, Rosalind." His voice grew rough. "But I am tired of it being *me*."

Torrington paced back and forth, his coat flapping angrily with every step. "I have never"—the smoke in his voice broke apart as he paused and looked at her—"wanted *anything* half as much as you." He came to stand mere inches from her. "I desire you above all else."

She heard the truth in his words, though part of her turned away from it.

"I do not find this to be easy. Or amusing. I've spent far more time avoiding marriage than you have. I vowed never to wed again. It doesn't even matter to me if I produce an heir. But you—" His voice faltered, and one hand pressed over his heart. His eyes fluttered closed, dark lashes fanning over his cheeks. "I must have *you*," he said in a pained whisper. "I could have made this so much easier. Just ruined you. Forced you. But I had hoped—"

Torrington took a step away from her, his eyes opening to fix on the path beside them and the river. "You'll be my wife, no matter how much you abhor it."

"Bram—" Rosalind wiped a tear from her cheek, his admission threatening to undo her. Her heart ached painfully, the ever-present knot, tightening around her entire chest.

He shook his head, declining to look at her. "Good morning, Rosalind." Then he turned and moved down the path in the opposite direction.

Away from her.

15

Bram looked down at his hands, the knuckles cracked and bleeding from the previous day at Hagerty's. Thankfully, his gloves would hide the worst of it.

Leaving Rosalind in the park the other day, still flushed from her climax and spitting her objection to him, had left Bram feeling raw and broken. He'd gone home and, no matter that it was midmorning, had proceeded to work his way through an excellent bottle of scotch.

Bram prided himself on being able to maintain his charming demeanor even through the worst circumstances, but the thread had snapped. His emotions had threatened to boil over. The remainder of the day, as Watkins had hovered over him like a worried mother and Bijou had watched him with mournful eyes, Bram had considered why he refused to simply walk away from Rosalind.

One thing was certain—he had never felt for either of his wives what he did for her. Bram couldn't even describe this *yearning* for Rosalind. It was beyond his ability to do so.

More than desire. More than companionship. More than

a shared happiness over warm kitchens and the ability to make a proper trifle.

He had his friends. His family. His hobbies. A warm bed partner when he wished it. If something was missing from his life, or if there were times when he felt his solitude more acutely than others, Bram reminded himself he was luckier than most. His life was peaceful. Content. He was wealthy. Titled. There were worse ways to spend the remainder of his days. And if he felt lonely, well, he had Bijou. Until he'd seen Rosalind standing before the window at Thrumbadge's, digging through books on the wild goose chase he'd sent her on, Bram hadn't understood he wasn't completely happy.

"Are you sure, my lord, that you shouldn't stay at home this evening?" Bram's valet, Johnson, moved around him like a small planet orbiting the sun, brushing off a bit of lint here and there. The valet was staring pointedly at Bram's eye.

"I'm expected," he answered. "My eye isn't so bad." There was nothing to be done about the slight puffiness around his left eye or the small bit of purplish bruise beneath it. The very edge of his lip was cut but barely noticeable. There was a slight chance no one at Lady Richardson's dinner table would notice his injuries. Margarite and Hertfort, both of whom knew of Bram's affinity for taking out his frustrations in the boxing ring, would know exactly what had happened, but aside from shooting him looks of disapproval, they were unlikely to comment.

Bram left Johnson and made his way downstairs, strangely light of heart considering the marks O'Leary had left on him. It was the knowledge he would soon see Rosalind, Bram guessed. He missed her even when she was disparaging him. Especially then.

Stung by a bee?

Bram stepped into his carriage for the short ride to Lady Richardson's, settling back against the leather.

Possibly. But a bee wouldn't have caused a bruise. Bram drummed his fingers against one thigh.

Fell off my horse?

Bram was an excellent horseman. He hadn't lost his seat since he was little more than a boy. No one would believe that. Margarite might even laugh out loud if Bram gave that as the reason for his swollen eye.

Tripped over Bijou?

Hmm. That seemed acceptable. Made him look like a bloody idiot, but he doubted anyone would question him further. Bijou was always underfoot. He carefully touched the area around his eye, wincing slightly.

Watkins had helped him ice the area rather well, but the puffiness and the bruise remained. His butler had had the audacity to suggest he was getting too old to be visiting Hagerty's.

Bram had replied that Watkins might be getting too old to be *butlering.*

They had parted ways, an uneasy peace between them, but Bram stood a good chance of being locked out of his own house tonight, and no lamp left burning.

A short time later, he was shown into the foyer of Lady Richardson's home, the butler, Jacobson, making every effort not to look at or even notice Bram's injury. He failed miserably.

"Lord Torrington." Jacobson announced his arrival as they reached the drawing room.

His Grace, the Duke of Averell stood off to the side, surveying Bram with a raised brow before greeting him. The duke and he were acquainted, though not as well as he'd led Rosalind to believe. He wasn't sure whether Rosalind would ask the duke to intercede on her behalf and break the betrothal to Bram, which is why he'd visited Averell himself. He needn't have bothered. Lady Richardson had already paid a call on her relation to inform him Rosalind would be wedding the Earl of Torrington. She must also have related other pertinent facts because Averell had also been aware that Rosalind had been compromised and that she had discreetly gone into trade with a baker.

Bram made a note to never, in the future, underestimate Lady Richardson.

After the duke's greeting, Torrington was introduced to the Duchess of Averell, a tiny, dark-haired thing, rumored to be a brilliant pianist who had Averell wrapped around her pinky finger. Averell did not stray, so the rumor was likely true, much to the dismay of London's female population.

The stunning older woman in a wealth of pewter gray was the Dowager Duchess of Averell. Bram had made her acquaintance previously at some function or another before the death of her husband. Next to her, back ramrod straight, hands perfectly clasped in her lap, perched a slender young lady. She was introduced to Bram as Miss Olivia Nelson, ward of the dowager. Miss Nelson was the granddaughter of the Earl of Daring. How she had come to be raised by the Barringtons and not her grandfather was a source of speculation in London society because Daring's dislike of the Barringtons, particularly the dowager duchess, was well known.

The only person left in the room awaiting an introduction was the young lady with the bold, assured gaze. Lady Phaedra Barrington. There was gossip she liked to accompany the duke to Elysium in the absence of his brother Leo Murphy, which would be horribly scandalous if it were true. A bet had been made in Elysium's Red Book about what sort of disaster the youngest Barrington would drag her family into. Some of the choices included ruination, the wearing of men's clothing in public, dueling—because the gossips said Lady Phaedra had taken up fencing—or general misadventure of some sort.

Bram voted for general misadventure. Lady Phaedra didn't have the look of someone who would settle for anything ordinary. If the duke was wise, he'd wed his youngest sister off as soon as she made her debut, though given what he'd heard of her personality, Bram wasn't sure what sort of gentleman would take on Lady Phaedra.

Rosalind, his brazen baker, was not present in the drawing room. Perhaps she'd fled after all. He thought it likely she'd go to France if she ran away, though she didn't speak the language. She would look for another copy of the cookbook and find some corner in which to make her pastries.

He greeted his sister Margarite with a peck on the cheek, ignoring her pointed frown at the condition of his eye. Bram waited for Rosalind to appear, half-listening to his brother-in-law. Hertfort was pontificating on the bill he was sponsoring in Parliament.

"What happened to your eye?"

Bram turned to see Lady Phaedra looking up at him. There was a shrewd look in the blue of her eyes that belied her youth.

"Just here." She tapped at the corresponding place on her own cheek. "In case you've forgotten."

Direct. Blunt. All the Barringtons were like that. Rosalind came by her manner quite honestly. "I tripped over my dog." Bram decided to go with the last reason he'd come up with for his injury. "I hit the knob of my drawing room door as I fell."

Lady Phaedra leaned back a space. "If you say so, my lord. Looks to me as if you've been in a fight." She tapped a slender finger against her lips. "Did someone try to steal your purse?"

"No, my lady. As I said, I merely tripped over my dog. The room wasn't properly lit."

"Hmmm." She cocked her head. "I won't say a word. You can trust me to be discreet."

Bram rather doubted it.

"Boxing, then? You've the look of a boxer, if you don't mind me saying so, my lord. Though your nose is rather straight." She shook her head as if delving into a deep mystery. "Which means you must be quite good and swift on your feet if you've avoided breaking your nose thus far." She leaned in just a bit and whispered, "I bet your knuckles are a disaster."

Bram's sister had said much the same about Lady Phaedra. Not about her nose or knuckles, but the part about being a disaster.

Lady Phaedra gave a small roll of her shoulders. "Well, I don't find you the least ancient, if it helps. Rosalind implied you were wrinkled and elderly. Much like Lord Richardson, her father. My cousin doesn't wish to wed. She never has. Ros prefers to be in the kitchen with her baking tins." Phaedra patted his arm. "Has nothing to do with you. Pity you aren't a chocolate cake."

"How nice of you to let me know." Bram gave her an amused smile. Lady Phaedra, he suspected, liked to be shocking. But he sensed she was also trying to tell him something about Rosalind, in her own way. Bram just wasn't sure what it was.

"Rosalind requires a firm hand," Lady Phaedra said in a lofty tone. "One only a more mature gentleman can provide."

"You sound remarkably like Lady Richardson."

"Thank you. I've been practicing. One never knows when you'll have to imitate your cousin's matronly mother. You'd think Cousin Winnie would see that the last thing Rosalind wants is to be reminded of Lord Richardson."

Bram considered that for a moment while Lady Phaedra continued to study him. He didn't know very much about the deceased Lord Richardson, but perhaps he should make a point of learning about the man who'd sired Rosalind.

"Do you want to know *how* I know you've been involved in fisticuffs?" Lady Phaedra said, apparently done discussing Rosalind.

"I couldn't hazard a guess, my lady." Bram glanced over at Averell, feeling his disapproval from across the drawing room, most of it focused on his youngest sister.

"I'm taking fencing lessons." She lowered her voice. "Which may have evolved into some general lessons on boxing and defending oneself. His Grace doesn't know the last bit," she said, sneaking a look at her brother. "Would be best for both of us if you don't tell him. You might be the only gentleman marrying into the family the duke remotely approves of, and I would hate for you to lose your only advantage."

"I am the soul of discretion." Dear God. Bram had never thought to feel such pity for the Duke of Averell as he did after speaking to Lady Phaedra. "Where is Miss Richardson?"

Lady Phaedra lifted her gaze to the drawing room door. "She's just come in. Rosalind was finishing the chocolate toffee cake for tonight's dessert. My brother's favorite." She gave him a mischievous look. "Don't worry, my lord. He can't be bribed to stop your wedding with cake. Ros is all yours."

Bram choked which pulled the cut at his lip. "Good to know." He turned his attention to Rosalind as she entered the room, stunning in a peach and cream striped confection which hugged all her glorious curves.

The thump of his heart echoed loudly in his chest.

He hadn't seen her since their meeting in the park, thinking it for the best given their heated discussion and the fact he'd partially ravished her against an oak tree. After trying to blunt his emotions with scotch for a day or two, Bram had sent Rosalind a recipe for macarons. A peace offering of sorts to his brazen baker. He'd made notations on the recipe, including the history of the macaron as he knew it. Originating in Florence and thought to have been brought to France by none other than Catherine de Medici, macarons became popular when a group of nuns sold the dessert to support themselves. A sketch of a tiny nun graced the corner of the recipe.

Bram's gaze settled on Rosalind's mouth, unable to help himself.

She blushed immediately, the red stain spreading over her chest and mottling her complexion in an instant.

"Like a moldy cherry," Lady Phaedra said under her breath as she floated away from him.

"Miss Richardson." Bram made his way over to Rosalind and bowed low over her hand, holding her fingers far longer than he should have. Warm vanilla and the scent of sugar surrounded her. She'd very recently left the kitchens. He tried to focus on the freckles across her nose but found he could only think of how she'd looked in the park, riding his hand as she climaxed.

"Lord Torrington." Her eyes were luminous, shining like the chocolate he'd dribbled over her thighs in his kitchen. The connection between them sparked so fiercely, Bram was nearly blinded by it.

He *loved* Rosalind. Desperately.

Bram allowed the feeling to overwhelm him. His fingers trembled just slightly holding his glass aloft. He was drunk on the sensation.

Difficult, gorgeous creature.

"Thank you for the macaron recipe," she said. "I haven't attempted to make them. Yet."

Rosalind hadn't been visiting Pennyfoil. Bram knew because he was in contact with the baker. Lady Richardson had probably forbidden Rosalind, perhaps assuming wrongly that Bram would withdraw his suit if he knew. Or she feared a scandal. The knowledge tore at Bram, knowing how much Rosalind needed to create.

Rosalind pulled her hand away, but not before Bram noted how she arched in his direction. Her voluptuous form was thrilled to see him even if Rosalind herself was not.

"Why is your eye puffy?" She peered at him.

Direct, as always. Bram shrugged. "I tripped over Bijou in the dark. Clumsy of me."

"There's a bruise just beneath. Weren't you carrying a lamp?" She managed to sound concerned and insulting at the same time. "Was Bijou injured?"

"My mind was elsewhere at the time, and I merely forgot the light. Bijou is fine."

"Forgot? One doesn't forget a lamp in a dark room." Rosalind bit her lip. "Did you become dizzy, my lord? Were your ears ringing?"

Rosalind seemed overly worried he'd had some sort of episode. Was that what had happened to Lord Richardson?

"No, I merely tripped. And it isn't the first time I've forgotten a lamp." He shrugged. "Nothing more."

Suspicion gleamed in her eyes. "You *forgot*. Because your head ached or—"

"I haven't lost my wits, if that's what you're implying. I wasn't wandering about imagining I was at the Battle of Waterloo." He leaned in. "I'm not so addled we can't wed."

Her mouth parted in surprise. "That isn't—I merely wanted to ensure you weren't ill, my lord." A mulish edge took hold of her chin.

"Ill enough to miss dinner?" Bram pressed a hand to his chest, trying not to wince. He'd gone a half-dozen rounds with O'Leary. There wasn't a spot of skin left on him that didn't ache. "Don't be foolish. You won't get rid of me quite so easily."

Concern immediately colored her features again. She

stared at the spot on his chest where his hand had landed, almost as if she expected him to fall to the floor and collapse. "Do you need to sit?"

"Rosalind," he said in a low tone. "Cease your questioning. Nothing is amiss, I assure you. I have a bruise because I tripped over my dog and hit the doorknob. I wasn't foxed, so you can scratch sot off your list of things you don't like about me. Nor did I have a fit of apoplexy. My physician assures me that I'm quite healthy."

"You have a physician?" Suspicion and concern lit her face again. "He visits often because you have a condition which requires his attention?"

"Careful, Miss Richardson. I might start to think you care for me with all this fussing about. I assure you, I'm well. You'll have to endure me as a husband for a few years at least, I expect."

A panicked, fearful look flickered over her lovely features so quickly, Bram nearly missed it. Without thinking, his fingers latched on to a fold of her skirts and tugged gently. "What is it?"

Rosalind stared down at his hand. "It is only that I would hate for you to collapse before dessert. I've made a chocolate toffee cake," she said stiffly.

Bram reluctantly let go of the silk. He wished he could spirit her away somewhere, perhaps take her outside and speak to her in private. Comfort her, if need be. There was a fragility in Rosalind tonight, as though she might break if he exerted too much pressure.

When Jacobson announced from the door that dinner was ready, Rosalind allowed Torrington to lead her in, the tips of her fingers barely touching his coat. The sway of her hips had her skirts whipping seductively against Bram's legs, giving rise to all sorts of lascivious thoughts. It was all he could do to make it to the dining room before the vision of Rosalind licking custard off his finger assailed him.

Escorting Rosalind to her place, he ignored the self-satisfied smile on her lips when Bram found he wasn't seated next to her, knowing she'd purposely arranged it.

The smug grin soon faded when Bram was directed to sit across from her.

Lady Richardson, Bram thought once more, should never be underestimated.

❧ 16 ❧

Rosalind had been dreading this dinner since her mother had informed her of the intent to host the Barringtons along with Lord and Lady Hertfort. She wasn't sure how to behave around Torrington. Not after their encounter in the park and the things he'd said. How was it possible to long for someone yet want to escape them at the same time? She'd stayed away from the drawing room as long as she could, until Mother had sent Jacobson to search for her.

"I must have you."

Those words and the raw emotion with which they were spoken still haunted Rosalind.

The knowledge that Torrington was circulating in the drawing room with her family had made her impending marriage to him real. She'd even argued with Mother that her family could meet Torrington at the wedding. There was no reason to invite Tony, Maggie, Cousin Amanda, Olivia, and Phaedra to dinner.

Especially Phaedra.

Phaedra was bound to launch into improper dinner

conversation. Or whip out a sword from beneath her skirts and dazzle them all with her fencing ability. Worse, she might feel the need to engage Torrington in conversation and share some embarrassing incident involving Rosalind. Like the harp playing.

She'd made sure she wasn't to be seated next to Torrington at dinner. Not because Rosalind didn't want the warmth of him at her side, but because she *did*. Her victory, however, was short-lived. Torrington was placed directly across from her, which was far worse. Every time she looked up from her plate, Rosalind was faced with all his magnificence. It made it difficult to concentrate on the beef in pastry, one of her favorite meals.

Rosalind watched his graceful movements as he ate, looking for any sign Torrington might not be well. He caught her staring several times. The last time, he mockingly put a hand to his brow and pretended to swoon over the soup course.

She frowned at him, pushing down the fear leaching through her system, not finding his antics the least amusing. This was all his fault. Why had he needed to confess his feelings for her in the park? Up until that moment, Rosalind had continued to pretend. She pushed away the food on her plate, unable to enjoy the excellent dinner Cook had prepared. All of this made Rosalind incredibly annoyed, mostly at Torrington.

The duke conversed with Torrington at length, as did Cousin Amanda. When Phaedra flicked a bit of carrot at Olivia, who was seated next to him, Torrington reached out and caught it mid-air without halting his conversation. He told an amusing story, which had the table laughing, all except Rosalind who couldn't forget the way he'd clutched his chest earlier. Watkins said he'd been ill. Torrington had a physician who visited him regularly.

Worry left a bitter taste in her mouth.

When the dessert was finally served, she breathed a sigh of relief that the evening was coming to a conclusion. She looked down at the chocolate toffee cake and picked up her fork. Rarely had Rosalind ever refused dessert. Spearing a bit of cake, she held it up to her lips.

Torrington's foot nudged hers. "A hint of nutmeg, Miss Richardson," he mouthed from his place directly across from her, "means just that."

Rosalind nearly threw the forkful of cake at him. Had she not been so concerned for his welfare, she might have done so. Not for an instant did she believe he'd tripped over Bijou.

The entire evening had been nothing but intolerable.

Sometime later, when Torrington finally took his leave along with the other guests, he enfolded her hand in his, squeezing gently. "All will be well, Rosalind," he said quietly so only she could hear it. "I promise. There is nothing to fear."

She nearly burst into tears before reaching the safety of her room.

Rosalind didn't want Torrington to matter so much to her. Or for her to feel such panic at the thought he might not be well. Marriage to him was bound to make things worse. The desire between them had only grown and expanded over time. Rosalind had been reminded multiple times she would likely be a young widow, even by Torrington himself.

As if that were supposed to make her feel better somehow. Because it did not. It made Rosalind want to curl up into a ball beneath the covers of her bed and never come out.

I should have just gone to Paris.

Now as she sat before the window in her bedroom, clad in her nightgown, hair neatly braided, Rosalind tried once more to focus only on the establishment she hoped to create with Pennyfoil. She picked up the macaron recipe from where she'd left it, her eyes scanning the instructions Torrington had so neatly written out for her. There was a tiny nun drawn in one corner.

Rosalind drew in a halting breath.

"It was the risk you took, madam. At wedding my uncle who was so many years your senior."

Rosalind retreated to her bed, the recipe still clutched in one hand, the words of her father's heir still fresh, though she'd been only a child at the time. He had derided Mother's grief at the death of Lord Richardson, assuming it merely a ploy for money.

Rosalind had been barely five that fateful day when her father collapsed. He'd taken to his bed shortly thereafter and never left it again. He died when she was seven. Her memories of him were vague. Cloudy. But she remembered how Mother had stroked his cheek when she sat and read to him, curling herself around his decaying body. She'd wept nearly all the time, except in front of Rosalind's father.

Rosalind's determination to avoid the same fate that befell her mother had been for naught.

A sob choked her.

If she must wed it should be Delong. Or Cheshire.

Anyone but Torrington.

17

"Rosalind, you must come out." Theodosia, now the Marchioness of Haven, blinked at her through the lenses of her spectacles, holding out one gloved hand. "*Please*. Your mother will descend upon us at any moment. Or Tony might punch my husband. If Granby were here, my brother's attention might be elsewhere, but as it stands, it is firmly on Haven."

Rosalind looked down at the spray of flowers in her hand. "You don't understand."

"Tony's dislike? He refers to Haven as 'the parasite'."

She shot her cousin a rueful look. "You know that isn't what I'm speaking of."

"Ros, out of *everyone* in this church, it is I who understand. I didn't want to marry Haven. I stomped my feet. Threatened to join Leo in America—"

"When is he coming back?"

"Soon. His last letter was quite cryptic." She waved the small nosegay she held. "The point is, there are still some days I wonder if I should have just fled to New York, which I imagine you've already considered. Though, in your case, I suppose you'd choose the Continent. I didn't do so, and I don't regret my decision. Haven is incredibly trying at times, but he does have his moments." A dreamy look crossed her features.

Dear God. Is that what I look like when I think of Torrington?

The panic thickened in Rosalind's chest.

"Torrington will grow on you if he hasn't already." Theodosia rattled away, assuming she was being helpful. "I quite like him. Half the women in London are cursing you, I'll warrant."

Rosalind swallowed back the acrid taste in her mouth. She was terrified. *Bloody terrified.*

Theodosia took her hand. "My goodness, your fingers are like ice."

"Do you think Torrington looks healthy?" It seemed to be the only thing she could focus on at the moment.

"What? Of course he does. Torrington is . . . *magnificent*. I know you have reservations because he's older. As both our fathers were." Theodosia frowned. "And I know Mama didn't handle the loss of my father very well."

Cousin Amanda, the strongest woman Rosalind had ever known, had shattered into pieces at the death of Marcus Barrington. She'd become unrecognizable. A pale shadow of the capable force of nature Rosalind had always known her to be.

"Then you burned the cake." Theodosia paused and looked out the window. "Well, I think my mother's collapse reminded you—" Her eyes ran toward the ceiling as if searching for the right word. "Makes you feel—that you will be left *behind* by Torrington," Theodosia said cautiously, "because he is older. And you'll likely be a widow. Sooner than you wish." She bit her lip. "Like Cousin Winnie after Lord Richardson's death—"

"Enough, Theodosia," Rosalind interrupted. "You have

the oddest notions. I'm certain my mother collapsed in relief from no longer having to play nursemaid to my father. Imagine, having to wait on your elderly rake of a husband while your youth is torn from you."

Theodosia gave her a stricken look. "Oh, Rosalind. I don't—"

"This is the worst day of my life. I don't want to wed. No one is listening." She stared out the window of the tiny room at St. John's church. Rosalind's fingers tightened.

"Perhaps you should look at why the idea of marriage seems so abhorrent to you." Theodosia sat beside her.

"Because I want to bake. Create. You know I want my own establishment. It's all I've ever wanted."

"You've been telling me since we were children you didn't want a husband. It has only been since Romy became Madame Dupree's silent partner that you decided to find Pennyfoil."

"Untrue."

Theodosia took her hand. "When Romy tried to make a trousseau for one of your dolls, you tore the dresses apart. Do you remember?"

Rosalind felt sick to her stomach. "I merely pointed out none of the dresses were in black." She pressed a hand to her stomach, to stop the emotions from erupting. "And the colors she chose were terrible. I just want to make pastries. You can't possibly understand."

"I suppose not."

"At the very least, Mother should have allowed me to find a man who appeals to me."

"Am I to believe Torrington doesn't hold the least appeal for you? You allowed him to take all sorts of liberties, Rosalind," Theodosia said quietly. "If you find him so unappealing, what prompted you to do so?"

"He has recipes I want. For Pennyfoil's. I'm not giving

up." Rosalind narrowed her eyes. "Who told you Torrington took liberties?"

"I may have overheard my mother having tea with yours. And I doubt you let him ruin you for that stupid tart you're always going on about."

"Eavesdropping is a terrible habit," Rosalind snapped. "And the tart isn't stupid. It was revered by a king."

Theodosia rolled her eyes. "I do wish Romy were here."

"As do I." Rosalind stood and fluffed out her ice blue skirts, watching as the brilliants sewn into the skirt reflected the light streaming in through the small stained-glass window. Best to get this over with as soon as possible. She wanted to make macarons later.

❦

BRAM NEVER THOUGHT TO FIND HIMSELF BEFORE A VICAR again. He'd assumed if he and a vicar happened to be in close proximity, it would be because Bram was being put in the ground.

A rustle of skirts came from the back of the church. Rosalind, stunning in an ice-blue gown covered with brilliants, held the arm of the Duke of Averell. There was a slight tremble to her plump form as she saw Bram. The panic he'd sensed in her the night he'd dined at Lady Richardson's still hovered over her shoulders, making her wobble slightly as she took a step forward.

The duke whispered something in her ear.

Rosalind straightened and lifted her chin, gazing at Bram once more but this time with determination.

Ah, there's my brazen baker.

Bram didn't expect Rosalind to come running down the aisle to him, but neither did he want her fearful and cowed.

The only sign of her continued distress was the slight shake of the bouquet she held.

Averell brought her to stand before the vicar, giving her a not-so-gentle nudge in Bram's direction as he released her.

Rosalind scorched the duke with one scathing look. Whatever he'd whispered to push her down the aisle had worn off.

A sound of amusement came from Lady Phaedra who sat next to Lord and Lady Haven, Miss Nelson on the opposite side. Haven was watching Bram with a bemused look, probably hoping for an ally. He and the duke detested each other.

The weeping of Lady Richardson grew louder. The dowager duchess quietly admonished her and took her hand. The Duchess of Averell sat on the other side, gently patting Lady Richardson's arm. Rosalind's mother had begun leaking tears the moment she'd put her slippered foot inside the church. The intensity of her weeping had slowly increased in volume and intensity until now, it echoed throughout the entire church.

Averell took the seat next to his wife and looked at his family with resignation. A family populated by opinionated, slightly eccentric women who seemed to ignore the duke's guidance. Averell had Bram's sympathies.

Margarite, Hertfort, and their four girls all sat together. His nieces were all dressed in varying hues of pink and adorned with a flurry of ribbons. Cora, the youngest, impishly waved at him.

Bram winked and waved back before facing the vicar once more.

Rosalind stood next to him, her luscious mouth pursed into a tiny rosette. Bram took her hand, lacing their fingers together so that she could not pull away.

She glanced up at him, worry shadowing her eyes. Her fingers were chilled even through her gloves. The fear which clung to her wasn't of Bram, which he knew because she was holding on to his hand for dear life. But of something much more profound.

Bram raised her fingers to his lips and pressed a gentle kiss to her knuckles, ignoring the disapproval of the vicar. "Everything will be all right," he reassured her. "I promise, Rosalind."

The vicar cleared his throat. "My lord."

Bram answered automatically. He knew exactly what to recite back to the vicar. It was his third wedding, after all.

But this was the only time when he'd truly meant the words.

18

Rosalind sat back in the carriage, looking out the window at the house she'd called home for as long as she remembered. It wasn't Lord Richardson's London house. His nephew had taken possession of her father's home a week after Lord Richardson had died. This property was one Cousin Marcus, in his endless generosity, had given his dear cousin Winifred along with a large allowance. No relative of the Duke of Averell would be allowed to devolve into genteel poverty or be tossed into the streets. The neighborhood was even more fashionable than the one the current Viscount Richardson resided in.

In any case, Rosalind would never live here again.

Hands clasped in her lap, fingers twisted in agitation. Unknown to her mother or anyone else, especially the traitorous Jacobson, Rosalind had snuck out yesterday to visit Pennyfoil. Surprised at the sight of her, Pennyfoil had immediately stopped what he was doing and joined her for a cup of tea. The work area bustled with activity around her. Cakes were being made. The lemon torte. The ginger spice cake with pears she'd perfected only a short time ago. When she apologized for not bringing over any additional recipes, Pennyfoil had waved away her concerns.

"I don't think we need them."

Rosalind looked out the window as the carriage rolled in the direction of Torrington's home. What Pennyfoil meant, she supposed, was that he didn't need *her*. Worse, there was a part of her that didn't care.

"Are you well, Rosalind?"

"Perfectly, my lord."

"Bram." He drummed his elegant fingers against one thigh. "Are you upset because I thought there was too much nutmeg in your chocolate toffee cake?"

Honestly, Rosalind had more pressing concerns. She'd forgotten all about Torrington finding the cake over-spiced. "There wasn't too much nutmeg."

He shrugged. "I disagree. Have you tried to make the macarons yet?"

Rosalind narrowed her eyes. "I planned to do so tonight. A pleasant way to spend the evening. I already know my way to the kitchens."

"Unfortunately, you'll be otherwise occupied, Rosalind. You'll have to make the macarons tomorrow, perhaps. If I allow you out of my bed."

A delicious tingle ran down her spine.

"Or perhaps I'll assist you. I could eat the batter off your thighs."

Her pulse skipped a beat at the suggestion, bringing to mind all the things Torrington could lick off of her skin. Her breasts swelled, feeling heavy beneath the confines of her clothing. "You're provoking me."

"Is it working?" His gaze lingered on her mouth, as it so often did. She'd come to realize Torrington, for whatever reason, had an obsession with her lips. Deliberately, she worried her bottom lip with her teeth, watching as he took a deep breath and shifted.

Torrington took the edge of his coat and flipped it over so she could see the tenting of his trousers. "This is an amusing game, Rosalind."

"I think so. When did you decide to offer for me? I know you visited my mother after Lord Blythe's birthday celebration. You already had the papers ready. You decided before that."

He looked taken aback, not expecting the question. "Does it matter? Will the answer help you to hold on to your notion I was only looking for a brood mare? Keep the distance you struggle to maintain between us?" Bram sighed. "When I saw you at Thrumbadge's," he said quietly. "I knew what I would do. But I had the papers drawn up after the Ralston ball."

Rosalind did a poor job of hiding her surprise. "You knew you were going to offer for me."

"Eventually."

☙❧

I LOVE YOU.

Bram's heart beat out the words though Rosalind couldn't hear them.

"I thought we might suit but wasn't sure, and I didn't want your mother giving you to Cheshire in the meantime," he said. "Would you rather I had?"

She made a disgruntled sound. Her moods of late seemed to vacillate between panic, hostility, and longing. All directed at him. He wasn't sure what to do other than be patient while Rosalind worked through whatever troubled her.

Bram had first assumed that Rosalind's aversion to marriage had to do with the gentlemen in question being

Lady Richardson's choice. The relationship between Lady Richardson and her daughter was volatile at times, the result of two very strong personalities in constant conflict with each other. Then, Bram had surmised she just wasn't attracted to him. Neither was true. But once he understood how serious she was about Pennyfoil's, Bram could see why avoiding marriage made sense. Rosalind wanted to practice her talents. Have her bakery. And it was a rare husband who would allow his wife to be in trade. Bram understood.

But the fear he'd glimpsed in Rosalind couldn't all revolve around Pennyfoil's, especially since she had to at least suspect Bram would be supportive of her endeavors. There was more to her avoidance of marriage. Marriage could lead to many things. Affection. Closeness. And in some cases, love.

That was what Rosalind was escaping by making her tortes and pies. He just didn't know why, exactly. She pushed him away, lashed out at him so ferociously, because she *did* care for him. And Rosalind didn't want to.

The carriage came to a halt before his house, Watkins already standing at the door. Bram had given very specific instructions to his staff. He exited the vehicle and held his hand out to Rosalind.

"Welcome, Lady Torrington. My lord." The butler bowed.

"Watkins will show you up to your room," Bram said, nosing along the side of her ear. "Your maid will be waiting upstairs along with a hot bath. I thought you'd want some privacy. I've a few matters to attend to."

Rosalind frowned. "Very kind of you."

Bram smiled to himself. It wouldn't hurt for Rosalind, now that she was slightly aroused, to be left to contemplate her evening, which would not be spent making macarons. Besides, Bram would be in the kitchen, cooking dinner for them and preparing the *baiser du ciel*. If nothing else, his new wife enjoyed food, and he hoped a good meal would help calm her fears. "There's champagne with the bath. A wonderful vintage."

"But—"

Bram pulled her close and pressed a kiss on her temple. Her softness pressed into him for only a moment before he pulled away.

"I'll see you in a bit, my brazen baker. Enjoy the bath."

19

R osalind relaxed in the steaming water as her maid
bustled about, putting away her things. The ice
blue gown was already carefully brushed and hung,
the matching slippers with their spiraling design stuffed with
tissue paper and placed in the wardrobe. She took a sip of the
champagne, perfectly chilled, and surveyed the pale cream
and yellow walls, all smelling of fresh paint. A large vase of
flowers sat on a round table in a small sitting area surrounded
by two comfortable-looking chairs. In addition to the
wardrobe, there was a dresser and a vanity. Her cookbooks
were stacked on a bookcase. A desk held paper and ink.
Torrington must have had the rooms redone for her, because
the colors were nearly identical to Rosalind's bedroom at
home. Everything, including the bath and the champagne,
was perfect. And she *had* needed a moment to herself after
the ceremony and the wedding breakfast. It had been harder
than Rosalind expected to leave her mother, now alone
except for her servants.

She'd had time, while soaking in the bath, to consider the
wedding and the following breakfast in detail. Torrington's

nieces, all four of them dressed in near-identical gowns, had fluttered around their uncle, small faces full of adoration as he bent to speak to each of them. She'd seen Torrington draw his sister into an embrace and whisper something to her which made her laugh and swat him on the shoulder. He'd interrupted the rapidly escalating argument between Haven and Tony with a story about a place called Hagerty's, of which he promised to say no more until the ladies weren't present.

Phaedra whispered to Rosalind that Hagerty's was a boxing establishment. And not the sort of place most gentlemen frequented.

Rosalind declined to ask how her cousin knew of such a thing. She wasn't sure she'd care for the answer.

While she was loath to admit it, Torrington had charmed the Barringtons, and that was no easy feat.

Rosalind kept trying to rekindle her anger at Torrington but couldn't seem to do so when sitting in a warm, scented bath he'd ordered for her and drinking champagne. Her resentment toward him had faded dramatically since she'd overheard Lady Hertfort and Mother discussing her fate.

She swirled a finger in the now tepid water. There was no anger now. Anticipation, yes. Rosalind often imagined what lay underneath Torrington's finely tailored coats. The only thing she knew for sure was there would be no padding. She couldn't wait to see for herself.

Gertie stood before the tub, a fluffy towel opened wide for Rosalind. The maid dried her off with ruthless efficiency, glancing at the clock on the bedside table before rubbing another bit of skin. Once dry, the maid dropped a ridiculous scrap of lace, ribbon, and little else over Rosalind's head. Diaphanous and nearly see-through, the garment left very little to the imagination. One pull of the ribbon at her neck and the nightgown would fall from her shoulders.

Rosalind shivered at the thought. Of all the things she

feared, most she couldn't even put a name to, having Torrington bed her wasn't on the list.

"If that's all my lady, I'll bid you a goodnight."

"Actually—" She wanted to ask after Torrington.

But the girl bobbed and exited the room before Rosalind could utter another word, scurrying away into the depths of Torrington's house.

Frowning at the maid's odd behavior, Rosalind took a seat by the fire to give her hair time to dry and waited for Torrington to appear. Surely he didn't mean to leave her alone on her wedding night.

She glanced out the window. Or rather, her wedding *afternoon*. The sun had still not completely set. Standing, she went to her new vanity, a lovely carved bit of walnut, and straightened her things, though the maid had done so only an hour before. Pouring another glass of champagne, Rosalind resettled herself on the chair.

She eyed the door separating her rooms from Torrington's. No sound came from beyond the door. Rosalind stood and cocked her head to listen. The entire house was silent. There were no footsteps from servants echoing in the house.

Strange.

In fact, the only servant she'd seen, besides her own maid, had been Watkins. Rosalind had been so out of sorts upon her arrival, she hadn't bothered to consider why Watkins showed her upstairs instead of introducing her to the staff. She walked to the door leading to Torrington's rooms and knocked. Only silence greeted her.

Rosalind strode to her own door and stuck her head out into the hall. "Hello?"

The most delicious smell met her nose. Or smells. Something sweet mingling with the aroma of chicken, mushrooms, and onion. Her stomach grumbled in response.

She hadn't eaten much at her own wedding breakfast. Her

nerves had been too frayed. Rosalind hadn't even sampled the wedding cake because she knew it would be dry. If Mrs. Hadley, Mother's cook had made a moist cake, biscuit, or scone in the last ten years, Rosalind had yet to taste it.

"Watkins?" she said into the hall. If there were servants about, someone would answer. "Hello?" she said a little louder.

Nothing. The entire house was still.

If the smell of chicken hadn't reached her on the stairs, Rosalind would have assumed she was all alone in the house. Grabbing her robe, which the maid had left for her on the bed, Rosalind threw it over her shoulders, then cautiously made her way down the stairs.

"Torrington?" She peeked into the dining room, catching a glimpse of a large table completely absent of food. Rosalind started down the long hall in the direction of the kitchen, but a bark sounded to her right, followed by a low, masculine rumble.

Walking with more certainty, she passed the kitchen stairs and made her way to the end of the hall. A door stood ajar. Bijou barked again, sensing her presence.

Rosalind pushed the door open cautiously, really hoping it wasn't Watkins who was behind the door. That wouldn't be an appropriate way to begin her tenure as Lady Torrington.

The sound of claws clicking on the floor came closer, and Bijou's snout appeared, poking through the partially opened door. The small, wet nose nudged at her hand as Bijou's tail thumped in greeting.

"Bonjour, Bijou." Rosalind kneeled to scratch the dog between her ears.

"Very good, Lady Torrington." The smoky sound of her husband's voice held approval and something else. He had discarded his coat and waistcoat. No cravat. His shirtsleeves were once more rolled up his beautiful forearms.

Damn him. He had made himself irresistible.

The shirt covering his broad shoulders was unbuttoned. *Completely.* And pulled out of his trousers. The white fabric billowed around him as he wiped at his chest with a rag.

Rosalind's mouth went dry.

A great wealth of muscular torso was exposed, all dusted with a smattering of dark brown hair. He smiled at her before looking down once more, wiping at something only he could see. His trousers hung low, his hipbones stark against the smooth skin. The hair covering his chest thinned into a small point below his navel, disappearing into the edge of his trousers which were, thankfully, still buttoned.

Rosalind might have fainted if they were unbuttoned.

"Do you like the presentation?"

Like? She was dizzy with lust. A warm, slow prickle glided up and down her skin, softly brushing between her thighs.

"The dinner." He nodded to the two plates sitting on a small table set for two. "Admittedly, I don't do as good a job as Watkins. He can fold napkins into all sorts of shapes." Torrington grinned. "Swans and other intricate designs."

"Quite a skill." Rosalind couldn't take her eyes from him. Torrington was dazzling.

"I thought we would eat here rather than in the dining room."

Rosalind's gaze ran over the small, cozy room. A private parlor. Meant only to be used by the family or perhaps the lady of the house. The furnishings in here were slightly more feminine than in the rest of Torrington's home. The room had probably once belonged to his mother. A fire crackled in the hearth, keeping the air pleasantly warm. Two silver domes sat at the table along with a bottle of wine and two glasses. A third domed plate sat off to the side. A vase of roses was centered on the table, illuminated by two flickering candles.

He'd done all of this for *her.*

"I must have you."

Her heart fluttered louder. She couldn't even summon up the 'brood mare' argument without sounding like a complete idiot. Nor disparage him for being too old. Or call him a reformed rake when he was obviously as romantic as any young lady in her first season.

He dabbed at the fine lawn of his shirt once more, frowning at the stain. "Johnson will have a fit."

"Johnson?"

"My valet. He's very tidy. I meant to change shirts before retrieving you. Spilled a bit of the sauce on myself when I carried it up the steps." He gave her an apologetic smile. "Hopefully you don't find my appearance to be completely upsetting."

It was impossible for Rosalind's heart—or any part of her —to stay closed to this man. Not when he stood before her half-dressed after making her dinner while she soaked in a bath. Which he'd ordered for her.

But. But. But—

Rosalind pushed the voice aside. She didn't want to listen. Not tonight.

Her robe had fallen open, and Torrington's eyes slid over her scantily clad form, paying particular attention to her breasts and her bare feet. He set down the rag he'd been using to wipe off his shirt and came forward, absently tossing a scrap of something to Bijou. Chicken, she supposed.

"Does everything meet with your approval, Lady Torrington?" He looked down at her, curls hanging over his cheeks.

She nodded, closing her eyes as his lips brushed gently over hers. Rosalind reached up and grasped one curl, allowing the strand to twist around her finger. Like a bit of silk.

"Have we finally achieved a temporary truce of sorts?" he whispered against her cheek.

"Yes." Rosalind didn't want to think past tonight or even this moment.

His mouth claimed hers more fully then, moving over her lips, tasting her with his tongue until she opened beneath his gentle onslaught. He kissed her for a long time, long enough for Rosalind's mind to still, her fears vanquished in the face of Torrington's seduction. Tentatively, mindful of the last time she'd touched him and he'd shied away, Rosalind's hands slid beneath his shirt, drawing her fingers along the lines of his ribs.

A groan of pure want came from him before he carefully pushed her away. "I hope you like *coq au vin*. Chicken."

"I do." She couldn't seem to let go of him. Her cheek pressed against the crisp hair of his chest.

"Let me pour the wine, my love. I'm not going to ravish you until you have eaten something." His finger lifted up her chin. "You can let go." He pressed his lips to her temple. "I'm not going anywhere. I promise."

Yes, but you will.

Her fingers tightened on him before she firmly pushed the dark thought away. It had no place here. Not tonight.

"I like this tea cosy you're wearing, by the way." The low growl rolled over her skin, caressing her nipples, before Torrington's thumb followed, circling the tip of one. "Very pretty."

"It's a nightgown," she said with a smile, shivering with pleasure at his touch. "I think."

"More an enticing doily." He kissed the end of her nose before moving to one of the chairs and pulling it back for her.

Rosalind sat, feeling his warm fingers trail over her collarbone. He leaned down and nipped at the skin beneath one ear. "Are you cold?" he whispered.

"No." Her entire form was malleable. Warm. Whether

from Torrington's kiss or the champagne she'd already had, she wasn't sure. "Are you?" She nodded to his open shirt.

"I was going to change."

"There's no need." Her gaze lifted to his.

He sat down across from her, dark eyes flickering with hunger that was for far more than the *coq au vin*.

Rosalind wasn't the least ignorant of what her immediate future held. While her mother hadn't been entirely forthcoming about the marital bed, telling Rosalind only that 'Torrington would guide her,' Theodosia had been much more detailed in the basics of losing one's virginity. The books Rosalind's father had left behind, though helpful in explaining a variety of sexual acts, assumed all parties had already discarded their virtue and thus were useless in describing how it felt to have one's maidenhead breached.

Theodosia had found it painful. Romy, uncomfortable.

Torrington speared a bit of chicken along with a mushroom on the tine of his fork. "Open your mouth, Rosalind."

Rosalind squeezed her knees together to stop the spurt of moisture at Torrington's seemingly innocent words. She parted her lips as he commanded. Flavor burst on her tongue. The earthy texture of the mushroom, the savory chicken, the hint of wine in the sauce. She swallowed. "Delicious. You really could have been a chef, fooling everyone with a French accent."

A rumble of amusement came from his chest. "Do you find it odd I like to cook? I suppose it isn't very earlish."

"I don't think that's a word, Torrington."

"Bram. I find horseraces dull. Hazard a waste of time and money—"

"My cousin Leo says never to play hazard. The odds are always in favor of the house."

"Agreed. Balls are tolerable, I suppose, if you are forced to hand lemonade to the right young lady." His hand stretched across the table, his forefinger circling and stroking the tip of hers.

"And send her off to look for a rare French cookbook when you already own a copy." Rosalind raised a brow.

Torrington shrugged. "I was conflicted at the time." His gaze on her softened. "You enjoyed the chase."

The throb intensified between Rosalind's thighs, moving up and over her stomach.

"But back to being an earl. Earls like to hunt, for the most part. I don't care overmuch for the sport, though I'm an adequate shot. I know how to set a snare."

"So, if we were lost in the forest, you could potentially find me a rabbit *and* cook it."

"Exactly." He flashed a grin at her. "My father, once I grew older, didn't care to have me spending so much time in the kitchen, which is probably what drove him to take me to Hagerty's the first time. Boxing, at least according to him, was a much more appropriate pursuit."

"You mentioned Hagerty's when you dined at my mother's." Rosalind accepted another bite of the chicken. Torrington really was an incredible cook.

"I hesitate to call Hagerty's a gentleman's boxing establishment because I believe I might be the only title frequenting the place, but I learned to box there. Wonderful exercise. Helps with frustration." His finger caressed the tip of hers once more. "Especially that which is sexual in nature."

Rosalind's skin was warm all over. "Is that where the puffy eye came from, not Bijou?"

He nodded. "And when Watkins told you I was ill, it was nothing more than me going far too many rounds with O'Leary. He's a butcher. Big. Irish. I was a bit bruised around the ribs. Dr. Graw does visit me, but only as often as I visit Hagerty's. You needn't worry, Rosalind."

The relief that Torrington had never been ill was so

profound, Rosalind found her fingers twisting far too tightly around the knife by her plate.

Torrington's eyes flicked down to her hand. "Are you planning on stabbing me, Rosalind? I thought you liked the chicken. Is it because I called your lovely wedding ensemble a doily?" The half-smile clung to his lips.

"No, I was only surprised." It was on the tip of her tongue to demand he refrain from ever going to Hagerty's again before she caught herself.

"Now, the lessons I excelled at, as an earl, are the sort which will take place in our bedroom. Or possibly other locations." He gave a careless wave. "I plan on debauching you quite thoroughly. Perhaps we'll read your father's naughty books together and you can point out what you'd like me to do." He held out another forkful of the chicken to her.

Rosalind's mouth closed over the bite, heat flooding her cheeks as she thought of some of the acts those books depicted.

"Alas, I fear I will disappoint you in one regard. I was never a rake. Not really." He leaned back and took a sip of wine. "I never reached the heights of say . . . the Duke of Averell. Either of them, though I do adore women." He speared a mushroom and held it before her lips. "But only one woman at present. Or ever again."

Rosalind's heart, so determined to remain apathetic toward Torrington, pulsed and ached for him, nearly as ferociously as her body did.

"Anna, my first wife, was a lovely girl. But sickly."

"She died of a fever."

Torrington nodded. "We grew up together. I bore her a great deal of affection. More brotherly in nature. Lizabet." His handsome features darkened. "She was beautiful and as well-bred as one of those Pomeranians we discussed previously. She had lovers and so thought it wise that it appear I did as well." Another drink of wine. "But I did not *adore* either of them." His voice was soft, like a wisp of smoke.

"And what of Bijou?" Rosalind said in a teasing tone.

Bijou, curled up in one corner, lifted her head at the mention of her name.

"Who did you think I was speaking of?" Torrington replied, lips twitching.

Rosalind narrowed her eyes at him and sipped her wine.

They ate in silence for a few moments, the air in the small parlor growing thick with the hum of their desire for each other. Rosalind felt fear clutch at her chest, the absolute aversion to allowing herself to care so deeply for Torrington. She seemed powerless to stop it from overwhelming her.

Only think of tonight, Rosalind.

While she ate, the left side of her robe slid down, exposing her bare shoulder. She moved to tug the sleeve back up but stopped at the soft hiss of Torrington's command.

"Untie your robe."

She was about to argue but saw the way his eyes were heated, almost golden in the firelight. Another wash of arousal lashed her, making her fingers tremble. She stood and unbelted the robe, allowing the garment to fall to the floor.

Her nipples hardened to peaks beneath the small scrap of lace covering her breasts, begging for Torrington's notice. She wasn't sure what to do with her hands, so she placed her palms on the table and waited.

Torrington got up and came to her. His nose nuzzled along the side of her neck while a big hand cupped one breast. The other wrapped around the base of her skull, fingers sinking into her hair. Pulling her head back to expose the slope of her neck, his mouth teased gently at the sensitive skin, nibbling and sucking his way to the line of her jaw.

He took her hand and pressed it against the bulge in his trousers. "I assume you know what to expect, given your taste in reading. You aren't going to faint at the sight of my cock, are you? Well, you may if you find it so magnificent it takes your breath away."

Rosalind couldn't help it. She giggled. "No. I've seen drawings."

"Of course you have."

"Will you faint at the sight of my breasts?" Rosalind had always been somewhat ashamed of her breasts. They were monstrous things. Huge. Difficult to contain.

"Possibly," he growled, running his hand over the lace. "I've wanted your nipples between my teeth for quite a while."

"You don't find them . . . too much?"

A low sound of appreciation came from Torrington. "No, I do not."

She shivered, arching back against him as he rolled her nipples between his big fingers. One hand slid down the line of her hip, grabbing at her thigh, caressing the soft flesh. He palmed her mound through the lace, running his finger along her slit.

"It might be better if we blow out the candles." One of her hands self-consciously covered the small mound of her belly.

"Don't be ridiculous. I licked your quim while you sat atop the worktable in my kitchen, where my meals, *our* meals will be prepared. I'll probably do it again. And I've already seen your stomach." His nose nudged against her hair. "Besides, I like your generous figure. Lots of curves. Small hollows for me to explore. You're full of secret places." His fingers tugged at the soft hair atop her mound. Taking her chin, Torrington kissed her until she grabbed at the edges of his shirt and her legs wobbled. He lowered his mouth to one nipple, sucking the small peak into his mouth.

"Undress me," he said against her breast, tongue flicking

out at her nipple. "You said you wanted to see me naked, Rosalind."

He stood perfectly still as she slid the fine lawn of his shirt over his shoulders. "I'm sorry," she pressed an open-mouthed kiss on his chest, "about accusing you of wearing a corset." Her fingernail circled one of his nipples. "It's clear I might be in need of spectacles."

"Finally, you admit it."

"You are truly a spectacular example of an elderly earl." Rosalind grazed her teeth along the line of his ribs even as her fingers worked the top button of his trousers. "Do you want to put your cock in my mouth?"

Torrington went completely still. She'd shocked both of them with her brazen statement.

"You're always looking at my mouth." Rosalind continued to tug at the buttons of his trousers. "I saw the way you looked at me when I licked the custard off your fingers. And at the park." She looked up at him. "I'm curious. Tell me what to do."

Torrington closed his eyes, cursing before opening them again. He was looking at her as if he'd never seen her before. So full of male hunger she nearly regretted being so brave.

"Get on your knees, Rosalind."

Rosalind lowered herself before him, her hands sliding up his muscled thighs, grabbing at the flesh beneath the fabric of his trousers. The buttons slid free, and Rosalind tugged at the material until—

Oh. Goodness. She'd seen the drawings in her father's books, of course. Known what a man's appendage looked like. Knew to call it a *cock*. Rosalind had even studied the detailed description of how to perform the act of putting a man's cock in your mouth, especially after the custard tasting with Torrington. But—her fingers traced reverently down the long, thick length of him. Having no other man to compare him to, she wasn't sure if his size was normal or—her hand wrapped around him. The reality was rather daunting.

Torrington hissed. Loudly.

Her tongue flicked out, touching just the tip. There was a saltiness to him. An aroma of cedar and musk. She thought of how she'd licked the custard off his fingers.

Another groan and both his hands threaded through her hair, tugging at the ends. "Did you read about this?"

"Yes." Rosalind parted her lips and looked up at Torrington, never breaking eye contact as she slid his cock into her mouth. Her tongue swirled around the length, sucking and licking. Tasting him.

Torrington made the most interesting sounds, which made her own body ache in response.

Rosalind tried to recall what else she was supposed to do, but her own arousal muddled her thoughts. *Oh. Yes.*

"Jesus, Rosalind." Torrington gasped as she grabbed his ball sac, rotating it gently between her fingers. "I hope you brought those damned books with you. I think—" His words were cut off as her teeth grazed around his cock. His fingers fisted in her hair, pulling her away.

Had she done it wrong? Rosalind looked up at him. "Didn't you like it?"

Torrington went to his knees across from her. "You are a wondrous creature, Lady Torrington." He kissed her softly. "But I don't want this evening to end too soon, and it will if I allow you to continue."

They fell to the rug together, a mass of limbs and mouths, stroking hands and tongues. His fingers teased at the wetness between her thighs, making her arch against his hand. Bits of lace and ribbon were pulled from her.

Rosalind's legs parted further, allowing him access to all of her. She wanted him to touch her, kiss her, lick her. Everywhere. Her hands ran up his chest, the crisp hair sifting through her fingers. The warm feel of Torrington's mouth at her breast sent the pressure inside her to a feverish point.

His bigger body wedged itself between her spread legs. His marvelous cock, the saltiness of which she could still taste on her tongue, lay hot against her thigh.

Torrington lifted his head. "It hurts the first time."

"I know. I don't care. I'm ready. I feel as if I will burn into ash if you don't—ravish me, Bram."

"I know, my love." His thumb and forefinger gently teased the small nub hidden in her folds. He coaxed another kiss from her lips while the lower half of her body tightened beneath the ministrations of his fingers.

"Bram," she choked out, feeling pleasure rise in a huge wave where he held her just at the top before allowing the sensation to crash over her. Her hips bucked as each ripple of pleasure struck her. His hand fell away, sliding along one thigh to take firm hold of her hip.

Her eyes popped open, widening at the sensation of being stretched as he pressed into her. With each contraction of her body, he slid further inside her, until he finally wrapped one arm firmly around her neck and thrust forward.

Rosalind's body arched. Theodosia was correct. It did hurt. Quite a bit.

A cry shook her, though she tried to bite it back. Considering how lustful Rosalind felt nearly all the time around Torrington and her boldness in taking him in her mouth, it was a bit of a disappointment to know she would feel the same pain as any uneducated, unwilling virgin on her wedding night.

"I'm sorry," she whispered.

"Why on earth"—Torrington sounded as if he was struggling—"would you be sorry about anything?" He kissed the end of her nose. Her forehead. "Relax, Rosalind. Breathe." He stayed perfectly still. "I meant to do this properly in a bed. I have a nice one just upstairs."

The sting was starting to abate, though she still felt . . . stretched. Full. It wasn't unpleasant.

He pulled back a few inches and then thrust hard inside of her. This time, Rosalind instinctively raised her hips.

Torrington smiled down at her, curls in a riot around his features. He had one that was completely silver. The hunger that had etched his features only moments before softened to longing. The sort that made Rosalind's throat grow thick and her fingers tremble where she touched his skin.

Each stroke was slow. Sensual. Punctuated with his mouth pressed to hers. Or by the quiet nonsense he whispered in her ear, some of it in French. Her body clasped his tightly, but Torrington's pace didn't change. His hand moved to where they were joined, brushing and searching, finding the spot which gave her the most pleasure.

Rosalind's legs wound around his waist, fascinated at the way the gold in his eyes gleamed down at her with so much unsaid emotion. When he found his release, Rosalind held him tight, seeing the truth of his feeling for her in his eyes before he lowered back to her neck, breath rough and uneven.

Rosalind's own climax thundered through her. A low shuddering of pleasure which spread out across her limbs. Like dozens of stars shining before her eyes.

That horrible dark fear tried to invade Rosalind, but she wouldn't allow it. She'd promised herself, just for tonight, not to consider the future.

Torrington kissed her cheek, nose nuzzling into the warmth of Rosalind's neck. It was a lovely feeling to have the hairs of his chest chafe against her nipples while Torrington still pulsed inside her. He fell to the side, keeping her close, the rapid beat of his heart hammering beneath her cheek.

"Are you still angry?" The question rumbled from his chest.

Was she? It was hard to tell with his naked body lying next to hers, knowing he'd made her dinner and the Sun King's tart which she suspected was beneath the last uncovered plate.

"I don't know," she replied.

Torrington stood and went to the sideboard, where a pitcher sat.

Rosalind couldn't take her eyes off him. He was more splendid out of his clothes than in them. So much better than anything she'd imagined alone in her bed at night.

He brought the pitcher along with a napkin to her side. Dipping the napkin in the water, he carefully pressed the cloth between her legs, dabbing gently. "Better?"

She nodded. "You made the tart, didn't you?"

"I did. Do you want your dessert?" His eyes caught and held hers.

Rosalind took a shaky breath. "Just to be clear. Are you asking about the tart or something of a more sexual nature? I find that many things you say sometimes have a different meaning."

He laughed, a sound Rosalind adored more than any music she'd ever heard. "True. Very clever, Lady Torrington. But I am referring to what lies under the silver dome." The curls tilted in the direction of the covered dish. "But I must warn you, I am likely to change the meaning of many things without notice."

"Duly noted."

Torrington pulled on his trousers then picked up the tray and carried it to Rosalind. She was still sitting on the rug, bits of lace strewn around her. The nightgown was made for seduction, not durability, it seemed. He retraced his steps, picked up her robe, and held it up. "For all the good it will do. I've already seen everything." He winked at her.

"You've put on your trousers—"

"Which I'm happy to remove with only a word from you. However, I suppose it's better if you have no distractions when you taste the tart." With a flourish, Torrington took the dome off the tray, revealing the dessert.

Rosalind's hands raised to her mouth to keep from screaming in delight. "It's beautiful."

Crisp, perfectly cooked layers of fluffy pastry and brandied cherries were formed into a tight, elegant rectangle, all dusted with sugar. The smell alone made Rosalind's mouth water.

Torrington handed her a spoon. "Once you break into the *baiser du ciel*, you'll see. Go ahead." He watched her, smiling as she dipped her spoon, breaking the sugared crust. A thick, creamy custard laced with a layer of cherries spilled out along with a stripe of—

"Chocolate."

"Yes. Taste it."

Rosalind's eyes widened. It wasn't the same as the chocolate he'd used while making *pain au chocolat*. It was . . . exquisite. Richer. Darker, with hints of cinnamon, and something else she couldn't place. The mix of brandied cherries, chocolate, and the custard, which she recognized as *the* custard, was so unusual inside the pastry crust.

"It was first presented to the Sun King, according to rumor, just as you see it. A flaky pastry crust layered with cherries and powdered sugar. He was unimpressed until one of his mistresses"—Torrington paused in thought—"I can't recall which one, decided not to wait for Louis to sample the dessert. The surprise is when you break it open."

"It's marvelous." Rosalind licked her spoon.

He leaned forward and kissed away a bit of cherry

clinging to the corner of her mouth. "The story goes"—his voice lowered to that smoky purr she had come to adore —"they were naked in bed at the time. I'm certain Louis ate some of the tart off her skin."

"Really?" Rosalind widened her eyes. "He would have had to be very careful not to miss a bite."

Torrington's hand glided over her collarbone. "Oh look, there's another bit of cherry you've spilled."

Rosalind gasped as his mouth closed over her nipple where it poked through the lace. He sucked and teased until she'd forgotten all about the tart. She fell back, Torrington coming with her, his tongue never ceasing its seductive torture.

"Merely a nipple," he whispered against her breast. "Not a cherry. My mistake."

Her hand slid down his chest to his trousers, which he hadn't even bothered to button properly, feeling his cock twitch beneath her hand.

"I think, my lord, I would like my dessert now."

20

R osalind didn't want to move. She was warm. Cocooned. And everything smelled of cherries, chocolate, and sugar.

The lobe of her ear was caught between teeth and gently tugged on. Lips brushed over a hidden spot on her neck. A big hand cupped her breast, toying with the nipple. And something hard, warm, and rather large, was throbbing against the curve of her buttocks.

She rolled over just slightly to see Torrington absorbed in drawing his fingers over the slope of her breast. Squeezing the flesh as if he were testing the ripeness of a melon.

"Enjoying yourself?"

He flashed her a wicked grin. "I am. And by my count, you enjoyed yourself at least a half dozen times. Not too bad for a feeble lecher."

Rosalind giggled and swatted his hand away. "I never, *ever*, called you a feeble lecher, my lord."

After enjoying the *baiser du ciel* in the parlor, she and Torrington had made their way upstairs. They lay entwined on the bed in his room, far larger than the one in Rosalind's, staring at the fire. True to his word, Torrington had explored every curve, every hidden bit of skin Rosalind possessed.

"Fine. Ancient debaucher, then."

Rosalind had spent nearly an hour just running her fingers over every inch of Torrington's beautifully sculpted form. She'd traced the small creases radiating from his eyes, fingertips stroking down the line of his cheeks to the hard angle of his jaw covered by his beard.

"I think I've more than apologized."

Torrington's hand slid between her thighs, tugging lightly at the soft hair covering her mound. "Have you? I feel certain there's more to be done, Rosalind. You can start your apology tonight by reading to me from one of those books I've heard so much about. I want you in nothing but stockings. Maybe a robe thrown over your shoulders."

A gasp came from Rosalind as his fingers slid lower. She would lay naked on the worktable in the kitchen covered in custard if Torrington wished.

"I have something for you," he murmured into the curve of her neck.

"I'm sure you do," she breathed, arching her back against him.

"No, not that, Rosalind," he said in mock outrage. "Insatiable. That's what you are." But Torrington was smiling at her. "This is a wedding gift."

Rosalind sat up. "But I didn't get you anything." The anger at being forced to marry, the worry and fear before the wedding, had blotted out the need to purchase him a pair of cufflinks or a jeweled pin of some sort.

He leaned over to the table next to the bed and pulled open the top drawer, retrieving a small, leather tome tied with a red ribbon.

Rosalind went still. "The cookbook."

Torrington nodded. "You're my wife. This should be yours."

Rosalind took the book and held it against her chest in utter worship. The leather was ancient and worn, the binding cracked in several places. Opening the cover, she leafed through the pages, noting stains from bits of egg or cream. Tiny notes in French were written into the corners of the well-used pages in a feminine hand which could have only belonged to Torrington's mother.

"I won't let anything happen to it, Bram. Ever. I promise," Rosalind whispered.

"I know." Warm lips pressed to her temple. "Look to your heart's content, but unless you are going to surprise me with a sudden fluency in French, I'll need to copy the recipes into English for you. And Pennyfoil."

Rosalind's fingers tightened on the book at the mention of her partner.

"Yes, I know about Pennyfoil. No, Lady Richardson didn't inform me. I already knew about Mr. Rudolph Pennyfoil before your mother warned me of his existence. She suggested once we wed, that I forbid you to engage in such a scandalous venture, but Pennyfoil's other partner disagreed."

Rosalind's stomach pitched. Pennyfoil had replaced her so quickly and without her knowledge? How could he? It was her recipes which had made Pennyfoil's profitable.

"Stop frowning and clenching your jaw. I am the partner, Rosalind. Me."

"How is that possible?" A strangled breath fell from her lips. "How could you—"

"Before you throw the cookbook at my head"— Torrington nodded at the tome—"let me explain, my brazen baker. Pennyfoil did not betray you, in fact he went to great lengths in denying you were involved in his bakery. I explained that as your future husband, mindful of your reputation, that certain adjustments to your partnership would need to be made." Torrington held up a hand to stop her from speaking. "Allow me to finish. I have no desire to become involved in the management of your establishment unless you ask my opinion. Whether you wish it or not, you are now a countess, Rosalind. Discretion is necessary. Legally, Pennyfoil is *my* partner. I had my solicitor draw up papers to that effect. But in all the ways that matter, Pennyfoil's belongs to you. The law does not favor women. Nor society. This is the loophole Lady Andromeda used. Legally, it is the Duke of Granby who owns half of Madame Dupree's modiste shop. I've only done the same for you. And I bought the building you wanted from Ledbean outright."

"Bram." Her fingers gripped tighter on the book. The enormity of what he'd done for her wasn't lost on Rosalind. No one had ever gone to such trouble for her. Her heart beat fiercely for Torrington, so much so it was in danger of bursting from her chest. A terrifying fear suffused her limbs, though she tried to will it away.

"Keep in mind that technically Pennyfoil is leasing the building from *me*, but since your partner has informed me that you actually keep the ledgers, I will tell you that I expect the rent to be received promptly. I would hate to evict my own wife from the premises." A kiss pressed along the skin of her neck.

"You will really allow me to have Pennyfoil's. You won't stop me."

"No, my love. I will not. Just be a bit more discreet than you have thus far. I had no problem trailing you to Pennyfoil's. The Duke of Averell has asked that I prevent you from becoming another Barrington scandal, if possible." A half-smile tilted his lips.

"I can truly have Pennyfoil's," she said again, the words

trembling from her lips. "You've done all of this for me." Fear crushed her chest, swallowing the joy trying to fill her.

"Yes." His fingers closed around hers. "I will never *demand* from you, Rosalind. Mostly because you'll ignore me, and I will have wasted my breath. I may"—he trailed his tongue along the edge of her ear—"issue an order in the bedroom on occasion, but I expect you'll enjoy that. I will also not ask you to attend functions just for the sake of being seen, pretend to enjoy the opera, or have you pay rounds of calls, because then you would be forced to eat substandard pastries from someone else's tea tray and listen to tedious gossip you don't care about. You don't have to wear a corset if you don't want to. Or underthings. Honestly, I would rather you didn't."

"Bram." The name choked out of her. Rosalind's emotions, kept so tightly bottled up since yesterday, clawed at her skin. She shifted on the bed, every instinct screaming at her to get away.

"I told you I don't care if I have an heir for the bloody title, and I meant it. I hope we will be blessed with a child, but if we are not, I will still consider myself to be the luckiest of men. I only want *you*." He cupped her cheek. "I love you, Rosalind, with everything I am." He kissed her gently. "And I know you love me. We can be happy. *Will* be happy. I promise."

She shook her head violently, scooting away from him as she dropped the cookbook. "I can't—I won't be able to."

"Rosalind." Torrington reached for her wrist, but she jerked away.

The image of her mother, dressed all in black, clawing at the floor, skirts billowing like some horrible cloud of death, filled her vision. The words, wrenched from her mother's anguished chest, screamed in her ears.

"Let me go be with him. I beg you."

The doctor rushing forward to sedate Lady Richardson as

two footmen had to be summoned to haul away her mother's unconscious form. The butler yelling at someone to send for the Duke of Averell to fetch Rosalind. Then the later anguish of Cousin Amanda ripping apart the entire household at Cherry Hill, weeping hysterically as Cousin Marcus was buried. She had to be carried away because she refused to leave his body.

That's what Rosalind would become. A grieving anguished wraith. Because of Torrington.

"No." Hysterical sobs left her. "No. I don't love you. I won't. I can't."

She needed to bake. Lose herself in the comfort of the kitchen and make muffins. Or scones. A spice cake.

"You *do* love me." Torrington's voice was wounded. Hurt. He reached for her again, but Rosalind sprang from the bed, slapping away his hands.

"Stop, Rosalind."

Racing to the adjoining door between their rooms, Rosalind walked through and shut the door firmly behind her, throwing the lock, unable to look at Torrington a moment longer.

She took a step inside the rooms her husband had so carefully decorated for her, one hand pressed against her heart.

She needed to bathe. Dress. Visit Pennyfoil's.

⚜

BRAM SAT IN STUNNED SILENCE AS HIS NEW WIFE, WITH whom he'd just spent the last day in bed, locked him out of her heart and her life without another word. He'd never told a woman he loved her. Rosalind's reaction wasn't exactly what he'd been expecting.

He stood and padded naked to the door between their rooms, listening for Rosalind on the other side. Placing a hand on the door, he closed his eyes, willing her to come back to him. Her pain, her *fear*, was a palpable thing. Bram should have seen the truth sooner. Examined more closely Rosalind's distress at wedding him. Gone to Lady Richardson and asked about the death of Lord Richardson.

It wasn't *loving* Bram that had led Rosalind to flee him moments ago. That wasn't the problem at all.

A call needed to be paid to his new mother-in-law. Immediately.

"My lady, you have a caller."

Rosalind didn't even look up at Watkins. She was kneading a ball of dough on the work-table in the kitchen with mixed results. Bread wasn't really her area of expertise, but she found her interest in pastry to be lagging since her—*Argument? Dismissal? Fit of weeping?*—with Torrington.

She paused, sinking her fingers deep into the dough, feeling the familiar sense of loss, but it was much more muted now.

"I'm not receiving. Tell Lady Richardson I'll call when my schedule permits." Her mother had called at least three times in the last week, but Rosalind wasn't up for a barrage of questions about her marriage. She wasn't about to sit and sip tea with the woman who was responsible for this entire mess. After Rosalind's escape from Torrington and his unwelcome confession to her, her husband had not tried to speak to her again. In the last fortnight, Torrington hadn't attempted to approach or engage her in conversation. In fact, she'd barely seen him. He stayed out most nights or in the study with

Bijou. Rosalind spent her time at Pennyfoil's. They were well on their way to having a perfectly civilized marriage of convenience. Many couples lived separate lives. Her marriage to Torrington was no different.

Rosalind felt better. The longer she kept Torrington at arm's length, the stronger she became.

After a time, with proper distance between them, Rosalind thought they might resume the physical aspect of their relationship on a limited basis. After all, Torrington still needed an heir. She enjoyed sharing a bed with her husband. But that was all they would share.

Watkins cleared his throat. "It is Her Grace, the Dowager Duchess of Averell, my lady."

Rosalind dropped the ball of dough, giving it a look of disgust. Too much flour. The bread would be dense and chewy. Barely edible. "Her Grace?" She wiped her hands on her apron. Even Rosalind wasn't so bold as to turn away a duchess, especially not Cousin Amanda. Perhaps she brought word that Romy was finally on her way home from Italy. Or possibly Leo was coming back to London. He had to leave America at some point.

Rosalind ran up the stairs, handed her apron to Watkins, patted her hair, and sailed into the drawing room.

Cousin Amanda sat on the sofa in a gown of soft pearl gray, giving the appearance she was sitting in a misty cloud. The loss of Marcus Barrington lingered in every line of her body, like a heaviness which caused her shoulders to sag slightly no matter how much she might wish otherwise.

Rosalind had done the right thing in regards to Torrington. The evidence was before her.

"Ah, there you are, Rosalind. I hope you don't mind, but I asked your butler for tea."

"Of course not." She came forward and kissed Cousin Amanda's cheek. "How lovely to see you."

"But unexpected." A wry smile tilted her lips. "You thought Winifred had come once more to speak to you. She is smarter than you give her credit for. She asked me to call instead."

Rosalind's smile faltered. "I see. I can't imagine what Mother can be concerned about. She got what she wished. I'm married to Torrington."

Cousin Amanda laughed, a light, airy sound which flitted around the room like fairy dust. "Yes, a terrible fate indeed. Torrington is quite marvelous. Winnie did well in matching you to him."

"Not in my opinion, Your Grace."

"I recall, Rosalind, when you were a child, that Andromeda made a trousseau for your doll."

Rosalind frowned at the abrupt change of topic. Surely, Cousin Amanda hadn't called to merely reminisce about Rosalind's childhood.

"You complained, stringently, that there wasn't a black dress included. You stated, very stubbornly, of course, that *all* wives must have a dress in black for when their husband died. I believe you insisted to Romy that she rework your doll's wardrobe to *only* contain that color."

Unease filled her. "Theodosia reminded me of the incident. I don't recall it with any great clarity," she lied.

"Your mother wore black for an extended period after Lord Richardson's death. Far longer than necessary. Years." Her lips pursed. "You came to live with us at Cherry Hill for a time so that Winnie could . . . recover from her grief."

Rosalind's mother had nearly been sent to an asylum. Her physician had called it a complete and utter break of the mind due to shock. "She went mad, Your Grace, in her grief over my father. I think we can admit that to each other."

The dowager duchess looked away for a moment. "She loved him very much, Rosalind. And she had been so young when they wed. Barely more than a girl. Winnie didn't even know how to run a household. Nor did she have your practicality. Richardson was everything to her. A father figure. A husband. A lover." Cousin Amanda laughed softly and turned back to face her.

"My father was a flirtatious, elderly rake."

"Gently reformed, Rosalind. A leopard doesn't change his spots, not when those spots are sixty years old. He might have strayed on occasion, but not with his heart. He loved Winnie."

"She gave up her entire life to nurse him. He would demand she fetch him a pillow. Ask her to cut his meat. I was there, Your Grace."

"When Richardson became ill, Winnie *chose* to nurse him because she wanted to spend every last moment with your father. I suspect what you recall most is Winnie's collapse. It is a pity you cannot remember the joy your parents had between them that resulted in you."

Rosalind's fingers shook against her skirts, wishing she could shred the muslin. "She should have chosen a man closer to her own age. Instead, she was a grief-stricken widow before the age of twenty-five. That's what my father's heir hurled at her while Mother . . ." A tear threatened to fall from one eye, and Rosalind blinked it away. "She sobbed hysterically and begged to join my father." It had been terrifying for a child of seven to witness, seeing her mother awash in anguish as she pleaded with God to allow her to leave this life and join her husband. "When they dragged her away, I ran into the kitchens. I made a spice cake." A tear finally spilled down her cheek. "No one even came to look for me. Or cared where I was until you and Cousin Marcus came. I was alone."

"Oh, Rosalind." Cousin Amanda held out her arms. "Come here, my love."

"And you." Rosalind fell sobbing into her arms. "When

223

Cousin Marcus died you . . . weren't yourself. You wouldn't leave his body." She looked up at the dowager duchess. "Romy feared you would hurt yourself."

"I—was not—well for a time."

"Do you know what my father's heir said to her? That Mother had put herself in this position by being foolish enough to marry a man so many years her senior. She should have been expecting to be a young widow." The pain exploded across Rosalind's chest. "And I was *alone*. No one even looked for me. I thought my mother would die too." She wiped furiously at her cheeks. "I promised I would *never* allow that to happen to me."

Cousin Amanda held her close, brushing her hair back from her forehead. "I know, dear. I'm so sorry it took Marcus and me so long to come to you. We didn't know how bad— my poor Rosalind."

"Why couldn't Mother have allowed me to become a spinster? I don't want to collapse." She tried to pull away from Cousin Amanda, but the duchess wouldn't allow it. "Or fall into fits. Lose myself and nearly die of grief because I wed a man twice my age. I won't allow it."

"My dear, Torrington could fall off his horse tomorrow. Perish from catching a fever. Be run over by a carriage leaving his club. He could be twenty or sixty and still meet with an unfortunate accident. Age has little to do with it. Merely bad luck."

Rosalind sobbed louder.

"You are out of excuses as to why you must not love Torrington."

"I don't love him. I won't." She shook her head. "We will lead a separate existence."

"Do you think by staying apart from him you will spare yourself? Because you won't. It is far too late for that. You already love him."

Another choking sob left her. Then a horrible wail. "I'm so afraid, Cousin Amanda. Like a weight on my chest which never goes away."

The duchess pressed a kiss to her head. "Do not waste another precious moment on what may happen, Rosalind. It serves no purpose other than to keep you tethered to a perpetual state of misery. Fear. Even knowing how badly—"

Cousin Amanda trembled and hugged Rosalind tighter.

"I would still love Marcus. Every moment of my life with him has been worth it. I would change *nothing*. Not even the pain of losing him. You cannot live your life in constant worry. Have your bakery, with a healthy amount of discretion. Make the lemon blackberry cake my dear Marcus adored, as he did you. *Love* Torrington. Give him children if you're meant to. When the time comes, and you finally part, that love will sustain you."

❧ 22 ❧

Rosalind handed Watkins her cloak with a tired smile. The visit with her mother had been exhausting, but necessary. Cousin Amanda had insisted, after leaving Rosalind, that a call be paid on Lady Richardson the following day. And one does not disappoint a duchess. Mother hadn't known what her daughter had suffered in those months after the death of Lord Richardson. Her grief at her husband's passing had been so profound, there was room for little else. She wept at having failed Rosalind and begged her daughter's forgiveness.

Jacobson, seeing the excess of handkerchiefs and tears, had immediately shut the drawing room door.

Once the weeping had subsided, Mother implored Rosalind not shy away from the happiness to be found with Torrington. True to form, Mother had insisted she'd known from the start the earl would be a splendid match for Rosalind because, over tea one day, Lady Hertfort had mentioned her brother loved cookery far more than he did hunting, the theater, or anything else.

Torrington, Rosalind found out, had visited Mother,

inquiring into the events surrounding Lord Richardson's death. Her mother, bravely, had chosen to omit nothing, telling Rosalind's new husband everything that had transpired.

"He loves you madly, Rosalind."

Mother had then kissed her cheek and told her to go home to Torrington.

The panic and fear still lived inside Rosalind, having taken up space near her heart when she was a child, and was determined not to go quietly. It might always linger. But at least she now saw it for what it was: the terror of a young child.

And she could no longer be apart from Torrington. She loved him.

"Where is Lord Torrington?" she asked Watkins. "And Bijou? I expected her to greet me."

"The study, my lady."

Rosalind nodded and made her way to her husband's study. She and Torrington hadn't spoken more than a polite greeting to each other since the day she'd stormed out of their bedroom. He hadn't pressed her, perhaps sensing after he'd called on her mother that Rosalind needed time to sort things out. Torrington was a patient man. Seducing her with a collection of recipes had proven the truth of that. Any other gentleman would have given up on her.

The door to the study was ajar, and Torrington's voice came through the opening. He was speaking in a low, soothing tone to Bijou.

"My lord," Rosalind said from the door, clasping her hands before her.

Torrington was kneeling next to Bijou's pallet on the floor. His hair was mussed, curls spilling along his cheeks, the silver in his beard glinting in the light coming through the window. The chair beside him held his discarded coat and cravat. There was only a mild flash of surprise at her appearance, almost as if Torrington knew she would seek him out today.

"Hello, Rosalind. Madame Bijou is under the weather. I'm playing nursemaid."

Torrington kept his tone polite, as if they were merely acquaintances who had run into each other while walking in the park. Rosalind had done this. Forced her husband into distance. Running from the bedroom in tears after this gorgeous, splendid man had told Rosalind he loved her.

Her chest constricted, far more sharply than the tightest of corsets.

Rosalind came forward, coming to her knees to scratch Bijou behind her ears.

"Her back leg has been bothering her, so she needs to rest," Torrington said. "I often forget how old she's become." There was a hint of pain in his words as one elegant finger traced the white fur around Bijou's muzzle. "But I think some chicken will make her right as rain, am I correct, Bijou?"

Rosalind blinked away the tears threatening to spill down her cheeks. Was this why she had refused to have a dog or cat when she was a child? Because her heart wouldn't allow her to become attached? Because all she could see was the grief?

What a fool I have been.

She took a deep breath, drawing in every ounce of courage she possessed. "I love you, Abraham Landsdowne." The words crept out of her mouth slowly. Quietly. "I *love* you." The air halted in her chest. "So much."

Torrington's gaze stayed on Bijou. He was silent so long, Rosalind thought perhaps he hadn't heard her. "I know," he finally said. His fingers reached out to gently tug at her skirts.

Rosalind looked up at the ceiling of the study, wiping at the tears streaming down her cheeks. "I'm so sorry that I made a mess of things. That I hurt you. I never wish to cause you such pain again. You have—given me everything I ever wanted. *You* are everything I've ever wanted. Only I didn't know and I—I humbly ask you to forgive me. *Please*." Her voice grew scratchy. "Please forgive me. Because you are so bloody *splendid* for a feeble lecher."

"Ah, Rosalind, you were doing so well." The amber eyes were calm. Full of love for her. Endlessly patient.

"I am afraid, Bram." She lowered her eyes. "I can't help it. If anything were to happen to you." She pounded the spot over her heart with a sob. "It would destroy me. I won't be able to bear it."

"Yes, you will. Admittedly, it won't be nearly as much fun without me around." He reached out and pulled her between his thighs. Strong arms encircled her. "For instance, I'm certain there will be too much nutmeg in the chocolate toffee cake."

"There wasn't." She leaned back into him, hearing the beat of his heart beneath her cheek.

"I disagree." His arms tightened around her. "I will die one day, Rosalind—"

A horrid, ugly sound escaped her. She turned her head, pressing her face into his chest, fingers grasping at his shirt. Her breath came in spurts.

Torrington's fingers threaded through her hair, loosening the careful chignon at the back. "But just for today, *only today*, my love, you won't think about such morbid things."

"I won't?" She sniffed.

"No. Just for today. Today we will be happy. Maybe make the macarons. Spend the day in bed reading from your collection of erotic books." He pressed a gentle kiss to her cheek.

"My father's books."

"I disagree, Lady Torrington. I'm fairly certain they belong to you now. I'm sure there are lots of illustrations. Life can imitate art. Won't that be fun?"

Rosalind smiled into his chest, inhaling the cedar and clean linen scent.

"So, do we have an agreement, my brazen baker? *Just* for today, you will not think such awful thoughts. They are banished."

She nodded. "Just for today." She could do that. Put all those terrible feelings aside for now, as she had on their wedding night.

"Good. You may despair tomorrow, my love." Then he tipped up her chin and kissed her, wrapping his arms tighter around Rosalind to pull her further into his lap. Torrington murmured beautiful nonsense into her hair, a great deal of it in French, until she stopped shaking.

৩৯৫৩

EVERY DAY, TORRINGTON REPEATED THE SAME THING TO Rosalind as she awoke, whispering it to her as sunlight streamed across the big bed in his room. Her adjoining chamber, they'd both agreed, was more of an immense closet and sitting room, for Torrington refused to allow them to sleep apart.

"You may despair over me tomorrow, but not today. Today we won't think of it."

And every morning, Rosalind did as her husband asked, loving him more with each passing day. When the fear threatened to invade her heart, she pushed it aside, instead focusing on the flood of orders Pennyfoil's had received after Rosalind organized a small sampling of the King's Tart, the name she'd given to the extravagant *baiser du ciel*. Or spending hours poring over fabric samples and colors for Pennyfoil's while approving the renovations for the building her husband had purchased which would house her new establishment.

But mostly, it was Torrington and her own happiness that filled her thoughts.

Once a week, her husband made sure to dismiss the staff, including Watkins, so he and Rosalind could create something marvelous in the kitchen together. Usually, the evening ended with an excellent meal, some of which her husband ate off her naked skin.

When the summons from the Duke of Averell inviting them to dinner arrived some months later, enough time had passed that the fear in Rosalind bloomed less frequently. The worry would never completely fade, she surmised, but it no longer dictated her life. And when it did surface, Rosalind would retreat to the kitchens or Pennyfoil's and make pies or a cake until she could breathe again.

"Leo is home." Rosalind strolled into her husband's study, pausing to scratch Bijou's ear. She held up the note. "Our attendance at dinner is required"—she consulted the paper in her hand once more—"as well as a request for lemon torte and a chocolate toffee cake."

Torrington looked up from the ledger he'd been working on. "Thank goodness. I'm tired of earl duties. I'd much rather make a cake." He reached out a hand. "But first, come here, Rosalind." His voice lowered to a smoky purr. "Lock the door."

She turned, smiled to herself, and shut the door, locking it behind her. "I'm due at Pennyfoil's. We've a large order for Lord Rothwell." Her partnership with Pennyfoil, already successful, was rapidly becoming the talk of London, for all the right reasons. Pennyfoil's had become a destination, just as Rosalind had first imagined. And she had been endlessly discreet. No one suspected her involvement.

"Then I'll be quick. Come. Here." His gaze lowered to her mouth. "I have been thinking all morning of you naked, on your knees before me as you were last night."

"You're insatiable for an ancient rake." She giggled, her body warming as he grabbed her around the waist and pulled her to his lap. Cupping his face between her hands she whispered, "I love you madly, Bram."

"And I love you." He crushed her to him, kissing her until Rosalind felt pleasantly light-headed. "My brazen baker. There is something I do almost as well as making the lemon torte." Torrington pushed up her skirts. "Let me show you."
**

I hope you enjoyed reading **A Recipe for a Rogue** as much as I enjoyed writing it. **If you did, I'd love a review!**

If you want more Barringtons, keep reading for the next in the series **The Making of a Gentleman.**

Miss Olivia Nelson has never done anything reckless in her life.

Determined to be a perfect young lady amongst a field of wild Barringtons, Olivia strives for politeness. Modesty. Restraint. But when Lady Phaedra Barrington declares her to be boring and goads her into venturing to Elysium, Olivia reluctantly agrees.

Elysium, part gambling hell and part pleasure palace isn't the sort of establishment Olivia should *ever* visit. Her future will consist of paying calls, taking sedate walks in the park and marriage to a proper, somewhat boring gentleman handpicked by her grandfather. When a handsome stranger comes close to ravishing her on Elysium's notorious second floor, Olivia is thrilled to have done something daring.

Until she finds the same man seated across from her at the Duke of Averell's dinner table. *Winking* at her. A proper gentleman, one with an ounce of decorum, would pretend not to recognize her. Or remind Olivia of what transpired at Elysium.

But Mr. Benjamin Cooke, Olivia soon finds out, is definitely *not* a gentleman. He's ruthless. Unprincipled. Brilliant.

Attractive. And *worst* of all, American. Cooke wants Olivia with a determination that is as thrilling as it is terrifying.

Now Olivia is faced with an impossible decision.

Will she be bound by duty? Or sacrifice everything to follow her heart? **CLICK HERE FOR THE MAKING OF A GENTLEMAN.**

AUTHOR NOTES

I really enjoyed writing the love story of two foodies who find each other. While most upper-class women of the time didn't pursue a career, I wanted all my Barrington women to have another passion besides marrying. Thus, Rosalind became a baker/pastry chef.

The word 'recipe' came into usage in culinary texts sometime in the late 18th century although many books still used 'receipt'. After doing my research (and being a modern reader who found the use of 'receipt' in place of 'recipe' to be jarring), I opted to use the more modern word 'recipe'. Dozens of old 'cookery' books are available online and the term is used interchangeably. Additionally, I chose to use more modern versions of certain kitchen terms when I felt necessary.

The rare French cookbook only for nobility, *Cuisiner pour les Rois,* the decadent custard, and the king's tart Torrington tempts Rosalind with are all the products of my fertile imagination.

Pain au chocolat is referred to as *chocolatine* depending on what part of France you are visiting according to various sources. The delicious chocolate filled pastry may or may not be completely French in origin. Some food historians believe the idea of wrapping chocolate in a pastry came from Austria and surfaced in France sometime in the 1830's. I included *pain au chocolat* because it is my husband's absolute favorite. Here's a fun article if you want to read further: https://www.theguardian.com/lifeandstyle/shortcuts/2018/may/28/chocolatine-pain-au-chocolat-war-over-pastries-left-nasty-taste-in-paris-france

Macarons (not macaroons) are thought to have been brought to France by Catherine de Medici when she married Henry II. Two nuns seeking asylum during the French revolution started making macarons to pay for their room and board and the small cookie became famous. There is a difference between a macaron and a macaroon (something I didn't realize until I did some research). You can read more here https://macaronqueen.com/blogs/news/the-history-of-macarons

Lastly, I receive a lot of comments about whether a woman could own property, a business, form a partnership, etc. I've given all of my Barrington women a loophole, so to speak as well as very understanding husbands, but the reality was far different for most women. You can read more here. https://hist259.web.unc.edu/marriedwomenspropertyact/#:~:text=This%20law%20actually%20gave%20women,occupation%2C%20and%20keep%20any%20inheritance.

ALSO BY KATHLEEN AYERS

The Beautiful Barringtons

The Study of a Rake (Prequel)

The Theory of Earls

The Design of Dukes

The Marquess Method

The Wager of a Lady

A Recipe for a Rogue

The Making of a Gentleman

The Arrogant Earls

Forgetting the Earl

Chasing the Earl

Enticing the Earl

The Wickeds

Wicked's Scandal

Devil of a Duke

My Wicked Earl

Wickedly Yours

Tall Dark & Wicked

Still Wicked

Wicked Again

Printed in Great Britain
by Amazon

11496734R00138